"We might as well have this out," said Mara.

Susan stared at her blankly.

"You can't go on being fooled forever," said Mara in a low, tense voice. "If it hadn't been for you, Dirk and I would be married by now."

Susan, appalled, said nothing at all.

"I'm in love with Dirk," Mara went on, "and in the end I mean to have him back. Don't you know why he married you?"

"Of course I do," Susan said.

Mara went on as if she had not spoken. "He married you because of the diamond. Because he wanted that fortune in his hands and you could lead him to it."

Susan closed her ears. If she believed that, she could never trust Dirk again!

Phyllis A. Whitney

BLUE
FIRE

FAWCETT CREST • NEW YORK

For Morea

BLUE
FIRE

1

He saw her almost at once. In spite of the confusion spilled across the South Side tracks, where there had been a minor collision, she was easy to spot. A chap at the Chicago *Bulletin* had said she was out on a job and had mentioned the accident. If the need was urgent, she could be found there. "Look for a half pint of girl with a full quart of . camera," he had directed. The urgency was not that extreme, but Dirk had come nevertheless with a curious wish to see her unguarded at work in her own environment.

The August afternoon had turned drizzling dark and this was not a section of Chicago that set its best foot forward. Gray was the predominant key for mist-blurred trains and tracks and milling people, for the sky and the lake and nearby buildings. Despite the soupy murk, he found her easily, hopping around through the crowd like a lively sparrow, pausing for a camera shot here, ducking out of the way of an ambulance attendant there, her orange scarf a tongue of flame that made its wearer easy to follow. Her hair was tucked under a shapeless brown beret, a trench coat engulfed her slight person, and flat-heeled loafers carried her in agile leaps as she searched for suitable camera angles.

Dirk lighted a cigarette in the shelter of a tilted boxcar and watched with a mingling of amusement and interest. The accident was apparently not serious, so she should be through with her duties soon. No need to get on with it immediately—he would bide his time.

Strange that he should remember so clearly the last time he had seen her. She had been seven and he sixteen. That morning she had been clambering about on an arm of rocks that thrust out across the sand of Camp's Bay at the other end of the world. She had held a camera in her hands that day too—a child's box camera. And she had insisted on taking his picture. Perhaps he remembered that long-ago morning at the Cape Peninsula so well because no one since that time had ever regarded him with the same warm adoration that lit-

9

tle Susan van Pelt had shown toward a somewhat uncertain young man of sixteen.

He continued to watch the girl with the camera, wondering what his best approach might be. Perhaps he'd better not tell her at once who had sent him here, or why.

Having taken her fill of pictures, the grown-up Susan swung her equipment over her shoulder and started toward him across the tracks. She still moved with the news photographer's watchful eye for an unexpected picture, so that she did not look too carefully at the rails and crossties under her feet. The toe of one small brown loafer caught in stepping over a rail and she went sprawling before Dirk could spring forward to catch her. It was an ugly fall, but she was up before he reached her, looking first to the safety of her camera.

To Dirk her anxiety, her look of near fright as she turned the camera about, examining it for injury, seemed a bit extreme. Probably it was borrowed from her paper and expensive to replace in case of serious damage. Only when she had made sure that the bulky camera had received no hurt did she pull up her plaid skirt to examine the bloody smear across one knee, where cinders had torn stocking and flesh.

"Ouch!" she said. And then more gently as if in afterthought, "Damn!"

Dirk hid his amusement at such hesitant profanity and stepped to her side. "That was a nasty spill. May I help? Let me take that camera and get you out of here."

The odd, trembling fear was fading and the look she gave him was straight and clear, her brown eyes enormous in her small, pointed face. A faint sense of shock went unexpectedly through him. She had been a homely little thing, with freckles on her nose and eyes too big for her size when he had first known her. She was not pretty now, but here was a face to arrest a man and make him look again. There was still a shadow of freckles and the mouth was generous and mobile. In the bulky trench coat her figure was invisible, but her ankles were good and small boned, her wrists fragile for the load of that heavy camera. Her mother had been a small woman too, he remembered—an American, and something of a scatterbrain.

She resisted when he tried to take her camera, but accepted the help of his arm, limping for a few steps until she forced herself to walk steadily.

"I'm all right," she said. "I've got to get these plates back to the paper right away." Her accent was wholly American. There was no trace of English or Afrikaans left in it.

10

"Let me take you there," he said. "We can find a cab on the next street. Think you can walk that far?"

"I can walk," she assured him, and her gaze came wonderingly back to his face. The brown eyes, hazel flecked, searched puzzled for an answer. "I know you, don't I? I've met you somewhere?"

They had reached the sidewalk and he raised a finger to a cruising taxi, postponing a reply. The girl hesitated only a moment and then got in when he opened the door. As the cab headed north, she dabbed gingerly at her raw knee with a handkerchief. Then she pulled off the ugly beret and ran a hand through her cropped hair. He started at the sight. Strange that he had remembered her eyes and forgotten her hair. It was a bright color, just short of true auburn, but with fire in the chestnut. She wore it shorter than he liked. She must be persuaded to let it grow, he thought, as if it were ordained that he should influence her life.

"Tell me where we've met," she persisted, studying him again.

The cab was following Michigan Avenue now, and luxury shops rimmed the boulevard like shining beads on a gray thread. In the tall buildings ahead lights gleamed in a thousand windows, brightening the mist with their glow.

"I'll give you a hint," he told her. "Can you picture a wide beach with very white sand and a piling up of big flat rocks cutting out toward the sea? Can you remember a line of peaks leaning all one way and repeating themselves against the sky?"

She gasped and one hand flew to her lips. "The Twelve Apostles! South Africa, of course. And you're Dirk—Dirk Hohenfield!"

"So you do remember," he said, a little surprised at his own pleasure.

Her eyes danced into eager life. "Remember? Of course I remember! How could I not? I was madly in love with you then. You were a smattering of all my heroes rolled into one, including Paul Kruger and Cecil Rhodes."

A faint smile curled her lips and he had an odd wish to see her smile with gaiety, to laugh aloud. Her face was not a gay one in repose.

He took her hand, the left one, and pulled off the worn pigskin glove. At least there was no ring on the third finger. That should make the old man's wishes a bit easier to gratify.

"You slapped me with this hand once," he reminded her. "I

11

can remember how surprised I was that such a little girl could slap so hard. Your right hand was holding a doll, I believe."

"I remember too," she said. "You hurt my feelings. You made fun of my dear Marietjie and I had to make you think I hated you."

"But you didn't." He spoke with confidence. She, at least, had never sensed his uncertainties, or the resentments of a brooding, sensitive boy. "What a funny little scamp you were. I liked playing hero for you, even if I didn't deserve to have you feel that way."

She withdrew her fingers and unwound the orange scarf from about her neck as if she sought some occupation for her hands. The elusive smile had vanished.

"Did my father send you for me?" she asked directly, and the gentleness was gone from her voice and manner.

"I'm on a combination business trip and holiday," he told her, but she would have none of that.

"If he sent you for me, the answer is still no. I'm twenty-three now. I hadn't heard from him for sixteen years until he wrote recently, following my mother's death. I don't know him. I don't want to know him."

"We must talk about that," he said. "Will you let me come to see you? For my own pleasure," he added hastily as he saw refusal coming. "This evening, perhaps? Will you have dinner with me?"

The hint of resistance melted and she relaxed in the seat beside him. "I should have known who you were the moment I heard you speak. I haven't heard the accent of South Africa in years, yet every word comes back to me."

"I'm no South African by birth," he reminded her quickly.

She nodded. "Yes, I know. Your father was German, wasn't he?" In spite of himself he stiffened, and she must have sensed his withdrawal.

"Why don't you come to my place tonight?" she asked. "I'll fix supper for you, if you like. It will be easier to talk than in a restaurant. Have you been in Cape Town lately?"

"I live there now," he said. "I work for your father, Niklaas van Pelt."

The cab had stopped for a red light that halted the wide stream of Michigan Avenue traffic. The bridge was just ahead, with the Near North Side beyond. They were almost there.

"He must be terribly old—my father," she said. "In his seventies? He was close to fifty when he married my mother. She was young—too young for him." The girl turned her direct look upon Dirk. "How did he learn that Mother had died?

He's never shown any interest in us before. How would he hear?"

"Your father has friends in America," Dirk told her casually. He must be careful now, make no slip about the letter which had alerted the old man to his wife's approaching death. It was clear that the girl knew nothing of her mother's letter.

Susan seemed to consider his words, neither completely accepting nor denying.

"He hurt her so much," she went on, her tone youthfully bitter. "My mother was sweet and gay and fun-loving. I can still remember the cold way he treated her when he didn't approve of her frivolity. He broke her heart—and her spirit too. That's why she ran away from South Africa and took me with her."

Dirk watched the cars slipping past, not looking at the girl beside him.

"My father did something wicked and went to prison for it, didn't he?" she said, sounding prim and disapproving, like a child who has been taught to parrot grown-up words.

The cab pulled up to the curb and Dirk opened the door and stepped out, relieved to bring a halt to her words.

"We'll return to this tonight," he said, and helped her to the sidewalk, camera and all.

She gave him her address, and he walked with her to the door and into the echoing cavern of a vaulted lobby. For just a moment he held her hand lightly and looked into brown eyes that had a shading of grief in them.

"Until this evening then," he said. *"Tot siens*—till we meet again."

At the homely Afrikaans farewell, tears came into her eyes and she blinked them back furiously. "Perhaps I shouldn't see you after all. I don't want to remember too much. Remembering hurts."

There was, he found, a somewhat surprising tenderness in him toward her, and he smiled, knowing that she would not withdraw her invitation. She turned abruptly and walked toward the elevators and he stood looking after her. The jaunty set of her shoulders seemed touchingly deliberate. She swung the shapeless beret from one hand, guarding her camera with the other, and the bright fire of her hair shone in the lighted lobby. He watched her until she disappeared through an elevator door.

Then he left the building and strode along Michigan in the direction of his hotel. He was ready now to question the tremulous letter her mother had written—all that sticky sentiment about her innocent and helpless chick with no nest egg to save her from harm. This girl was far from helpless, and yet there was about her an air of innocence that was as unexpected as it was appealing. He could see a streak of her father too, which gave her a stubborn resistance. She might be harder to convince than he had expected, but he would give it his best try, for more reasons than one.

A subtle excitement had begun to stir in him and he whistled as he walked along the avenue. Had there been any about to recognize the tune, they would have known it for an old riding song of the Boers. All about a young man who was willing to ride his ten-pound horse to death on a night-long journey in order to be with his love in the morning.

> *I'll think of my darling as the sun goes down,*
> *The sun goes down, the sun goes down,*
> *I'll think of my darling as the sun goes down,*
> *Down, down below the mountain.*
> *I'll ride, I'll ride, I'll ride, I'll ride,*
> *I'll ride all night,*
> *When the moon is bright . . .**

The girl felt the excitement too. Through the rest of the day she thought a great deal about Dirk Hohenfield—and about what little she knew of the past.

Her mother had been born in Chicago and had lived there after her parents' death. Her one excursion out of the country had been with a world-circling musical troupe for which she had played the piano. When the tour had ended in financial disaster, Claire had stayed on in South Africa. There she had married and remained until something she would never talk about had terminated her life with Niklaas van Pelt. This was at the close of the war and she had been able to return to the States and the city she knew best—Chicago. At home, with a small daughter and herself to support, she had held various positions as receptionist and hostess—a type of work that required good looks and a charm of manner that Claire was happily able to supply.

* From "As the Sun Goes Down." New words and new music by Josef Marais. Copyright 1956 by Fideree Music Corp., New York, N.Y.

Her mother's illness and untimely death only a few months before had left Susan with a devastating sense of loss. She had always been a rather lonely person, but that had not mattered so much when there was someone to whom she could devote herself. Now there were reminders on every hand of the companion she had lost, and there was no one who needed her.

During the past year or so she had made friends in her newspaper work, it was true, but that rather sophisticated world was still new to her. She wanted very much to belong to the fourth estate, but she suspected that her coworkers did not yet take her seriously. There was no one to whom she was truly close.

Dirk Hohenfield's sudden appearance was like having a rocket shoot across a bleak horizon. Like a rocket he would soon be gone, but for a little while she would delight in his presence and even in his link with a place she had never been able to forget.

It was understandable that the day dragged and that she was preoccupied with her own thoughts until the moment when she could get away. Then she stopped at a grocery store to shop and went home to the little apartment on the Near North Side that she had shared with her mother. In the tiny kitchen she went to work, feeling happier than she had for a long time.

Now she could think without interruption of the man who was coming here tonight. She did not know all the circumstances, but she knew her father had taken him as a ward when Dirk's parents had died. Apparently he had continued in a close relationship to her father after he had grown up.

When a casserole of scalloped potatoes was browning in the oven and the salad greens were ready in the refrigerator, the steaks prepared for broiling, she wandered into the living room to look about with a sense of dissatisfaction.

She would have liked Dirk to see her as she really was, and she was not a pastel-pretty person like this room that had so well suited her mother. But there was nothing to be done about the matter at this late date. She wrinkled her nose ruefully at the rose-pink cloth she had spread over a gate-legged table by the window, and at pink candles in rosebud-painted china holders. Without disloyalty she knew that these things were Claire and not Susan, and she could only hope that Dirk would understand.

How well she remembered the boy he had been—the very way he had looked the last time she'd seen him, his bright fair hair shining under the South African sun, his eyes as vivid a

15

blue as the Cape Town sky. They had clambered out upon a great stretch of rocks that reached into the Atlantic and he had been watchful of her, lest she slip and tumble into the water. She had wanted to take a picture of him with her small camera, but somehow it had never come out. He had teased her as he posed, and laughed at her, though never unkindly. With the single-mindedness of a lonely child she had looked up to him and there had been an aching in her beyond her years, sensing as she had that she was about to lose him out of her life forever. Such a loss seemed especially poignant for a child, moving at the bidding of adults and helpless to save what she loved.

By comparison, of course, Dirk had been grown-up—yet not wholly so. He was always willing to romp with her, and sometimes even to talk to her about his own adventurous dreams that still had about them an immaturity which she had been too young to recognize. Sometimes he told her of how he would be a great lion hunter when he was older, or perhaps he would find gold and become enormously rich. He had been the only person she knew with the spirit of adventure burning high in him—and thus akin to the heroes of the stories she loved to read.

Now he was here and real, they were both grown-up, and her feeling of excitement persisted and heightened.

A gilt-rimmed mirror over what had once been a real fireplace gave back her reflection and she studied it critically. Her beige dress with the green belt was right for so warm an evening, but she was uncertain of the green velvet band she had wound through her hair. Was that ribbon Claire or Susan? Sometimes it was very hard to tell.

She had just raised a hand to remove it when the sound of the buzzer startled her. Too late now—the ribbon would have to stay. She flew to push the button that would release the door catch three floors down.

"All the way up!" she called over the hall rail and heard the breathless sound of her own voice.

He came up bareheaded and the memory of the way he had looked in the sunlight that last day in South Africa was upon her again. Of course he was older now, but in so many ways the same. Still breathless, she retreated to her doorway, trying to hide this betrayal of her own eagerness. She must not let him think her too absurdly young and expectant.

He climbed easily and reached her with no loss of breath. His eyes were as intensely blue as she remembered them—no less so in the man than in the boy. There was an eagerness in

him too and her heart thumped foolishly at the kn⌐
This meeting could mean nothing, she reminded hersen.
rocket could not stay its flight, and Susan van Pelt woula
never return to South Africa.

In his arms Dirk held an extravagance of yellow roses and
she took them from him, letting her pleasure shine in her
eyes. He followed her into the apartment, looking only at her.

"There were no proteas to be had," he told her.

The word, so long forgotten, brought a bright recollection
of South Africa's flower—the fabulously beautiful and exotic
protea that grew there in endless variety.

"Please sit down," she said, shyly formal. "I'll be only a
moment. I want a vase for these roses."

In the kitchen she filled a pale-green vase with water and
arranged the flowers tenderly, her fingers a little clumsy with
excitement, fearful as always lest she break something. That
moment with the camera today had frightened her badly. Her
neurosis! she thought wryly, and hoped Dirk had not noticed.

When she carried the vase back to the living room to see it
on the coffee table, she found him standing before a row of
photographs on the wall. It pleased her to see that he had sin-
gled them out for his attention, since these pictures were
Susan and not Claire.

There was one dramatic shot she had taken of a fire which
had damaged a West Side tenement some months ago, another
of an excursion boat loading children at a Chicago River
landing. And one of a snowy night on Michigan Avenue with
shop windows magically ablur through the storm. The one she
liked best, however, was a study of an elderly newspaper dealer at his sidewalk stand. The play of light and shadow was
exactly right, the composition perfect. She had been proud of
the result and pleased to sell it to a national magazine.

Dirk studied the pictures and she was glad of the opportunity to study him. The charm he had held for her as a child
was still there, but magnified as the boy had matured into a
man. How very attractive he was, not only because of his fair
good looks but in the kindness he showed her, in the quick intelligence that was so evident in him—all adding up to an appeal so strong that it dismayed her a little.

"Do you enjoy this sort of work?" he asked, still considering the pictures. "I should think it might be hazardous and a
bit rigorous for a woman."

"I love it," she said fervently, but she liked the fact that he
was thinking of the girl behind the photos. "Before I went to
the newspaper I sold photographic supplies in a store in the

17

ver really liked that. I always wanted to be out
...s."

...e good," he said, and she warmed to his approval.
...ed to look directly at her and there was an appraisal
...yes that made her a little self-conscious. She chose a
cha... in a shadowy corner and let him take the sofa facing the
light. She did not want to be looked at and measured too
closely, but only to look, to fill her eyes with the bright dazzle
of him. This moment was one she would treasure and remember when he was gone.

"There's a great deal to photograph in Cape Town," he reminded her, a faint amusement underlying his tone as if he
sensed something of the effect he had upon her and rather enjoyed it.

But that was a road she would not follow. "It's no use," she
said firmly. "I'm not going back if that's what you mean."

"Have I asked you to?" The timbre of his voice had
changed with the years. It was no longer a boy's voice, but
that of a man, deep and vibrant. "I told you I wanted to see
you for my own pleasure first of all. The rest can wait a bit."

She brought him a drink and as they sipped companionably, she asked him about his work for her father in Cape
Town.

"You were always going to be a famous hunter someday,"
she reminded him. "Or discover a fabulous vein of gold."

He laughed aloud, pleased that she remembered. "I'm
afraid my present hunting is on the prosaic side, though it has
its moments of interest. After—what happened—your father
sold his home in Johannesburg and moved to the Cape Town
house, where he has lived ever since. He has become an exporter of native craft work and has two shops as well. His
store in Johannesburg is particularly fine, and there's a smaller one in Cape Town. My hunting these days consists of
going out to places he can no longer reach—in the Transkei,
Zululand, Northern Rhodesia. Your father's standards are
high—we don't look for cheap things, but for real native art
work. It's remarkable how keen he has remained, how alive
he is."

She did not want to hear about her father. "I can barely remember the house in Jo'burg," she said. "It was always the
Cape Town house I loved best. Protea Hill! Such a lovely
name for it. When we went there for the December holidays
in summer I had a room with a wonderful view."

Dirk set down his glass, his eyes holding hers. "A view

18

that's still waiting for you, Susan. I doubt that it's changed in the slightest."

"I know," she said. "The mountain wouldn't change."

She excused herself, went off to the retreat of the kitchen to put the steaks under the broiling flame and toss the salad. But he would not remain a guest in the parlor. He joined her and carried in plates and glasses as though he enjoyed helping her, though he must be accustomed to servants.

When they had settled down to the meal, she asked him more about his own life so that he would open no further dangerous doors.

"What did you do before you went to work for my father?"

His smile was rueful. "When I finished school I got the diamond fever so you see it was diamonds by then, instead of gold. I did a little prospecting on my own, though not very successfully. Your father still owned land around the Kimberley area at that time and he told me I could have anything I discovered there. He was mainly interested in quenching my fever, I suppose."

He reached into a pocket and drew out a leather wallet. From an inner fold he took a small packet of paper.

"I still have one of the stones I found at that time. I've kept it for a lucky pocket piece and to prove I've been a digger."

She bent her head to watch as he unfolded the square of paper, and was aware of his own fair head so close to hers that his breath touched her cheek.

"There," he said. "I'll wager that's like no diamond you've ever seen."

The tiny stone shone orchid pink and translucent against the white paper and was irregular in form. The rough natural shape of the diamond was revealed, but it lacked the brighter sparkle of a cut diamond.

"This is what they call a fancy stone," Dirk told her. "Fancies are odd, off-color diamonds. Perhaps pink or green or yellow. Sometimes even black. This one isn't large enough or perfect enough to be of any great value, but I have a certain sentiment about it. Of course it's uncut, or I would have been breaking the law by bringing it into this country. Only uncut stones come in duty-free."

Susan picked up the little stone and nested it on her palm, seeing not the diamond but a very young man with a hunger for adventure in his heart, working for a dream that had never materialized.

"I thought De Beers owned all the diamonds in South Afri-

19

ca," she said. "How is it you were permitted to do any prospecting on your own?"

"The syndicate owns the important holdings," he explained. "But there are still diggers who work their own claims and sell what little they find to De Beers. As a matter of fact, it's against the law to possess an uncut diamond in South Africa unless you are an authorized person. As a licensed digger who found this stone myself I'm able to keep it." He returned the pink diamond to the paper and folded it away in his wallet. "Have you ever heard of the Kimberley Royal?" he added.

She shook her head, fascinated by this talk of diamonds and of a South Africa she had long ago put away from her and reconciled to painful memory.

"The Kimberley Royal was one of the great finds," Dirk said. "A remarkably beautiful and valuable stone. Bigger than the Hope diamond and nearly flawless. I saw it once as a boy. The very machinery that sorts diamonds these days may crush or damage the unusually large stone, but that's a chance that has to be taken. The present system is geared to a realistic commercial output. It takes, on an average, four tons of rock to give one carat of diamonds. But now I'm getting a bit technical."

She did not mind. She loved to listen to him and she gave him her absorbed attention all through the meal. Later, when he had gone, she would think about everything he had said.

When dessert was finished and she had cleared away the dishes, they sat among the pale pinks and baby blues and drank large cups of American brewed coffee. But now Dirk seemed restless, as if he felt time was slipping away and the subject for which he had really come had still not been opened between them.

In this mood his appeal for her was more disturbing. There were contrasts in this man, vibrant changes that would ask much of any woman who cared for him. But the thought of caring for him seriously was ridiculous and she dismissed the notion impatiently. She must be on guard against herself if her thoughts followed such a course.

He set down his cup and moved about the room again, glancing once more at the photographs, picking up a small carved antelope figure from the bookcase and holding it out to her with a smile.

"So you still keep a bit of Africa around?"

"It's an impala," Susan said, the remembered name coming back to her unbidden.

He studied the stripe-grained golden wood of the carving,

turning it about with experienced fingers. Tall lyrate horns rose from the slender, gracefully turned head. The ears were pricked, the muzzle delicate, the eyes long and luminous, even in a wood carving. The figure was at rest, its forelegs curled beneath the body, the haunches smoothly rounded, with the strong, hindquarters of a leaping animal. The curving grain suggested the haunch stripe of the impala and about the whole was an air of life and sensitive alertness, as though the creature might at any moment leap from its oval stand and go flying out of Dirk's fingers.

"A good piece," he said in approval. "The artist has caught the feeling of a wild thing, even at rest."

Susan stared at the figure. Until Dirk held it up the carving had meant nothing in particular to her and she had not thought of its name in years. Her mother had never connected the carving with South Africa. Yet suddenly knowledge was there, rising without warning from the forgotten past.

He set the figure down, moving closer to her, and this time he picked up a book from a table at her elbow and turned it over with a low whistle of astonishment.

"You want nothing to do with South Africa, yet you read the books of John Cornish?"

"Someone on the paper recommended it," Susan told him, a little startled by his tone. "The jacket flap says that his mother was an American, like mine, and I believe he lives in America now. Except when he's off to get material for a new book. That one is about Algeria."

Dirk turned the book over and studied the face pictured on the back of the jacket with an air of displeasure.

"Cornish used to write about South Africa," he said. "That's where he grew up. In fact, it was an article of his that helped to send your father to prison. Did you know that?"

She had not known it and she sat staring at him in silence.

"Cornish is back in the Union now," he went on. "The Johannesburg papers were running pieces about him when I left. I even ran into him one day there in the Carlton Hotel. It was not a fortunate meeting. I hope he'll stay away from Cape Town."

She wanted to ask more about John Cornish and her father, but remembered in time that these were matters in which she had no interest.

Dirk put down the book and came toward her, stood over her, so that she had to look up into his face. "Why are you so afraid of returning?" His gaze commanded her, yet there was a gentleness in him that kept her from turning away.

21

"My mother told me a few things about my father," she said. "He really cared very little for us. There's no reason to go back just because he's lately changed his mind about seeing me."

"But it was your mother who ran away at a time when he needed her most," Dirk said.

Indignation flared in her. "That's not true! He didn't need her, didn't want her. She was thinking of me, of getting me away from what might happen to us because of him."

He countered calmly with a question and she saw pity in his eyes. "Didn't she ever tell you why your father went to prison?"

"She said it was best that we both forget. For years it's never been mentioned between us. Anyhow, all that has nothing to do with me now."

The truth behind her willing ignorance was something she could explain to no one. There was about it a faintly nightmare quality she knew better than to rouse.

"I know enough," she hurried on. "My father must have been an important man in his day. Mother told me he was well-known in the diamond world—one of the most valued men with De Beers. He ran for the South African Parliament at one time too, didn't he? He was a leader, a respected person. Yet he threw it all away. Threw his family away—everything!"

"Listen to me," Dirk said, and the gentleness had gone from his manner. "It's time you knew the story. It's true that he broke the law, and no one knows why. But he's paid for that mistake a good many times over. So it would be a fine thing if his daughter—"

Susan jumped to her feet, familiar panic rising in her. "I don't want to hear!" she cried. "If you go on, I won't listen."

He looked clearly astonished at her show of emotion. Quietly he sat down on the sofa, and drew her to the place beside him, put a quieting arm about her shoulders. She shivered at his touch, all too conscious of his warmth and nearness. It was dangerous to get too close to a rocket. The tears she had been holding back since her mother's death welled up in her eyes. Softly, helplessly, she began to cry. He turned her head so that her cheek was against his shoulder and his fingers smoothed the bright hair back from her warm, damp brow.

"I'm sorry," he said. "I'd forgotten that you've had a bad time lately. I'm not sure what it is you fear and I suspect that it's unreal. But I won't trouble you about it now."

She suffered herself to rest against his shoulder for a few blissful moments and then raised her head and gave him a wavering smile.

"There—I'm all right now. And terribly ashamed. I didn't invite you here to be cried on." She blew a nose that she knew was pink, dried her eyes, and silently despised herself.

Dirk glanced at his watch and stood up. "I mustn't forget that you're a working girl and probably have to be up early in the morning. I appreciate your good dinner. It's been wonderful to see you again, Susan."

He was impersonal now and almost brusque. She knew she had sent him away with her tears, her nonsense. "Wh-when are you returning to Cape Town?" she asked, her voice fainter than she intended.

"At the moment I'm not sure," he told her. "This assignment may take me longer than I'd expected. To be perfectly truthful, I'm going home just as soon as you're ready to go with me."

He waited for no answer to that, but kissed her lightly on the cheek and took his departure before she could summon words to answer him. She stood frozen in the doorway, and listened to the sound of his steps as he ran lightly down the turning stairs. Before he reached the bottom he began to whistle and the tune touched some chord of memory in her mind. When the street door opened and closed, she went back into the apartment and stared about her vaguely. Somehow the place had a different look to her now. The valentine touches no longer mattered. Dirk had known they had nothing to do with her.

On the table lay the book by John Cornish. She picked it up and, as Dirk had done, turned it over to study the face portrayed on the book jacket. The picture was a candid shot and she had not thought it professionally good. It showed the rather brooding face of a man in his early forties or late thirties—a face with a strong bone structure beneath the flesh, the eyes deeply set beneath heavy brows. The mouth was straight and unsmiling, with a relentless quality about it, yet there was a mark of sensitivity to the lips. It was a face worth photographing skillfully, and this had been a haphazard shot.

What role had this man played in her father's life? She knew of him only as a highly respected writer on African affairs. Today America regarded him as an American. She put the book aside abruptly. She did not want to read John Cornish after what Dirk had told her about him.

She reached for the carved impala and sat on the sofa hold-

ing it tightly in her hands as if for comfort. She knew very
well what it was she tried to postpone, to fend off. In spite of
the fear that had its roots in her half-forgotten childhood,
there was a faint edge of eagerness encroaching upon her resistance. Was it possible that she might in the end give in and
go back to South Africa with Dirk Hohenfield?

She shook her head stubbornly, fighting off the thought.
No, certainly she would never go back. Not if it meant any
contact with Niklaas van Pelt, who was her father.

The tune Dirk had been whistling still haunted her memory, running through her mind over and over again. The words
came back to her suddenly.

> *I'll think of my darling as the sun goes down,*
> *...Down, down below the mountain.*

2

Afterwards Susan would always think of the days that followed as the time of the pink diamond.

In the beginning she tried to steel herself against Dirk and
his confident, persuasive ways. But she could not refuse to see
him, did not want to, and with each new meeting her defenses
crumbled a little more. He behaved as if all the time in the
world were at his disposal and he could afford to wait. The
late August days were hot in Chicago and some evenings,
when she was free from her work on the paper, they would
walk down Michigan Avenue together or perhaps find their
way to the lake front along Grant Park. During these walks
he would often speak of South Africa, of Cape Town, and a
long-forgotten homesickness began to stir in her. With it there
came, in spite of herself, a softness and a yearning that
warned her of what was happening.

She had fallen in love two or three times before, rather
foolishly. There seemed in her a perversity that drew her to
someone who, for one reason or another, could not possibly
consider her seriously at the time. It was almost as if she had
protected herself by the very impossibility of the person on

whom her attention focused. As if she bided her time, playing at love, waiting. She did not want to go through this again. Dirk would soon be off to Cape Town and she must stay on here. With such reminders she tried to fight the softness in herself.

It was during this period that headlines began to shout of new violence in South Africa. Trouble had erupted fiercely in one of the squalid locations near Durban, and Susan showed Dirk the paper as further buttress against her returning to Cape Town.

"I don't think I'd want to live in South Africa now," she said. "There are so many terrible things happening there."

"This is in Cato Manor, where there's always been trouble," Dirk said. "It's a thousand miles from Cape Town."

"But there's been trouble in Cape Town too," she reminded him. "You can't shrug Langa aside."

"No one's shrugging it aside. Listen to me, Susan. You're talking to a South African now. The press here is never fair to us. Living in a place isn't like reading headlines. You'll find it's business as usual in Cape Town. The coloreds are on our side and you'll see very little agitation. It's an explosive and complex problem. Don't try to judge it sitting here in Chicago."

He was right, of course, and she let the matter go.

The time came, however, when Dirk dropped his pretense that the passing days were of no consequence.

"Susan, Susan, you must hurry!" he said. "If we wait too long we'll miss springtime in Cape Town. September and October are the most beautiful months in South Africa—we mustn't let them go."

One evening at her apartment, when she had given him dinner again, he spoke to her more brusquely than ever before.

"I must get back to Cape Town," he told her. "Your father needs me and I have my work to think about. This afternoon I booked my flight home. I'm leaving for New York at the end of the week."

A darkness of despair welled up in her and she found herself remembering that other departure when it had been Susan van Pelt leaving South Africa. But then she had been a child, helpless to stop what was happening. It was far worse to be grown and equally helpless. Yet because she was grown she must hide her feelings somehow. By an effort she kept her voice steady as she answered him.

"I'll miss you," she said and was proud of the fact that she

25

spoke lightly when there was so much hidden pain beneath the words. "But of course you must go. There's nothing but wasted time for you here."

He had taken a restless turn around the room and now came back to her with an unexpected light in his eyes, alive with all the dynamic energy that was so vital a part of him. He stood over her as he had done that first time he had visited her here and held her attention by the very force that seemed to move him.

"Believe me, Susan, I didn't ask for this to happen," he said. "It's going to complicate my life quite frightfully. I'm not sure I'm pleased about it. Yet I think I knew it was going to happen that first day when I stood on the tracks and watched you hopping about with a camera that was almost as big as you were."

She stared at him in dismay, not knowing what he meant, and he took something from his pocket and dropped it almost casually into her lap. It was a small blue and gold jeweler's box and she looked at it without touching it.

"Open it," he commanded.

She put a finger to the metal catch and raised the lid. A ring lay against the white satin—a thin gold ring with a polished pink stone in the raised setting.

"The jeweler said it was unheard of to mount an uncut stone," Dirk said, "but I thought you might like it that way. A bit of polishing has given it more of the look of a diamond. It means something to me this way—uncut. Does it fit, I wonder? I had it made for a very slim finger."

She looked up at him, unable to believe what was happening, and was startled to see the anxiety so clearly evident behind his quick impersonal manner. He was tense and a little fearful, not at all in proud control of his own emotions as she had believed. She found what she saw in his face more endearing than anything else might have been, and she held out her hand.

"Put it on my finger, please," she said.

All the angry impatience drained out of him and with it the uncertainty, leaving the engaging younger Dirk she remembered. He sat beside her and took the ring from the box, slipped it onto the third finger of her left hand. There was only tenderness in his manner, and a pleading.

"Now my luck is in your hands, darling," he said. "Treat it gently."

Not until she was in his arms did she truly believe in what was happening.

"I booked places for two on that flight to South Africa," he told her. "And space for two on the plane to New York. Though I've been terribly afraid I was going too far. Now there's the matter of your passport and inoculations, a marriage license, and all the rest. Let's go to New York and get on with it. Let's not waste another moment."

Get on with it they did. She would never have believed that she could break all the threads of her accustomed life with such dispatch and so joyously. Fortunately she had already packed or given away most of her mother's things. The apartment was sublet to a friend on the paper. Dirk drove her across the state line for a quicker marriage than could be arranged in the city, and Susan found herself on the plane for New York with a man who was now her husband.

In spite of the breathless quality of all that was happening, there was time for the happiness that lay between them. This, Susan knew, was what she had been waiting for all these lonely years. This was the answer to her nostalgia, to her sense of something left unfinished. She knew why no one else would ever do. In her was some guiding force wiser than conscious thought which had waited only for Dirk. Whatever South Africa held for her, she would now be able to face it because Dirk was part of her life, she of his. This was the most satisfying thing of all—his need of her, so tenderly clear.

Only now and then did she remember Niklaas van Pelt and try to bargain a little.

"If you're marrying me just to take me home to my father, you're making a mistake," she told him, teasing a little. "I still haven't promised to see him, you know."

Dirk was offhand. "We'll talk about that when the time comes. I've written Uncle Niklaas airmail about our change in plans. Though if I thought you were serious about the accusation you've just made—"

She kissed him warmly to prove that she had not been serious. His reassurance was hardly necessary. It was clear in his eyes, in his touch, that he was a man in love.

Their days in New York shone through a haze as pink as the diamond on her finger. She glowed with happiness and contentment and Dirk said she grew prettier every day.

The only part of her old life that she had brought with her was her own small 35mm. camera and Dirk humored her in her picture taking.

"So I've married a career woman, have I?" he laughed when she insisted that camera and light meter accompany her on their daytime jaunts. She explained gently, but with a cer-

27

tain firmness, that there was no reason why she should not continue to sell pictures to American and British magazines and papers. The eyes of the world were turned toward Africa these days.

She particularly enjoyed taking pictures of Dirk—shots that showed his bright, laughing quality and ignored the captious side that occasionally showed itself in an unexpected moment. At times she suspected that something was worrying him, something he kept from her, and that some problem awaited him in South Africa. She suspected that it might well concern her father. Perhaps he would disapprove of this sudden marriage of his ward to a daughter he did not know—the daughter of a woman who had left him. She hoped she was wrong if this meant hurt and a difficult situation for Dirk. But for the moment she could only try with all her heart to adjust to these moods of Dirk's and keep from questioning him. She did not, however, want to record such shadows with her camera. These were the sunny days, and must be captured as such.

It was still September, still spring in South Africa, when they boarded the big American plane at New York's International Airport. Even by jet it was a long and wearying trip, and Dirk had allowed for stopovers in Accra and Brazzaville. They left French Equatorial Africa in the early morning and set down in Johannesburg in midafternoon. Jo'burg was the port of entry—the City of Gold, "Goli," as the dark people called it—a relatively young and booming metropolis of great wealth and great poverty.

When they had gone through immigration and passports and baggage had been checked, they sat in the busy waiting room before huge bay windows of glass and watched planes taking off for every part of Africa and the world. They were truly in South Africa now, and Susan saw the SLEGS VIR BLANKES signs for the first time. Signs that were translated as "Europeans Only," "European" meaning "white." She winced at the signs just as she would have winced at similar signs in the American South.

All signs were given in the two languages of the country, and so were the announcements over loudspeakers. Susan had forgotten her Afrikaans, but as she listened, the sound of it began to return and it seemed not unfamiliar.

Once, to her surprise, Dirk's name was paged over the loudspeaker and he hurried away to pick up the message. When he returned he looked a little angry.

"Was it word from my father?" she asked.

"No." He shook his head. "It was merely a warning."

The word startled her. "A warning?"

"Oh, it's not as bad as all that," he said, managing a smile. "Someone thought I ought to know that John Cornish is going to Cape Town. He'll be aboard our plane."

He said nothing more and seemed to lose himself in his own remote thoughts, so that she was left wondering. Why had it seemed necessary to let Dirk know that Cornish would be aboard their plane? If the harm John Cornish had done lay in the past, how could his presence in South Africa affect her father now? And why had Dirk used the word "warning"?

When their flight to Cape Town was called, they started across the tarmac to a plane with a springbok symbol marking the nose. Suitably enough, since the South African gazelle with the curving horns had the habit of springing high into the air.

"I feel as though I were going too fast," Susan whispered, clinging to Dirk's arm. "Some of me is still back home. I haven't caught up with me yet."

Dirk did not hear her. He was watching a man up ahead mounting the steps to the plane.

"Look quickly," he said. "The tall chap up there wearing a gray topcoat—that's John Cornish. He'll be aboard, all right."

She looked in time to see the tall man vanish through the door. The glimpse of a straight back told her little and he was out of sight by the time a stewardess showed them to their seats.

"Do you know him well?" she asked, letting Dirk help her with her seat belt.

"I knew him as a boy," Dirk said.

"How well did he know my father?"

"Actually, he knew him very well. Cornish grew up on a veld farm near Kimberly and your half brother Paul was his closest friend. They were in the war together—as commandos."

"Tell me about my family," Susan said. "I know so little. It doesn't seem real that I've had half brothers and a half sister. I know the eldest boy died as a child, but I'm not sure about the others."

"Your sister married and went out to Australia to live," Dirk said. "Paul died in Italy during the war. Cornish was wounded at the same time and was shipped home to recover. He had a bad time with his leg and that put him out of the fighting. He still limps a bit. When he came home he went into the field that always interested him, journalism. Your fa-

29

ther eased his way more than once. Which made it all the harder for Uncle Niklaas to take when Cornish turned on him a year or so later."

The plane was taxiing into place for the take-off, and Susan forgot John Cornish and all that concerned him. In the days when she had lived in South Africa, the Blue Train had still been the main luxury accommodation, taking a good many hours to cover the thousand miles to Cape Town. Now the airplane was the popular and luxurious means of transportation.

The sign of the springbok was everywhere in the plane, woven into the green aisle carpet and into the seat covers. But this was a springbok turned Pegasus and Susan had yet to catch her breath. She was experiencing not only the normal difficulty of today's air passenger in keeping up with the speed of her flight but also the feeling in her own case of rushing too rapidly back into the past.

They flew over the crowded huddle of Johannesburg, where the white man had space and the black man did not. The strange yellow-white mounds of gold mine dumps loomed below, square with slanted sides, and then the plane was away, and Susan looked down upon open country. The green faded quickly and the veld spread below, a bare and tawny land, not yet wakened, as it would be briefly, by the touch of spring.

Africa had surprised her because, except for the equatorial belt, there had been so little jungle green. So much of the land was tan and dull gold and sometimes reddish. In the past it had been wholly lion country, of course, and that was still its color—the tawny yellow of the lion.

Dirk read a magazine, hardly glancing out the window at a view long familiar, but Susan, in the window seat, could not take her eyes from the scene that swept below the plane. Nothing as yet had brought a sense of recognition, but she knew that would come eventually. Ahead in Cape Town the mountain awaited her. She had never forgotten the mountain. Sometimes it came into her dreams, pressing vastly above her as if it would crush her by its very mass of high-thrust granite.

Before they reached Kimberley, dusk hid the land and in the great spreading darkness below there were few lights to be seen. The distances of Africa were immense and so often empty of human life.

"Talk to me," she pleaded, slipping a hand beneath Dirk's on the arm of the seat between them. "Africa frightens me a lit-

30

tle. It's rushing toward me over the years. Right now there's nothing but space and emptiness around me, but when I come down Africa will be waiting. And I'm not ready for it." She tried to laugh, but there was a catch in her throat.

He put aside his magazine and covered her fingers with his own. She leaned back in her seat and let the new delight of sensation that his touch could arouse sweep away obscure fears. For now, this was enough. Love was her protection for whatever awaited her in South Africa.

"What do you remember best about Cape Town?" he asked quietly, as if by the very softness of his tone he would avoid rousing her sleeping fears. "What do you remember of your father?"

She closed her eyes in order to invite the pictures. The mountain was there so easily, whenever she summoned it. And glimpses of the house in Cape Town—Protea Hill. She could remember Dirk too, flashing and out of the pictures with his bright fair hair and blue eyes. But when she tried to think of her father, to recall his face or even to summon back the look of her mother as she had been sixteen years ago, the vision blurred as if she had dropped pebbles into a pool, causing the surface to waver into distortion. With every throb of its engines the plane was hurling her toward her father and, though she had made no promise to see him, the inevitability of their meeting was there like a wall against which she was sure to fling herself. She dreaded the probable crash, and dared not think about it.

"Don't ask me to remember now," she said. "Let all that take care of itself when the time comes. Tell me about you instead. How did my father happen to take you as his ward?"

Dirk's fingers released her own and he stared unseeingly at the magazine in his lap. "My father, as you know, was a German," he said at length. "He was interned and I never saw him again because he died before the war was over. He had worked on the farm for your father. Afterwards my mother died. Of grief, I've always believed. Niklaas van Pelt took me into his home. It was a simple enough thing."

He spoke without emotion, yet Susan sensed a depth of feeling that denied the simplicity he claimed. There were dregs of painful memory in Dirk. She must learn to know these things a little at a time. The very learning meant a loving exploration. Only in the closeness of marriage could the delight of knowing another person be fully plumbed. But such

31

a plumbing could not be managed quickly. Falling in love was one thing. *Loving* was another. There must be growth and time for growth.

"Perhaps we should both leave the things that hurt alone until we really want to talk about them," she said. "I won't ask you again. I'll make a pact with you on that. There's plenty of time."

Dirk looked past her out the big oval of the window. "We're over Kimberley," he said, "and coming in for a landing."

The distraction served and she hardly noticed that he had agreed to no such pact on his part.

A stewardess announced that they would have approximately forty minutes on the ground and then the plane was taxiing along a runway of the small airport.

Dirk flung Susan's coat about her shoulders as they left the plane and she was grateful for its warmth. The spring night was cold, the air sharply invigorating.

MIND YOUR HEAD—PASOP U KOP. She saw the sign between two small buildings as they walked from the plane to the fenced enclosure where passengers might wait. After a look about inside the small restaurant, they returned to the brisk clear air and stood beneath the stars, content enough to be close to the earth for a little while.

Others from their flight stood about talking, or merely waiting, and Susan noted the smartness of South African women. They wore the furs and expensive suits and spiked heels of New York or London or Paris. Looking at them one felt merely a sense of recognition. Common fashions had a way of pulling the world together. One might trade hemispheres and seasons these days with scarcely a sense of the scene having changed. Only something inside her rushed and rushed, trying to catch up.

She had forgotten their fellow passenger until she saw John Cornish standing by the enclosure fence not far away. She recognized him at once from the photograph she had seen. Dirk saw him too and quickly turned his back toward the other man.

"He may try to speak if he sees me," Dirk said. "I'd rather avoid him. If he should come over and I have to introduce you, I shan't mention that you're Niklaas's daughter. Let's not get his journalist's nose pointed in our direction any more than it is."

Susan nodded her agreement, but she still felt puzzled. She saw Cornish leave the fence for a turn about the enclosure, saw him start past them, then glimpse at Dirk's averted head and stop.

"He's seen you," she murmured to Dirk and sensed the stiffening that went through him.

As the writer approached, she looked at him with frank curiosity and saw that he was to a great extent like his picture. There was a touch of gray in his dark hair and a craggy look to his brows and nose and well-defined chin. There was the same somber, relentless cast to his face that the picture had revealed, and even though he smiled as he held out his hand to Dirk, his expression did not light to true friendliness.

"What luck," he said. "I've been hoping to run into you again."

Dirk's hesitation was momentary before he took the other man's hand, but Susan suspected that Cornish was quite aware of his reluctance. He turned a look of surprise upon her as Dirk introduced her as his wife.

"You've married an American girl," he said. "My congratulations, Hohenfield."

He held out his hand to Susan and she was aware of the substance of his fingers as he took her own. They were lean and hard and there was a hint of wiry strength in their pressure. She remembered that this man had been a commando in the war and the knowledge was not reassuring.

"What luck to run into you," he said again to Dirk. "I've been hoping to see you. The letters I've written Niklaas van Pelt haven't been answered. I've done all I can with my book in Pretoria and Johannesburg. I'm going to Cape Town now and see if I can persuade van Pelt to see me. Will you intercede for me, Hohenfield?"

Dirk's shrug was casual as if he were close to the edge of being rude. "As you know, Uncle Niklaas makes his own rules. If he has determined not to see you, then I expect that is the end of it."

"It's not the end of it as far as I'm concerned," the other man said coolly. "If you're unwilling to give me your help, then I must do without it."

"Exactly," Dirk said.

The moment was sharp with antagonism on Dirk's part, though this fact seemed to slide off John Cornish as if he were totally indifferent to discouragement. Susan had the dismayed feeling that Dirk was quite capable of causing a scene if he lost his temper, and she spoke hurriedly to stave off a possible explosion.

"What sort of book are you writing this time, Mr. Cornish?" she asked with a little rush of false enthusiasm she did not intend.

His attention was clearly focused upon Dirk and there was the alertness in him of a man who could think and move quickly if he had to.

He answered without looking at her, almost absently. "It's a book about diamonds and South Africa."

"Another one?" Dirk's blond brows rose derisively. "Isn't there a surplus of books about diamonds already? Books on everything from the history of De Beers to diamond smuggling!"

John Cornish answered impassively, and there was something a little frightening about his refusal to take offense or yield his stand. This was a man who would make an implacable and dangerous enemy, Susan thought.

"It's possible that I have a different approach," he said. There was a pause, as if some crackling significance hung in the air between them. Then he turned to Susan with an air of having answered Dirk and dismissed him. "Kimberly is the right place for this talk of diamonds. You must come back another time and see something of the mines."

"I'd hate to go down into a mine," Susan said quickly, wanting to oppose this man because Dirk opposed him.

"Mines are only the beginning of the story," Cornish said. "The real excitement lies well aboveground. I suppose it's a truism to point out that diamonds are harmless enough in themselves. It's what men do with them that breeds the trouble. And that's what my book will be about."

A loudspeaker called them back to the plane, and Dirk took Susan's elbow, turning her away from John Cornish. But the other man came with them, walking along toward the plane as if he sensed no lack of welcome. Susan was aware of his slight limp, though he kept pace with them easily.

"I shall hope to see you in Cape Town," he said in the tone of a man who expected to be asked to tea.

Dirk made no answer and Susan walked uneasily between the two. This interchange had seemed to threaten her father in some way and she sensed that Dirk was resisting the other man's fixed purpose with an inward anger and stubbornness of his own. But none of this made sense to her and in any event it was not her affair. As long as possible she meant to avoid seeing Niklaas van Pelt. And in all likelihood she would never meet John Cornish again. It was ironic that she who so longed to avoid Niklaas should be confronted by a man whose only purpose seemed to be to force a meeting with her father.

When they were once more airborne, Susan gave herself over to the wifely duty of soothing Dirk's irritation.

"I don't blame you for disliking that man," she said. "The very fact that he would choose to be a commando makes me feel uncomfortable about him."

Dirk did not take to such soothing. "Why should you feel uncomfortable? It requires courage to make a commando. Some of the first commandos were ancestors of mine—on my Afrikaner mother's side."

When she glanced at him blankly, he went on.

"That's where the word comes from. The men who went along with the voortrekkers as fighting men, as guards, were called commandos. It was a designation of bravery and honor."

"You sound as though you were defending John Cornish," Susan said in bewilderment.

"I'm defending him only on the score of an unreasonable feminine attack," Dirk said. "I have no use for him and I mean to keep him away from your father. But not, my darling—" he gave her a quick, exasperated look "—not because he was briefly a commando in the war."

Susan lapsed into hurt silence, convinced for a moment that men were given to being unreasonable, ungrateful and unfair. But when the numerous dinner courses began to be served she recovered in spite of herself, and Dirk seemed to regret his sharpness.

"We're both tired after a long trip," he said penitently. "John Cornish isn't worth quarreling over."

One of the likable things about Dirk was his regret when he had hurt her and the eagerness with which he made up for any momentary loss of temper. She knew that he was volatile and high-strung; indeed these very qualities were part of the attraction he held for her, part of a personality that would never be stodgy and dull. She must learn to wait for the gentler mood, the contrition that would always come if she gave him time.

She quickly regained a happier state as Dirk began to describe the dark invisible land over which they were flying. They were above the tawny veld that bloomed so briefly in spring with a vast carpet of wildflowers. The veld with those unexpected hills that from the plane looked like no more than small bubbles thrust up from the landscape. He complimented her on remembering that "veld" was pronounced "felt" in the proper Afrikaans way.

He told her of the mountains that rose where the land descended from the high central plateau of Africa to a lower plateau—like giant steps descending to the sea. And at last of the jagged peaks that guarded the Cape Peninsula and the final downward drop to the level of the Atlantic.

Now there were lights to be seen below—the clustered lights of towns—and all through the plane passengers began to stir and take down their parcels, put on their coats.

"Someone may meet us," Dirk said. "I wired your father the plane we would take."

Susan glanced at him in surprise. They were coming down now, descending in a gentle slant.

"Do you mean that my father might come to the airport?" she asked, disturbed at the thought. "You should have warned me. I—I'm not ready—"

"I doubt that Niklaas himself will come," Dirk said, and there seemed a sudden tension in him that she did not understand. He reached for her hand where it lay on the seat arm between them. "Susan dear—" he began and then broke off.

"Is something wrong?" she asked in dismay. "I mean about my father? Something you haven't told me?"

His fingers tightened upon her hand. "Darling, will you trust me? Just trust me, that's all. As long as you're with me, we'll work things out, I promise you."

Lights were rushing toward them and in a moment the runway markers were flying past and the plane's wheels had touched the concrete with a faint jar.

Susan could feel the thudding of her heart as the plane rolled to a stop and she got into line in the aisle to move with Dirk toward the exit. This was not really Cape Town yet, she reminded herself. Malan Airport was at a distance from the city and not even the mountain could be seen through the darkness. The moment of recognition could not come until morning and she would be better prepared for it then.

They did not see John Cornish among the passengers as they went through the barrier gates and into the broad main hall of the handsome building. Dirk moved toward the luggage pickup without so much as a glance about to see if anyone had come to meet them. Susan went with him, keeping close to his side, feeling that she was truly in a strange land now. The tension she had noted in the plane was still upon Dirk, and an impatience too, as if he were braced for something which might prove to be an ordeal and which he resented having to face.

As he pointed out their bags and was handing over the checks, Susan saw a man and a woman approaching the luggage counter. The woman had seen Dirk and she walked with a purposeful step that carried her directly toward him. She was young, less than thirty perhaps, and strikingly attractive, with a complexion that was clear and glowing. Bareheaded, she wore her heavy fair hair coiled in a loose knot at the nape of her neck. A smartly styled tan coat hung carelessly from her shoulders and her slender feet were encased in high-heeled brown pumps. Susan's eye for pictorial detail registered her as remarkably photogenic.

Just behind followed a light-skinned colored man in a chauffeur's uniform. A man who was possibly about Dirk's age. Again her quick eye noted detail—the fact that he was fine looking and carried himself well. Yet she had seldom seen a face so carefully devoid of feeling, so guarded in expression.

Susan touched Dirk's arm and he turned and saw the two as they reached him. The air of defensive waiting was still upon him, but he made an effort to appear friendly.

"Mara!" he exclaimed. "I wondered if you would come. This is my wife, Susan. Miss Bellman. Good evening, Thomas. Will you help us with the bags?"

The colored man answered his greeting with a touch of finger to cap and stepped up to the counter to reach for the bags Dirk indicated. Mara Bellman smiled brightly at Dirk.

"Congratulations and all that sort of thing," she said, and turned her violet gaze upon Susan. "Welcome to Cape Town. I'm your father's secretary and general assistant. I'll have to confess that Dirk's marriage has taken us a bit by—surprise."

Susan tried to return her smile, but her lips felt stiff. "I suppose it has taken us by surprise too," she admitted.

She wanted to ask about her father's reaction to their marriage, but a restraint lay upon them all, something unspoken but real, and she said nothing.

"Let's get along to the car," Dirk said. "We're both fagged and this is no place to talk."

Thomas picked up the bags and started toward the doors. They followed him into the cool night air, walking briskly toward the car. But now, having dismissed her father in her own mind, Susan slipped a hand through the crook of Dirk's elbow, drawing him back.

"Tell me," she whispered, "which way is Cape Town?"

He understood and his impatience faded. "It's that way. To our right. You can see the lights. By daylight you could see the mountain from here. But that will have to wait until morning. At least there's the Southern Cross. Do you remember it?"

He pointed and she looked up at the dark, star-tossed sky, her eyes searching eagerly until she found the constellation—like a small kite in the heavens. Not particularly impressive, yet capable of rousing in her a choked sense of emotion. She could recall a dark night away from the lights of the city, and someone showing a little girl the Southern Cross for the first time. Had it been her father?

The old, unappeased longing, the nostalgia, was upon her again—for what she could not tell. Dirk felt her shiver and slipped an arm about her.

"Come along, darling," he whispered.

She went with him toward the car. The sense of space rushing dizzily away had ceased. She was here and Cape Town was waiting for her.

It has to go well, she told herself. We must make it go well. But the uneasiness would not leave her.

3

During the drive Mara made an attempt at light conversation, though Dirk helped very little, lost again in his own thoughts. Her accent was wholly South African, Susan noted, with much of the English in it, yet with a slurring of syllables that she remembered from the past.

Dirk broke into the middle of Mara's words as if he had not noticed that she was speaking.

"What did Uncle Niklaas have to say about our news?" he asked.

Mara was quiet for a moment. Then she began again, as if summoning up her bright, animated tones. "He hasn't talked about it, actually. But at least he has been making preparations and giving orders madly. For tonight you are to be taken directly to the hotel. You're to come to see him late tomorrow morning, Dirk. That will give you time to move out of the hotel and into the Aerie before you come to his place."

"The Aerie?" Dirk sounded surprised.

The movement of Mara's blond head in assent was graceful, but there was a hint of spite in her voice. "He thought you would want to be by yourselves. And the Aerie is vacant. Not too far away either. It should be convenient."

"At seventy-odd," Dirk said to Susan, "your father has lost none of his tendency to highhanded action. But at least this will spare us the need to do any house hunting immediately."

"What is the Aerie?" Susan asked.

"It's a smaller house your father owns," Dirk said, "and not as pretentious as it sound. Sometimes he houses visiting buyers there. One of the things you'll have to get used to in Cape Town is the way we name our houses, instead of giving them numbers. If a stranger wants to find a house, all he can do is ring bells along the street until he locates it. This house is furnished and in good repair—I had a look at it myself not long ago."

"We've added a few touches to make you more comfortable," Mara told him, still brightly vivacious. "We moved down some extra furniture from Protea Hill and we've fixed up a little office with your desk in it, Dirk. And your clothes have been sent down, of course. The servants won't be there till tomorrow, which is why you can't move in tonight."

"You have been busy," Dirk said, his tone dry. He turned to Susan. "We're following Rhodes Drive. The road curves around Devil's Peak just above us on our left. The mists have started down, so you can't see the peak tonight."

She knew her directions now. The unseen mountains curved like a broken amphitheater, she remembered, with Devil's Peak and the Lion's Head making the two opposite wings and reaching down toward Table Bay. Though the sky was still starry, clouds blanked out the peaks and to her disappointment she could not see Table Mountain itself—the mountain of her memory. Nevertheless, she knew it stretched hugely between the two wings, forming backdrop and stage. Cape Town itself filled the spectators' seats and spread around the Lion's Head to the suburbs on the sea. Cape Town tonight was a panorama of brilliance fanned out below the drive, extending to the far rim of lights that edged the bay.

It was beautiful, but it did not speak to her. She must still wait until tomorrow for a glimpse of the mountain. Only then could she know she had come home.

The car, a right-hand drive, had been following the left side of the road in the British manner. Now it turned left through tall Grecian columns that marked the impressive entrance to the hotel. It climbed the curving drive past centered palm trees and came to a halt before the front door. They were close beneath the mountain now, but the mist had thickened,

39

reaching down the lower slopes, and there was nothing to be seen except the bright pink hotel façade looming among the palm trees.

Mara came into the lobby with them and stepped efficiently to the desk to make sure that all was in order with their reservation. When Dirk was signing the register, Susan walked a little way into the lounge to look about.

This was the after-dinner hour and men and women of varied ages, the women well cloaked against the chill in mink stoles, were enjoying coffee at small tables scattered through the long, high-ceilinged room. The well-bred atmosphere of an English novel prevailed, except that these people seemed more sensitive to the cold than any true Englishman would have been.

Once assured that all was well, Mara bade Dirk and Susan a somewhat hurried good night and returned to the car. A boy took them upstairs in the small lift. Their room had a surprisingly cozy air about it, and less of the impersonal quality of most hotel rooms. After the chilly halls, the warm glow of an electric heater made them welcome.

There was still a strangeness about Dirk. Susan wanted to cry, "We're here!" and go straight into his arms the moment the boy had gone. But now he kept his distance and made an effort at casual conversation that held her away.

"I'm fond of this hotel," he said. "They go in for old-fashioned British comfort of the sort that used to be demanded by officers who served in India and spent their holidays in Cape Town. There was no nonsense about those old boys when they wanted something."

He was still much too keyed up and clearly as afraid of silence as Mara had seemed to be in the car. But Susan could hold herself away from him no longer, and slipped her arms about his neck.

"What is it?" she asked, her cheek against his. "Ever since the plane started down you've been waiting—as if you expected something unpleasant to happen."

"It has happened," he told her. He held her to him briefly and kissed her cheek, but the evidence of being wound up did not leave him. He had withdrawn from her in some strange way and instinct warned her not to push him when such a mood was upon him. Whatever was wrong, he would not talk to her now. And for the moment, in spite of her disappointment in this entire homecoming, she was almost too weary to care.

It was wonderful to get out of her clothes and into the

white-tiled bathroom. She turned on the oversized taps in the enormous English tub, dropped in the big chained plug, and gave herself up to the luxury of steaming hot water. Afterwards she crept between sheets warmed by a hot-water bottle, and pulled the blankets and slippery satin puff over her. She was sound asleep by the time Dirk came to bed, and she slept longer than he did the next morning.

She awakened lazily to the waiter's knock and watched him bring in a breakfast tray with covered silver dishes and a coffee pot. He set up a table in discreet silence and bowed himself away. Dirk was up and already shaved, his fair hair sleek and darkened from the water, his skin glowing above the towel wrapped around the neck of his terry-cloth robe. Susan lay watching him through half-closed eyes, savoring the novelty of wifehood, wishing he would forget about breakfast and come to tell her how much he loved her. His manner, however, was brisk and impersonal.

When the waiter had gone, he poured a cup of coffee, weakened it with the usual English touch of hot milk, sugared it too generously, and brought it to her.

"This will wake you up," he said, plumping her pillow so that she could sit up in bed. "I ordered breakfast up here so we could make an early start. How are you feeling this morning?"

She wasn't sure as yet, but she tried to answer cheerfully that she was fine. The diluted coffee was a little sickening to her taste, but she did not want to offend him by pouring it out and starting over with a strong black cup that would shock her awake. Somehow he could never believe that she liked her coffee black or that she preferred to get up and wash and dress before she had anything at all.

He turned to the window to fling draperies open to the daylight, and she watched hopefully. If the day was bright and sunny, perhaps her spirits would rise correspondingly. But from the bed she could see now that the sky was white with solid clouds, the early morning gray and drab.

When she slipped from under the covers and went to the window, she found that their room faced the bay, with the mountain out of sight behind. To her left the Lion's Head was hidden by clouds—an omen of continued bad weather, she remembered—and mist curled along the flank that stretched toward the bay and was known as Signal Hill. The red roofs and white houses of Cape Town lay spread beneath the window, with the big buildings of the downtown section making an island in themselves near the shore of Table Bay. But there was no bright color in the scene today, no sunshine to cheer her, no lifting of her spirits. And no sense at all of recognition, of coming home. Shivering, she turned back to the electric heater.

Dirk was serving a portion of omelet onto her plate, offering toast in the silver rack that assured its arriving cold.

"Let's hurry a bit," he said, the touch of impatience in his manner no longer hidden. "I'd like enough time to get you over to the house and settled before I go to see your father."

She sat down obediently and tried to eat. But the sense of things going wrong made a lump of discouragement in her throat and it was hard to swallow.

At least Dirk had made no suggestion that she go with him to see Niklaas van Pelt, and she was grateful for that.

While she was dressing in a gray-wool suit against the chill that the electric heater did not entirely dispel, the telephone rang and Dirk answered it. Miss Bellman was waiting for them downstairs with the car and the news gave no lift to Susan's spirits.

As they went down and out to the car, she felt increasingly depressed. Nothing seemed auspicious for the beginning of their married life together in Cape Town. Nothing was going right or turning out as she had hoped it would.

This morning Mara was alone and at the wheel of the long gray Mercedes. Susan and Dirk joined her in the front seat and once more Susan was aware of the girl's vital beauty, her assurance and air of efficiency. She seemed enormously alive, and by contrast Susan felt drained of vitality.

"Your car's ready for you whenever you want to come to Protea Hill to drive it away," Mara told Dirk. "I suppose you'll pick it up this morning when you come to see Mr. van Pelt?"

Dirk nodded. "I'll be glad to have it back. Susan, unfortunately, doesn't drive. Her education has been neglected."

Susan smiled weakly and gave her attention to this old section of Cape Town through which they were driving. The streets were narrow and took unexpected turns up and down steep hills. White cottages, built in the old Dutch style with gabled fronts, were visible on every hand, and there were glimpses of lacy wrought-iron balconies and fences that suggested Spain more than Holland. Rain drizzled across the windshield and mist still shrouded the mountain. Everywhere people were hurrying to work and there were many dark faces among the light. In their dress the people on the sidewalks and in the double-decker buses looked like those one saw in New York or Chicago. This might have been a rainy day anywhere, except for an occasional native blanket or Moslem veil. Whatever lay behind headlines which had been shouted across the world was not visible on the surface this morning in Cape Town.

The car was taking a general uphill course in the direction of the Lion's Head and at length it pulled up before a two-story stucco house with Spanish arched windows and a red-tiled roof.

"I've found a cookie for you," Mara said as they got out of the car, and Susan remembered the familiar name used for cooks. "And a Bantu boy for the yard. By tomorrow I'll have your housemaid and I'll bring her up myself. Hope you can make do till then."

They would barely be able to endure, Susan thought wryly, and reminded herself at once that these were different ways and she must be grateful for all that Mara was doing to make them comfortable.

"You've been efficient, as always," Dirk said pleasantly, covering Susan's silence.

Mara got out of the car in her brisk way, slamming the door after her. She seemed displeased as she went ahead of them through a gate of iron grillwork set in a white stone wall. Following her, while Dirk watched the Bantu boy unloading the bags, Susan noted a small bricked courtyard with a delphinium border. The steps to the arched door were shallow and at the top she walked directly into a wide hall with a darkly polished floor, its gleam unhidden by rugs. At the rear a staircase railed in iron grillwork turned at right angles and disappeared toward the floor above.

Mara ran ahead up the stairs to fling open doors in the upper hall. Moving after her more slowly, Susan had the increasing sense that this was wrong as a homecoming. Dirk was not even at her side. Another woman showed the way, another woman had made all the preparations of welcome, had arranged both flowers and furnishings. She tried to brush such unreasonable resentment aside. Later there would be time to acquaint herself with the house and make it her own and Dirk's.

Upstairs Mara had chosen a room for them and furnished it with linens and freshly hung curtains and draperies. Her high heels clicked across the polished wood of the floors as she explained this and that, and called orders to the Bantu boy to bring up the bags.

43

"You may have a little trouble getting him to understand," Mara said, speaking to the boy in Afrikaans. "But Cookie is one of our coloreds and she knows English, so you can get her to translate. If you'll excuse me, I'll run down and show Dirk his office."

Susan thanked the native boy as he set the bags down in obedience to her gesture, and he went away, moving quietly on bare black feet.

The bedroom was pleasantly spacious, but undistinctive, with twin beds, dressing table and bureau, a wardrobe closet. Like fashions in clothes, furniture also pulled the hemispheres together, making it easier to forget other differences. Only the wardrobe closet—a wide armoire—set this room apart. Yet there was, Susan felt, a wrong note about the whole. The over-flowered draperies did not quite harmonize with the spreads. The furniture seemed placed without thought for balance. It was as though an unfriendly hand had arranged everything on a purposely jarring key.

There were windows on two sides, so at least there should be a fine view on a clear day. Now they overlooked a world of mist. Leaning on the sill of a window on the garden side, Susan found that the house was perched high on the lip of what appeared to be a dry, woodsy ravine. Beneath her window stretched lawn and garden, with a retaining wall at the back. Beyond, the hill dropped steeply away to the deep recesses of the ravine. There mist wreathed the flat, parasol tops of a thick stand of Mediterranean pines. Some distance below were other houses on the far side where the hill climbed up from the slit of the ravine. "Aerie" might not be a very original name, but Susan could see that for this house it was appropriate.

She pulled off the small soft hat she had traveled in and ran a comb through her russet hair. Then she went out of the bedroom and down the stairs.

Mara and Dirk stood near the front door, engaged in earnest conversation, speaking softly as if what they discussed was private. Some instinct of warning halted her on the stairs. She remembered Mara's forced volubility in the car yesterday and Dirk's rising uneasiness as the plane came in to land. Then too there was Mara's almost officious manner of taking over the preparations in this house, and the jarring touches Susan had sensed in the bedroom. The work perhaps of a woman whose intent was not wholly amiable? Disturbed and alert now to anything that might lie beneath the surface, Susan went down the stairs.

44

Mara heard her step and looked up, her lovely face blank of any emotion. Whatever her words had been with Dirk, their import was not visible in her expression.

"Mr. van Pelt expects to see you tomorrow, Mrs. Hohenfield," she said matter-of-factly. "Suppose I call for you in the car right after lunch?"

The tide of warning did not subside in Susan. This was too sudden, too soon. She would not be managed like this against her will and she did not believe a visit to her father had been the entire subject of this whispered conversation.

Before she could object, however, Dirk spoke quickly. "That will be fine, Mara. My wife will be ready."

The other woman gave Susan a bright, slightly vacant smile and went to the door. "I'll leave you then. You won't need the car to get over this morning, Dirk?"

"I know the way on foot," Dirk said, his voice dry.

Mara ran down the flagged walk and got into the car. With a careless wave of her hand she pulled away from the curb.

"I will *not* be ready," Susan told Dirk in a low, indignant voice. "You had no right to arrange this without consulting me. I'm not ready to see my father."

Dirk closed the door upon the damp mists. He put a hand beneath her small stubborn chin and tilted it upward.

"I'm sorry, darling. This has been a bleak homecoming for you, hasn't it? I know you didn't mean to see your father so quickly. But it's better to get it over with and put it behind you. He expects you."

She refused to be appeased. "I don't like that woman! I don't like it a bit that she has arranged everything in this house to please herself. And now she's trying to manage me!"

To Susan's surprise Dirk put his head back and laughed. "I do believe you're jealous," he said.

She stared at him angrily, realizing that she was off on the wrong foot but not knowing how to make a graceful recovery.

He put an arm about her and drew her to him as they started upstairs. "You have my permission to put her down all you like," he said. "She's a bossy piece, and if you don't care for her arrangements in this house you have only to change them. Otherwise, don't give her a thought."

The relief that flowed through her washed away her anger. If he felt like this, then Mara didn't matter at all.

Upstairs in the bedroom Dirk returned to the subject of her father. "Don't forget that this meeting will be as much of an ordeal for your father as for you. Especially since he won't be able to see you."

45

Susan turned from arranging her toilet articles on the dressing table. "Not see me? What do you mean?"

"You know that he's blind," Dirk said.

"Blind? Of course I didn't know!" Susan stared at him in dismay. "You never mentioned it. You never told me—"

"How could I, when you always stopped me from talking about your father? Besides, I'd supposed—"

She walked away from him and stood at the window that overlooked the ravine and the parasol tops of the pine trees. But she saw nothing of the view before her. As though a curtain had been rolled up, her father's face had flashed back into her mind more clearly than at any time since Dirk had found her in Chicago and wakened long-suppressed thoughts of Niklaas van Pelt. Her father's eyes had been gray, with a direct, penetrating look about them. They were eyes that could see through you quite clearly—or so she had believed as a child. It had always been difficult to keep a secret from him or to deceive him in any way. Her mother saw only what she chose to see, but Niklaas van Pelt saw the truth. And with every child that was sometimes a thing to be hidden. It seemed unbelievable that so clear and vigorous a look was now quenched forever. She would need to fear his eyes no longer. She had been fearing them, she realized. Yet the thought brought her no relief, only a sad stabbing of pain.

"I'm sorry if I've shocked you," Dirk said gently. "I had no idea that you didn't know. After all, he's quite an old man now, and he has been accustomed to being blind for many years. It hasn't changed him, except that sometimes he must be more dependent than he likes to be. But that is what I am for—and Mara too."

As he spoke he moved in and out of the adjoining bathroom, putting his shaving things in the cupboard over the washbasin, setting a bottle of shaving lotion on a shelf. Susan followed him into the room that was so much larger than most American bathrooms, and reached for a glass. Shock had left her a little sick, though she was not sure why. Long ago her father had been dismissed from her life, from her affection and her fears. Why should it matter now to learn suddenly that an old man whom she no longer knew, who was nothing to her in a personal way, had long been without his sight? Why should the knowledge give her this feeling of faintness?

She reached for the cold-water faucet to fill the glass, but somehow her grip was insecure and the glass flew out of her

46

hand, struck a corner of the wash basin, shattering on the floor. She stared at the debris with a sense of horror that was out of proportion to the damage done.

"No harm," Dirk said. "The glass doesn't matter. But perhaps you'd better sweep it up so we won't step on it later."

Awkwardly she obeyed. There was a hand brush in a cabinet and she knelt on the floor, sweeping the bits of glass into a pile. Her fingers were shaking ridiculously, though she tried to hide their trembling from Dirk. Her tendency to drop things and then be upset out of all proportion to the damage was a senseless weakness of which she was ashamed, and she was glad that Dirk was preoccupied and did not seem to notice.

When he was ready to leave for her father's, she went with him to the door and he kissed her, tweaked her ear affectionately, and went off down the street. She watched him out of sight, not altogether reassured. In more ways than one she had behaved badly this morning and the knowledge depressed her.

The cook, a small, brown-skinned woman with a *doek* about her head—the white kerchief draped in the special manner of South Africa—came in to ask about lunch. Susan tried to be friendly, but the woman seemed uncertain of a strange American, and ill at ease. She must fix whatever she liked, Susan told her. Whatever was available. Such vagueness in an employer was clearly unfamiliar to the woman and again Susan felt inadequate. How could she manage to cope with the duties this house would demand when she was at a loss when it came to so small a task as giving directions to the cook?

When the woman had gone doubtfully back to her kitchen, Susan began to look about the downstairs portion of the house. The dining room seemed dark on this gray day and she spent no time there, but went on to the living room. This promised to be cheerful and attractive. A big bay window with a cushioned seat beneath it overlooked Cape Town. There was a higher, wider view to be had here than she had seen this morning from her hotel window. The room possessed a small fireplace too and, while the furnishings were undistinctive and lacking in color, a good deal could be done with personal touches.

Pictures always helped bare and characterless walls. This, at least, was a start she might make in the right direction. There were a few of her mounted photographs in her bag upstairs. Dirk had objected to their weight but she had wanted them with her. They would help to make her feel at home. Glad of a purpose to occupy her, she ran up to the bedroom and got the photographs from her bag.

Four of them, well arranged against the end wall, would lighten the room with their white mats and lend a spot of interest that would not be wholly impersonal. She carried the stack of photographs—some eight or ten in all—down to the living room and spread them out on the floor. There she knelt before them to make her choice.

A little pang of homesickness went through her at sight of these Chicago scenes and she braced herself against it. She was where she wanted to be—with Dirk. Wherever he was, there she would make her home.

News pictures seldom came out best for her. She liked to try for good ones, but she knew she was still very much an amateur. Sometimes such a picture was inherently dramatic because of the circumstances involved. But when she was photographing a person it was possible to take more care and obtain a more striking graphic effect. She picked up her favorite picture of the aged newsdealer at his stand and studied it with pleasure.

A sudden ringing of the doorbell made her jump. She dropped the picture and stood up as if she were a child discovered playing with forbidden toys. Unaccustomed to servants, and not sure of her own role, she wondered if she was supposed to let one of them answer the bell. But nothing happened and there was another ring. Probably neither the yard boy nor the cook was expected to answer the front door, and she would not have a housemaid until tomorrow, Mara had said. She went to the door herself and opened it.

Silhouetted against the gray morning stood John Cornish, tall and angular and grave. He said nothing for a moment, his deepset eyes observing her as though he might expect some show of displeasure.

"G-good morning," Susan faltered, taken aback. After the antagonism that Dirk had shown toward this man in the Kimberley airport, Cornish was the last person she had expected to see, and so quickly, on her own doorstep.

"Good morning," he said. "May I come in?" His mouth was straight and unsmiling, his look knowing as if he fully understood the predicament he placed her in.

She did not move from the doorway. "Dirk isn't at home. If you've come to see him—"

"I haven't," he said calmly. "I've come to see you, Mrs. Hohenfield."

48

She knew very well that Dirk would not want this man in his house, but there seemed no way to refuse him entry without being ruder than she was able to be. Had he found out that she was Niklaas van Pelt's daughter and come on that account to further his aims?

Wordlessly she gestured him into the hall and took his damp coat to hang on the hall rack. Then she led the way reluctantly into the living room where her pictures lay spread across the floor. When Dirk found out about this visit, she would be in for his displeasure, she was very sure. She hated to try his patience further. Why did John Cornish have to add to her problems on this gray, uneasy day?

4

"I won't keep you guessing," Cornish said as he followed her into the living room sidestepping the pictures. "I don't suppose you've had an opportunity to meet Mr. van Pelt yet, but of course you will be meeting him shortly."

So he didn't know her identity as yet. She invited him to a chair, sat down on the window seat, and waited in silence for him to go on.

"Your husband seems to have prejudiced himself against me without a hearing," Cornish continued, watching her keenly from beneath craggy brows. "But you are an unprejudiced newcomer on the scene, and an American besides. Is it possible that you might hear me out on this?"

"What has my being an American to do with it?" she asked.

He permitted himself a frosty smile. "I live in America now, you know. And I've found American wives often given to independent thoughts and decisions of their own."

She did not want to be an American wife, she wanted only to be loyal to Dirk, and this man's presence in the house already involved her in something close to disloyalty. She must be rid of him quickly.

"All this is my husband's affair, not mine," she told him. "If you are here to ask me to intervene and try to arrange a meeting for you with—with Mr. van Pelt, you're asking the impossible."

"I see." The look of appraisal was still in his eyes and she had the sudden instinct that he was here not merely for the obvious purpose which he had stated but for some further reason that he did not mean to tell her. She suspected that he had never believed she would really go against Dirk's wishes. The uneasiness she felt in his presence increased.

He glanced at the photographs which lay spread in a row near his feet. "Interesting," he said. "Do you mind if I look?"

She shook her head helplessly. It was clear that telling him she minded would do little good.

He picked up the picture she had taken of a fire on Chicago's West Side, and held it up to the light, studying it. "What a good shot. Fortune certainly played into your hands."

She prickled to her own defense. "Even shots of dramatic circumstances don't always come out well. A news photographer has to be quick to see a picture, and he has to have the patience to wait."

"Granted." He set the photograph down and picked up another—the one of the newsdealer that she liked best. "A good friend of mine in New York does news stories on assignment for a big magazine. I've gone the rounds with him a few times and he has helped me with occasional photos for my books. I find there's a similarity in some ways between the journalist's approach and a photographer's."

Casually he carried the picture over to her. "Take this shot, for instance." He held it out for her to see, though she knew it by heart. "Here you didn't quite wait for the story, I think."

She could understand very well why Dirk did not like this man. He was a person who did not hesitate to speak his mind, no matter what toes might be stepped on.

"What do *you* think the real picture should have been?" she asked stiffly.

He tapped the photograph with one long finger. "This is good composition and interesting in itself, but not particularly revealing. You've caught a well-balanced shot of an old man with a tired face working behind a stack of newspapers, but you haven't told us much about him. You didn't wait for the moment when his expression would light up and come to life —either over a sale, or in disgust at a customer, or some other way that might show what he's like as a person."

"Doesn't his face show that?" Susan demanded. "After all, he has lived his face."

Cornish shrugged. "You're annoyed with me, aren't you?

Not that I blame you. I had no business popping off like that."

"I sold the picture," Susan said more quietly.

"You should have, of course. It's worth printing." He leaned toward the row of pictures and replaced the one he held. "You're very good, you know. Don't take the words of an amateur critic too seriously. If you keep on you'll be able to laugh at the critics."

She wanted to resent his words, to consider him rude and officious, but he gave her a slow, grave smile that lessened the somber quality of his face, and she felt herself unexpectedly disarmed. It was true that he spoke from a position of greater maturity and experience. However, her very softening toward him put her on guard again. It was his purpose, of course, to disarm her.

"How did you know where to find us?" she asked. "How did you know I would be alone?"

His sardonic left eyebrow quirked. "A good reporter never reveals his private sources. It wasn't particularly difficult to manage. Do you mind if we talk a bit about Niklaas van Pelt?"

She saw that she was neatly caught and must either be as rude as she should have been in the first place or hear him out. At least she would not tell him that Niklaas was her father. His private sources had not revealed everything and she wanted no place as Niklaas's daughter in this book John Cornish was writing.

"I'd like to finish my work here as quickly as I can," he went on. "That's why I've let no grass grow under my feet. I want to get out of South Africa and back to the States."

"You were born here, weren't you? Isn't South Africa your home, even more than the States?"

Cornish frowned. "It was Mr. van Pelt we were going to talk about."

"You were going to talk about him, not I," Susan said.

"Exactly. As I mentioned in Kimberley, I'm writing a book about diamonds and what they can do to men. It's the men I am interested in more than the diamonds. One of the men who had an influence on the diamond business, and was affected by it in turn, is Niklaas van Pelt. He belongs in the book. His name will run through it and he will have a chapter given over to him, whether he likes it or not."

"As I understand it," Susan said quietly, "you had a hand in injuring him rather seriously some sixteen years ago. Haven't you done enough?"

He was silent for a moment and she sensed again the re-

51

lentless determination in this man, though exactly where it led she was not sure.

"If what happened can stand unchallenged, then that is what I shall write," he said. "But there were certain aspects of the affair that I have never understood. Perhaps van Pelt can be persuaded to talk about them now."

He would have gone on, but Susan heard the sound of a key in the front door and knew that Dirk had come home.

"Here is my husband," she said. "You had better talk to him."

Cornish stood up. "I doubt that he'll listen to me, but I will see you again."

Before she could say that she had no intention of seeing him again, Dirk was in the room. At the sight of John Cornish he threw Susan a questioning look and faced the other man, antagonism bristling as it had before.

"What do you want here?" he demanded.

Cornish answered without hesitation. "I want an appointment with Niklaas van Pelt."

"You'd better realize," Dirk said, his voice tight with anger, "that I will arrange no such appointment. Mr. van Pelt does not wish to see you under any circumstances."

"He has answered none of my letters, and I quite understand how he may feel," Cornish said calmly. He went into the hall, took his coat from the rack and bowed gravely to Susan. As Dirk opened the door for him, he paused for a moment longer. "Nevertheless," he added, "I will manage to see him."

Susan returned to the living room and stood staring absently at the row of pictures on the floor. She felt not a little frightened by the anger in Dirk's face. Anger that might now be directed at her. She braced herself against whatever was to come. In some long-ago time she had learned to retreat from angry words, to shut herself away in a world of her own making where violence could not reach her. But Dirk's anger was cold and nonexplosive—the outburst did not come. Perhaps the deepest anger was always deadly cold, and all the more alarming for that very fact.

"Susan—" his very tone was chill—"I will not have that man in my house. He's not to be trusted. Whether you care about your father or not doesn't matter. I am deeply concerned about protecting him from the harm this man may do. Cornish spells disaster for all of us. Do you understand me?"

She looked at him distantly, unable to return at once from

the inward retreat to which she had withdrawn. For a long moment he faced the remoteness in her eyes, then he went abruptly from the room and she heard the sharp closing of the door as he left the house.

She pressed her fingers to her temples and felt the pain of sensation flooding back. What was happening? What had gone so wrong between herself and Dirk that suddenly they did not understand each other? Why had she not gone to him quickly and promised whatever he wished, since that was all that really mattered?

Something nebulous and threatening seemed to crowd about her, gathering like mists on the mountain, menacing all her new-found happiness in some dreadful way. If Dirk stopped loving her, there would be nothing left—only empty loneliness again, and all her hopes ended. Yet at the core of her there was a small, hard spot of anger—not cold like his, but hot and bitter. She could not be wholly meek in her loving. If she had the scene with John Cornish to relive, she would be forced to do again as she had done and ask him into the house. There had been no harm in her action, no complete justification for Dirk's attitude toward this man.

Unless? "Disaster for all of us," Dirk had said, and the sharp chill of his voice seemed to linger in the room.

With a sweeping gesture she gathered up the photographs and carried them upstairs. She did not want to hang any just now. There was no comfort for her in looking at them.

When Cookie came to tell her that lunch was served, she went downstairs and sat at the dining table alone. It was hard to swallow, and sugar beans, cooked with meat and served over rice, tasted as flat as her spirits. Which was not Cookie's fault. She tried to pretend an appetite she did not feel, and lectured herself firmly as she ate.

John Cornish had spoken of her as an American wife. The fact that she had married a South African husband must also be considered. The English husband and the Afrikaner and Dutch and German husbands were not, as she must never forget, entirely like the American husband. The Old World still held the man to be master, and perhaps in the long run that was a better and more satisfying thing for any woman. She knew that Dirk liked in her the very youthful qualities she was inclined to regret, and that he did not enjoy any tendency to oppose him and go off on some headlong tangent of her own. It was up to her to learn how to be a South African wife and suppress her occasional headlong American impulses.

Dirk remained away all that day and into the evening. Susan went early to bed between chilly sheets, not yet being hot-water-bottle minded.

It must have been after midnight when he came in. He undressed quietly and she pretended to be asleep. In spite of her good resolutions, her wounded spirit resisted him, turning from him, yet longing perversely to have him break down her resistance.

He did not come near her, however, and she heard his even breathing in the next bed while she lay awake for a long while. At some time during the late-night hours she fell into an uneasy slumber, but she was awake again at dawn, to find a cold clear light seeping into the room.

She knew she would not sleep again, so she slipped out of bed in her thin nightgown and went to a window, heedless of the cold. There she parted the draperies so that she could look out. The window faced at an angle across the irregular amphitheater of mountains and town, so that the Lion's Head, the right wing, was out of sight, just behind the house. The broken pyramids of Devil's Peak rose straight ahead on the far side of town. She had to turn to her right a little to view what all Cape Town affectionately called "the mountain," and with her turning the full impact of it struck boldly across her vision.

The mists had blown away and the dawn sky was clear, with a rosy tinge beyond Devil's Peak. No cloud "tablecloth" lay over the mountain's top this morning. It stood clear in awesome power, its great mass stretched behind Cape Town, its head a long straight line ruled against the sky. The light of dawn struck across the rocky face of sheer precipice and set it glistening. Thirty-five hundred feet it rose, so massive and close that every cleft and ravine and steep fall of rock was visible in detail. Here the black gods of old Africa had lived in times long past before the white man had come to the continent. And here they would live when the white man's power was gone.

Upon Susan the impact was tremendous. She had no thought for the chilly room behind her or the cold pane of glass beneath her fingertips. She had half expected to find the mountain dwarfed when set against her childhood recollection, but the reality was more impressive than her memory of it.

She had come home. This was the Cape Town she had loved, with Table Mountain ruling the sky and Devil's Peak raising its jagged head across the valley. She liked best an older name for the peak—the Wyndberg. What a home for storms it was, when great winds beat across Cape Town winter and summer. Today the white houses and red roofs no longer looked dim and gray. There was a clean, well-washed gleam to them, untouched by industrial grime.

She did not hear Dirk when he left his bed, did not know he was near until he put his arms about her and drew her slim body against his own. For an instant she stiffened, and then warm love flowed through her and she was alive again.

"I'm sorry, darling," he said softly and kissed the place where her short hair curled above her ear.

She forgot the mountain and turned her face to him. Relief was a wave engulfing her, carrying her free of darkness. She put her arms about his neck and pressed her cheek against his own.

"Dirk, it's been dreadful! You went so far away and I didn't know how to reach you."

"I know," he said. "There's a devil of perversity that gets into me at times. And you closed yourself away from me behind those wide eyes of yours. We mustn't let this happen, sweet. You know I love you. Never forget it."

And he knew how much she loved him, she thought. He did not need to hear her say it. It was something she told him with her hands framing his face, with her lips upon his own. The embrace was all the sweeter because she had been for a little while so frighteningly far away from him.

Before they went back to the warmth of blankets, she turned once more to the mountain. "I remember what they call it—the Old Gray Father. Oh, Dirk, it's good to be home again! Yesterday I couldn't find myself. I couldn't find you and I was afraid."

His hands pressed her shoulders gently. "Do you see the ravine that cuts down the hill below us? The house you lived in as a child is just across. Your father's house. Can you find it there, lower than we are, on the opposite hill?"

Her gaze swept the width of the ravine and moved along the hill beyond to a white house with red-tiled roof and the intricate lacework of wrought iron around its porches and balconies. From this angle it did not look altogether familiar, but she knew it was the house she had visited with so much joy as a little girl and dreamed about with longing through the Johannesburg winter.

"Your father expects you today," Dirk said. "Mara will come for you this afternoon and you mustn't be afraid."

"Will you be there?" she asked.

"Probably not. There's work for me away from the house. But you mustn't disappoint him. He's counting on this."

The picture of an elderly blind man, grown pitifully helpless, had taken hold of her imagination and she had been able to put aside the disturbing memory of a piercing look that saw everything and a judgment that could be merciless.

"I'll go," she promised. "But remember that I'm doing it for you, more than I am for him."

He laughed and there was something exciting in the sound. He tousled her short hair almost roughly and tangled his fingers in it as he kissed her again.

"You're to let your hair grow," he ordered. "I want to see it down to your shoulders. I don't like being married to a crop-haired boy." He picked her up and she clung to him as he carried her back to her bed.

Afterwards she lay awake for a time, a dreamy contentment upon her from which all fearfulness had fled. She loved him so very much. She wanted only to please him, to serve him, to be what he wished her to be. The ancient longing of Eve, of Woman, possessed her and she wanted—for the moment—nothing else.

Even after she rose for the second time, even after Dirk had gone to work, the sense of having at last come home remained with her. When she was alone she went lightheartedly to every window in the house and looked out upon the clear bright day, savoring each remembered view. Behind the house the Lion's Head was free of clouds, raising its nubby rock top from the hill that separated Table Bay and the ocean beyond.

She even got out her camera and checked her film supply, tried a shot or two from upstairs windows, just to get her hand in again and because every view filled her with delight. Once more she felt alive and eager to plan.

Dirk had said there was a downstairs bathroom she might fix up for a darkroom, if she liked. She must purchase supplies, set herself up in business, as it were. This morning she could even remember without resentment that John Cornish had said she had talent. Perhaps she might take a few pictures around Cape Town that he would approve of. If she ever saw him again—which was unlikely. Knowing now how Dirk felt, she must take no more chances. If he came to this house again, she would not be at home to Mr. Cornish. The spell of the repentant Eve was still upon her.

5

In the afternoon Mara came over, bringing the new maid—a dark-skinned girl named Willimina Kock. "Willi" for short, Mara said. The girl had a gentle manner that was appealing, and she spoke English naturally as a language she had grown up with. Mara gave orders briskly about Willi's duties as if she hardly expected Susan to know what they would be. The girl said, "Yes, Miss Bellman," quietly and went to change into her working clothes.

"She'll manage quite well for you," Mara said casually. "She's had a bit more education than is necessary, but she needs the work. If you're ready now, we'll get along over to the house. Your father is waiting for you."

Susan felt like saying, "Yes, Miss Bellman," to all this brisk efficiency, but she suppressed the urge. Undoubtedly this handsome, blond young woman was hired for her ability to handle such matters with authority.

When Susan had put on her coat, she slung her camera over her shoulder, hoping to find an occasion to use it later. As they got into the car and drove along the short, narrow street to a sharp turn, Susan glanced at her companion speculatively.

Today Mara seemed less brightly vivacious than she had been before, and while she was courteous enough, there was a chill behind her manner, and perhaps disapproval. Did this, Susan wondered, reflect Niklaas van Pelt's feeling about a marriage between his long-ignored daughter and his ward? At any rate, remembering Dirk's laughter at Mara's expense, she would not be troubled by her today.

Though the van Pelt house was not far across the ravine, it was necessary to follow the road uphill to the place where it bridged the cut and go the long way around down the other side. From this approach the house looked more familiar to Susan. It was built in a fat L, with lacy iron railings along the upstairs and downstairs verandas. The short part of the L extended toward the front and was capped by a peaked roof, red tiled. Under the eaves were old-fashioned gingerbread curlicues. A low stone wall, painted white and topped with more of the fanciful iron grillwork, was further fortified with a high box hedge, behind which towered a huge rhododendron bush.

Mara turned the car into the driveway and ran it around to the garage in the rear.

"I'll take you in," she said shortly, and Susan let herself out of the car and walked beside the brisk-moving Mara toward the front of the house.

There were a few flowering shrubs, Susan noted as they walked through the yard, but the rare proteas her father had once raised and which gave the house its name were no longer in evidence.

As they neared the steps wings of nervousness began to flutter inside Susan. This sudden attack of anxiety was nonsense, she told herself. It was ridiculous to be seized by a groundless fear that bordered on panic just because she was to meet this old man whom she really did not know.

Mara seemed unaware of Susan's uneasiness. She went up the front steps and across the wide veranda, with Susan following after. The front door had narrow panes of glass running down a strip on either side. The sight brought recognition. Susan could remember a child peering out at the street through one of those panes on a rainy day when she could not go outside to play.

A maid, wearing the usual white kerchief, opened the door at Mara's ring and they entered a wide hall, with a stairway running up at one side. A small Oriental rug lay against the dark floor, and a chest of drawers made of some dark, handsomely grained wood stood against the wall, a ladder-backed chair beside it. On top of the chest brass candlesticks flanked a tall Chinese vase filled with glowing pink flowers.

"If you'll wait here a moment," Mara said, "I'll tell him you've arrived."

Susan was glad enough to wait in the dim light of the old-fashioned hallway and try to get her own bewildering emotions in hand. Something in her accepted the house in warm recognition, remembering the hallway, the very stairs, the glimpse of a dining room beyond, with more flowers on a long sideboard. Yet when it came to facing the man who was her father she could feel nothing except a tendency to panic and she did not know why.

The colored maid took her coat, but Susan kept her camera over her shoulder as if its very presence helped to identify her with a world she knew and belonged to. When the maid had

58

gone she turned to the vase of flowers with a further sense of recognition. So spring proteas were blooming in Cape Town. The waxy petals of this variety were thick-fleshed and stiff, the centers a solid, prickly mass. Woody stems supported the blossoms and the green leaves were waxy like the blooms. She touched a tentative finger to a leaf, knowing that the surface would be faintly sticky.

Behind her, at the far end of the hallway, the assured click of Mara's spiked heels sounded and she turned about.

"Come this way, please," Mara said. She had taken off her coat and wore a blue knitted suit that revealed her figure effectively.

At the rear the hall turned at right angles, ending with an open door. As they approached the door, Thomas Scott came out, carrying a sheaf of envelopes. Susan said, "Good morning," and he bowed his head, murmuring a scarcely audible response. For an instant she was aware of dark eyes that held a hint of anger in them. Mara paid no attention to him as they went through the door of Niklaas van Pelt's study.

Now the sense of engulfing recognition brought with it a dread that was nearly overpowering. There was something disturbing about this room, some association it held for her. Yet it was a pleasant room, with French doors opening upon a terrace, the walls done in soft grays and grayish greens. It was not the colors of the room she remembered, however, or even the pictures on the walls. These things had been changed since her childhood. The great desk of native stinkwood stood in the same place. The heavy dark bookcases were the same, and the slippery chairs that were difficult for a child to sit upon without sliding. All these she saw at a glance as a background for the man who occupied a great red leather armchair behind the desk. Toward him she had no feeling of recognition at all, and the very fact helped to quiet the fluttering of anxiety as she faced him.

"Here is your daughter, Mr. van Pelt," Mara said.

The old man behind the desk barely lifted his fingers in a gesture of dismissal and Mara went softly away, silencing her clicking heels, closing the door without a sound behind her.

"Susan?" he said. There was a resonance in the deep voice that was not unmusical, but there was no warmth in the sound, no eager greeting. It was merely a question addressed to a yet-unsensed presence.

"Yes," she said, equally cool. "I am here, Father."

He reached toward a chair beside the desk and removed a heavy silver-headed cane that leaned against it.

59

"Sit down, please," he said.

She obeyed, her eyes never leaving his face. It was a thin face with deep grooves in the cheeks. The beaked nose was the same, strong and aggressive. But the keen eyes she might have remembered were hidden behind dark glasses. His hair had grown grayer than she recalled, but it was not yet white, and it still grew thickly back from a fine brow. She knew him and she did not know him. Around her the room watched and bided its time.

"I am glad you have returned to South Africa," Niklaas said, his tone formal. "Though it is a surprise that you return as the wife of Dirk Hohenfield. That is something I neither planned nor expected."

"I'm sorry if you're not pleased," she told him. "I know you like to plan all matters close to you yourself."

She had not meant to say that. The words had presented themselves unbidden and they sounded rude in her ears. But there was no way to take them back.

A flicker of some expression that was not a smile crossed his face and was gone. "I see you are still outspoken. You were a gentle child, yet you had a surprising way of speaking your mind at times."

"I had no business saying that," she apologized. "Dirk has been like a son to you for years, and you don't know me. There's no reason why you should be pleased to see him marry me."

"Your voice is a woman's voice," he said, as though he had listened only to the tone and not the words. "But the image in my mind is of a straight-haired little girl with bright reddish plaits, brown eyes, and a stubborn chin. I must change that picture."

For the first time she sensed what he might be experiencing and was moved. She at least could see the change in him, she could comprehend the fact that they were strangers. He could see nothing of the far greater change in her.

He put out a hand and touched her shoulder, felt the strap of the camera, followed it down to the case, and she knew he was seeking to replace his eyesight by means of his fingers.

"What is this?" he asked.

"A camera, Father," she told him.

"Yes, of course. Dirk has said you were working at picture taking on a newspaper in Chicago, and that you wanted to keep it up."

He touched her shoulder again, reached upward lightly to her short hair and then withdrew his hand as if the feel of it

60

distressed him. Tears stung her eyelids. Tears of pity for a once vigorous man who was no longer whole.

He made no further exploration through his fingers, but sat back in the deep chair, his hidden eyes turned in her direction, his expression impassive, remote. She had the feeling that he had put her aside as someone he did not know. A silence grew between them, as if he withdrew into his own darkness and forgot she was there.

Waiting for him to speak, she looked about the room and saw the touches of Africa that were new since she had been here as a child. On the wall behind her father hung a mask carved in some dark-brown wood: a face with the thickened lips and flattened nostrils that made it almost a caricature, yet a face that possessed dignity. The earlobes were elongated, with tubes of ivory thrust through them, and the eyes were lost in hollows. Yet there was a vitality here that made one know a man like this had lived in proud authority and been respected by his fellows. In a corner of the room stood a native assegai, and against one wall a tall, cylindrical drum waited for fingers to beat old rhythms upon the tightly drawn skin.

But the silence grew too long and Susan stirred uneasily, finding herself at a disadvantage. After all, he had summoned her here; she had not asked to come. He had no business treating her as if he had gone away and left her here alone.

"Why did you want me to come to South Africa?" she asked him boldly. "Why should you want to see me when so many years have passed?"

He seemed to return from a distance as he touched a paper on the desk before him. "Your mother did not tell you she had written to me? She did not tell you what she asked of me before her death?"

Susan was startled. Her mother had written to Niklaas van Pelt? And without letting her know! She felt shocked and a little betrayed.

"I didn't know she had written," she said. "What did she write to you about?"

Raised blue veins marked the hand with which he pushed a letter toward her across the desk.

"Here it is. Read it for yourself."

She picked up the sheet of airmail paper almost reluctantly. The sight of her mother's rather childish handwriting opened a wound that was far from healed. The letter began on a slightly frantic note, and she sensed the despair with which it had been written. The doctor had felt it wiser to keep the truth from Claire, and Susan had agreed. But now it seemed that her mother had not been fooled after all. The letter began with the statement that she had not much longer to live, that she had never asked anything of Niklaas for the child before, but that she must ask it now. When she was gone Susan would have no one. Claire's own family was long dead. There would be no one to advise the girl, protect her, care for her.

Susan looked up from the letter at her father. He had withdrawn again. The blank, smoky surface of the glasses told her nothing. From a humidor on his desk he took a cigar and snipped the ends, then lighted it with the ease of a man long used to managing all small actions by touch. Susan watched in uneasy fascination, as she considered the words she had just read. Her mother's concern in the letter was touching, but not very realistic.

"You needn't have sent for me because of this," she said. "I'm not so helpless as she represents."

He puffed his cigar and said nothing. She read on. Now her mother was speaking of some personal matter that lay between herself and her husband. Susan did not understand and read the words through a second time:

I know you always thought it my fault that the Kimberley disappeared. You believed I tricked you. You believed I was a thief. How could I bear that, Niklaas, when I truly did not know what happened to the stone? How could I stay on in South Africa as your wife when you thought I had betrayed you in such a terrible way? I told you the truth—though you never believed me.

Susan looked up from the letter. "What is she talking about?"

"Have you read it through?" her father asked.

Her eyes returned to Claire's words sloping along the page:

At the time I had a feeling that the child knew something about the diamond. That perhaps she had witnessed something, or was unwittingly in possession of some knowledge about it. But she was in a wildly distraught state during the period before we left the country. When I tried to question her she would only sob hysterically. The only thing to do was get her away from South Africa where she would not have to grow up under a shadow.

I encouraged her to forget. I taught her never to look back. Just as *I* had to forget and never look back. It was the only way. Though many a time I've wondered what might be locked away in her childhood memories—something she might know without knowing that she knows it. Perhaps you can draw it out of her, if ever you see her again.

There was nothing of further consequence to the letter. It closed stiffly, formally, and then the writer hurled herself into an emotional plea for Susan's welfare in a postscript that was typical of Claire.

Susan put the letter back on the desk within reach of his hand. "I don't know what she meant by all this. I've never so much as heard of a lost diamond."

"She was referring to the Kimberley Royal," Niklaas said. "One of the famous diamonds of South Africa. It disappeared many years ago and that was the end of it."

His tone was even, without emotion. He felt for Claire's letter and returned it to a folder while Susan pondered the words she had read. A glimmer of the reason for them was beginning to form in her mind and she spoke the thought aloud.

"I believe I know what my mother meant to do. She couldn't be sure that you would interest yourself in me after all these years. So she tried to offer you a clever bribe. At least she must have thought it clever. She could weave the most fantastic notions at times."

"I don't understand," her father said.

"I know it sounds a little silly," Susan said apologetically, "but I knew her so well. It's exactly the sort of thing she would dream up. If she could convince you that I knew something about this lost diamond, then perhaps you would interest yourself in me. You might go out of your way to take me under your protection. Isn't it possible that is what she intended?"

Once more the silence between them lengthened. He did not answer her suggestion. He neither admitted nor denied. Yet the more she thought about it the more logical such reasoning seemed. It would never have occurred to Claire that Susan might hate to be brought to South Africa by means of such a ruse. Or that it might be a tiresome and disturbing thing if her father and others began prodding her into trying to remember something she could not possibly remember, never having had any knowledge of it in the first place.

Apparently the ruse had worked. Niklaas van Pelt had sent for his daughter promptly. Even Dirk—who had undoubtedly read this letter—had asked her back in Chicago if she had ever heard of the Kimberley Royal. But Dirk had not been truly interested, she remembered thankfully. He had not pushed the matter and never returned to it.

If this was why her father had called her home, she wanted only to escape his presence and end this disillusioning interview.

"Apparently you don't agree with this reasoning," she said. "And if that's the case there's nothing more I can say. I had better be going."

He heard her rise and reached for the silver-headed cane beside his chair as he stood up. He made no effort to keep her, but held out his hand. She put her own into it, aware of the sensitive touch of his fingers, as though he were again using them to see, learning the fragile structure of her bones, the span and length of her hand. But he did not ask her to come to see him again, nor did he suggest another visit. Because of Dirk she would undoubtedly be forced to visit this house from time to time, but there was nothing left between them of a father-daughter relationship.

Mara came to meet her as she left the study, and Susan glanced a bit wistfully up the stairs. There was in her a greater sense of recognition of the house than of her father. She would have liked to wander upstairs, to return to the past through its rooms and corridors. But this was not something she would ask of Mara Bellman.

"Thomas can drive you home if you like," Mara offered.

Susan shook her head and patted the camera slung at her side. "Thanks, but I want to walk. Perhaps I'll find some good shots along the road."

Mara saw her to the door and Susan was glad to be out on the steeply slanting street again, climbing toward the high place where the road rounded its horseshoe curve and turned toward home on the higher level of the opposite hill.

More than anything else she wanted to be alone. An unexpected sense of pain and disappointment filled her. In spite of her efforts to convince herself that her father meant nothing to her and that she could expect little from this meeting, there must have been an unaccepted hopefulness in her based on the memory of a child's deep affection for her father. The fact that her mother's ruse had succeeded and he had sent for her, not out of a like, remembered affection but only because of her value to him in the possible recovery of great wealth, left her with an aching sense of disappointment.

Where the street began to curve Susan once more had a clear view of the mountain and she paused to gaze sadly up at it. The climbing houses ended well below the highway that cut horizontally along the mountainside, leaving a visible gash. Above the road the slopes were grassy, steepening as they extended upward to the level where rocky buttresses began. How blue and clear the sky was above the mountain this morning. In other parts of Africa the sky had seemed surprisingly white and thin. But the skies of South Africa could blaze with a deep-blue light.

To distract herself in this moment of painful disappointment she snapped a picture of the mountain. As she did so something moving at one end of the great fall of rock caught her eye. A tiny cable car was swinging up the face of the cliff, its support invisible, as if nothing suspended it between mountaintop and earth. She watched it travel clear to the small white block that was the building at the top where the cable ended. She must go up in that car one of these days. She would get Dirk to take her. For some reason no one had ever taken her up there as a child.

As she moved on toward the Aerie, she thought of how clean the streets of Cape Town seemed, and how pleasantly old-fashioned in this section. The white gabled houses still echoed the Dutch architecture, and the white stone walls, or picket fences with gardens beyond, seemed extraordinarily neat and well-kept in the true English manner. In one yard a poinsettia bloomed, and in another mountain mimosa, sweet-scented and pale yellow, sprinkled petals over the wall and upon the sidewalk.

But her surroundings could not hold her attention for long because the thought of her mother's letter was still upon her. There had always been a gentle fiction she had kept up to please her mother: the fiction that it was Susan who was dependent and helpless and Claire who cleverly solved all their problems. This had cost Susan little and it had helped Claire to build up the picture of herself that she found it necessary to harbor.

In reality, Claire had never had any notion of the physical difficulties of Susan's work or of the predicaments in which her daughter sometimes found herself in an effort to serve her paper. To Claire, being respectable had always been of the greatest importance. Underneath she might sometimes be as eager as a child for the gratification of her own wishes and pleasure. Yet all must be conducted with an air of gentility and decorum. She would never have been one, Susan recognized, to stand beside a husband who had disgraced himself, and thus disgraced her as well. Yet in the end Claire had been truly concerned about her daughter, had tried to ensure her future. And in a sense she had succeeded. At least the bait of the diamond had succeeded, Susan thought bitterly. It had caused Niklaas to act.

She wished now that she had asked her father more questions about the Kimberley Royal. In itself the story seemed unbelievable. Had there really been some suspicion on her father's part that her mother might have taken the stone, or was that still another of Claire's fancies? Had her father's imprisonment had anything to do with the disappearance of the diamond?

She had no answer for any of these questions.

The road climbed beneath the Lion's Head and she looked up at it, looming against the sky. The Lion overhung all this part of town, claiming ownership, as Devil's Peak on the far side of the amphitheater was ruler there. Yet both must pay homage to the more massive mountain bridging the space between them.

Tonight she would tell Dirk about this meeting with her father, ask him the questions that troubled her. The thought of Dirk brought something of her courage surging back. After all, what did Niklaas or his motives matter? She must forget, suppress, the child in her who had once so loved her father. She had Dirk now. With him she could be complete.

Her steps quickened. He would be in for dinner before too long and the warm memory of their reconciliation this morning hurried her toward home.

6

Dirk came home late and hurried to shower and change before dinner. Again Susan had left the meal in the cook's hands, but tonight the food tasted wonderful. *Bobotie*, meat balls with egg and curry, baked in a square English pie dish, was a favorite of Dirk's, he told her, and she found the well-spiced flavor delectable.

The table looked attractive with the white candles the new

maid, Willi, had set in silver holders that had been a gift from Niklaas van Pelt. Blue cornflowers had been massed in a small bowl in the center to give an accent of color.

It was pleasant to have Dirk telling her about his work tonight. He had persuaded Niklaas to put in a stock of handsome silver jewelry, he said. Not work from the reservations this time, but fine silver craft done here in the Cape, some of it set with semiprecious stones mined nearby. He had brought home one of the pins for her and she unwrapped it from the tissue in delight. Cut into a raised silver oblong were tiny figures copied from ancient cave paintings: a naked running figure with a bow and arrow, another leaping with a spear upraised, and between the two human figures a doomed impala in graceful flight. She pinned the brooch to her blouse, touched by his gift.

John Cornish was not mentioned, and the meal went off without variance.

Willi served at the table so quietly that they were hardly aware of her. When she was out of the room Susan told Dirk that her father had shown her the surprising letter Claire had written him before her death.

"You knew about the letter, didn't you?" she asked. "You must have known about it when you met me in Chicago."

"Yes, I knew," Dirk agreed. "Your father showed it to me before he sent me to fetch you home."

"But then why didn't you tell me about it? Wouldn't it have been fairer to me if I had known?"

"Fairer, perhaps. But not so useful in furthering my purpose." There was both amusement and affection in his smile. "You were being a bit obstinate and I didn't want to add to my own handicap. If you'd suspected that your father had an ulterior motive in wanting you here you might never have come."

"But of course my mother's ruse about the diamond was nonsense," she assured him. "That was something she thought up to make certain my father would interest himself in me. And it seems to have worked." She couldn't help a tinge of bitterness in her tone. Dirk was undoubtedly right. If she had known about the letter she would have been much more set against coming.

Dirk reached across the table for her hand. "Think of it this way—it might be of real service to your father if you could recall anything that would give him a clue about the Kimberley."

Clearly he had not understood her point. "But, Dirk, that

was only a made-up story! I don't know anything about a diamond. My mother was full of well-meant little feminine tricks like that. It's exactly what she would have done—and thought herself very clever and helpful."

Dirk's smile lighted his face with the bright look she loved to see, but at the moment it irritated her a little because it meant that he did not really accept her theory about the letter.

"How could my remembering anything about a diamond benefit my father?" she demanded.

"That's a question I can't answer," he said. "But I have a strong feeling that it might."

She was on dangerous ground now, she knew. Always before, she had avoided probing too far because that way fear lurked like a shadow at the back of her mind, ready to engulf her if she looked too closely. But she could not go on being a child about this forever. She had to know. She moistened her dry lips with the tip of her tongue.

"Was it because of this lost diamond that he went to prison?"

Dirk shook his head. "No, oddly enough, the diamond had nothing to do with what happened. Even though the Kimberley was presumed to be in his possession at the time. It had been entrusted to him by its owner—a close friend of Niklaas's—to bring to Cape Town for a special exhibit. When it disappeared, his friend said nothing to the press or to the police, merely withdrawing his consent to have it exhibited. He was devoted to Niklaas and he did not let anyone know what had happened. So there was no prosecution, no public search, no fanfare. Not until years later when all the trails had grown cold did word of the diamond's disappearance emerge."

"But then why did my father go to prison? What was the offense that sent him there?"

"You should have asked me that in Chicago," Dirk said gently. "When I wanted to tell you, you wouldn't let me. Now your father has asked me not to go into all that past history, since you don't know about it. He feels it has no bearing on the present. If he decides differently he'll tell you himself. So that's the way it has to be, darling. I can't go against his wishes in this."

Willi brought in the dessert—an English dish called a "trifle"—made of sponge cake, jam and rich custard. It put an effective end to their discussion as she struggled to get it down.

Under the circumstances she could hardly insist that Dirk tell her what she wanted to know. He had not accepted her reasoning about her mother's letter and there seemed to be no way to convince him. In any case, it could not matter now that she was here. It was wiser to let the whole thing go. Besides, she was looking forward to her first evening at home with her husband and she wanted no friction to mar it.

After dinner, however, Dirk seemed restless, as if the idea of settling down to a quiet domestic evening were foreign to his bachelor nature. Willi lighted a coal fire in the small grate, and Susan set out some books and magazines invitingly, drew two chairs before the hearth. But Dirk did not notice her little byplay and she watched him, troubled, as he moved about the room, pausing at the bay window to look out at the lights of Cape Town, lost in thoughts he did not speak aloud. When the telephone in the hallway rang and he jumped like a cat, hurrying to answer it, she knew he had been expecting the call.

From the hallway his voice reached her, controlled and low. She rearranged books on a nearby table, making small sounds so that she would not hear his words. Dirk had enjoyed a life of his own for years before she had come into it. She mustn't expect his transition to be as complete and wholehearted as her own.

When he returned to the living room he looked both exasperated and angrily alive.

"I'll have to go out," he said. "There's no help for it. Do you think you can put up with a husband whose daytime work spreads into the evening hours?"

She was careful to smile, to hide her disappointment, but she would have been more reassured if he had offered some explanation about work so urgent that it demanded his presence after hours.

She went with him to the door, striving for an appearance of cheerful good humor, and he kissed her warmly before he hurried away.

When he had gone the house seemed still and somehow lifeless. Darkness created a seclusion of its own, a withdrawing from the life of the city all about, so that each home became a unit existing of itself, without relation to the whole. The Aerie's high perch made this seem doubly so.

At least she was not yet entirely alone in the house. Small sounds issued from the dining room and Susan crossed the wide hall and went into the room where Willi was tidying up.

Once more Susan had an impression of a consideration and courtesy that was natural to this pretty, dark-skinned girl.

69

Willi must be about her own age and Susan wondered about her as a person in the uneasy life of today's South Africa. It was clear that she was not typical as a servant, and Susan had wondered at Mara's choice of her for this work.

"Have you always lived in Cape Town, Willimina?" she asked.

"Not always, Mrs. Hohenfield," Willi said, setting the coffee service in place on the sideboard. "My parents were originally from the Cape, but they moved to Johannesburg when I was quite small. We returned here a few years ago." She glanced at Susan and then away, offering nothing more.

In Chicago Susan had known colored girls in school and had made friends with one who had worked on the paper. She liked what she had seen of Willi. She wanted to know her. And Willi would not take the initiative, so Susan spoke frankly.

"I've heard that the color bar is easier here in the Cape Province than it is in the Transvaal. Do you find that true?"

A spark of something quickly suppressed showed in Willi's eyes. "It is better here," she agreed and went on with her work.

"Are positions difficult to find?" Susan persisted.

The girl shrugged slender shoulders expressively. "So many come here hoping things will be better. There are dozens applying for every job. Especially in certain types of work."

Susan remembered her friend on the paper—a colored girl who was a graduate of Northwestern University. It had been hard for her too, even though opportunities were increasing. She and Susan had enjoyed several talks on the subject. But Willimina did not know her yet, and friendship could never be forced.

"At least you've been able to get in some schooling, haven't you?" Susan asked.

The look of spirit was there again in Willi's eyes. "A little. I wanted more, but it was necessary to help at home. Otherwise I wouldn't be—" She broke off, but the inference was clear. With the schooling she had wanted she would not have had to work as a domestic.

She took the bowl of cornflowers from the center of the table and placed it between candlesticks on the sideboard, then removed the tablecloth and folded it up.

"Is there anything else you would like me to do this evening, Mrs. Hohenfield?" she asked.

Susan shook her head. "I don't think so. Do you have very far to travel to get home?"

A flicker of surprise crossed Willi's face. "Miss Bellman said I was to have a room here. In fact, I've already moved my things into it."

Susan laughed. "I'm sorry, I didn't know. Perhaps you'd better tell me about the arrangements. Do the cook and yard boy stay here too?"

"No, they both go home to their families. Our house is a little crowded just now, so I was glad to have a room here. That is, if it is all right with you, Mrs. Hohenfield."

"I'll be glad to have you in the house," Susan admitted. "I've been thinking that it seems a bit empty when my husband is out. Where is your room, Willi?"

"I'll show you," the girl said.

She led the way through the kitchen, where the cook was giving things a last wipe-up, and went out through the back door. The night air was cold after the sun-warmed day, and Susan shivered as she hurried across the yard behind her. The girl stopped before a door that appeared to lead back into the house and pushed it open. It gave directly upon a small square room, meagerly but neatly furnished with bare essentials.

"I haven't had time to fix it up yet," Willi said. "I've brought some of my own things, but they aren't unpacked."

There was no door from the room into the house. The closest approach would be across the yard and through the back door.

"I should think this would be difficult in bad weather," Susan said. "Why didn't they have a door open directly into the house?"

"This is the way it is done here, Mrs. Hohenfield," Willi said, and looked away.

Susan understood. For years white people in South Africa had been living in a state of acknowledged jitters. And with some reason. All Africa was pushing at a door which was being held shut by a comparatively few white men in power— the descendants of the Boer settlers—the Afrikaners of the Nationalist party. It was these men who were calling the tune and making the laws. One of these laws, Susan remembered reading, was to the effect that servants were not to sleep inside the house of a white employer at night. It was necessary, everyone said, to take no chances. In Johannesburg many people slept with a gun on the bedside table. After the last demonstrations in Cape Town, Dirk said, there had been a run on the stores that sold firearms.

Not wanting to intrude on Willi further, Susan told her good night and hurried back through the kitchen, where the

71

cook was getting ready to leave. When Susan spoke to her the little woman darted a quick, birdlike glance her way, as if she were vastly curious about this stranger from America, and not entirely comfortable with her as a "missus."

When she had gone, Susan tried the door behind her and then laughed at herself. This sort of fearfulness could be contagious and it was a disease she did not want to catch. There was no reason why anyone should mean her harm. This was a lovely night with the stars bright and clear and she decided not to wander about inside the house in a lonely, tiresome fashion. Instead she would go outside and enjoy the evening.

She slipped into her coat, tied a scarf about her head, and let herself out the front door. Following a paved walk around to the side of the house beneath the bedroom windows, she found that a street light spread its radiance through the garden. Along one side ran a low stone wall and when she looked over she saw that the hill dropped away beneath, disappearing into the shadowy ravine, where pine trees clustered. Beyond she could see lights burning on the opposite hill, and was able to pick out her father's house.

She sat on the wall and watched the panorama of Cape Town lights spreading densely up from the shores of the bay, to thin out and lose themselves on the lower slopes of Table Mountain. Tonight the mountain rose in massive darkness against the star-flecked sky. Her eyes sought the Southern Cross and she was enchanted as a child to find it again. How far away America seemed, and how vast and troubling was this tip of the continent. All up and down Africa freedom was on the move. Yet here beneath this lovely, peaceful sky quiet was held only by force and by those who believed against history that they could turn back the tide that moved, not only in Africa, but across the world.

She thought of Willimina, remembering very well from her childhood the gentle, friendly, highly intelligent people who were known as the "Cape coloreds." These people were a greatly mixed race that might include Portuguese, Indian, English, Dutch, Hottentot, Malay, and a good many other strains. They had come to be set apart from the black population and had fared better in the Cape Peninsula than the "blanket native," so recently from the reservation.

Somewhere close at hand a voice began to sing plaintively, sadly, of a soldier from the old Transvaal and his longing for "Sari Marais." She knew the tune for a song of the Boer War that she had heard as a child. The melody deepened the sense of loneliness all about her, and when it ended the silence seemed intense.

She returned to the house, wanting now to wake it up with sounds of her own making so that she might shut away the haunting loneliness. She was not truly alone. Dirk would soon be home and she must find ways to be busy and happy when he was absent.

There were so many things she must do, changes she wanted to make. All through the house there were touches of Mara Bellman that she felt impelled to erase and replace with her own. Now this was to be *her* house.

When Dirk came home he found her sitting on the floor in the bedroom, surveying her handiwork. The dressing table had been moved to a new place where the light was better, the beds pushed closer together, the throw rugs on the floor set in a new pattern. She sat with her hands clasped about her knees as she contemplated further changes, and he laughed aloud at the sight.

"I didn't expect you to be at this sort of thing so soon," he said. "Though I've been told all wives go in for rearranging the furniture periodically."

He did not mention his appointment and she was careful to ask no questions. Just having him home was enough.

Nevertheless, her sleep that night was dream-haunted. Once she wakened cold and trembling, with an impression in her mind so vivid that it stayed with her for a long while before she went to sleep again.

In the dream a door had opened and she was walking through it with a feeling of hope and confidence. The room she stepped into was alive with a great glitter and dazzle. For an instant the flashing blue light seemed more beautiful than anything she had ever beheld. Then the brilliant fire turned evil and somehow cold. And she knew what it was. A monstrous flashing of diamonds surrounded her. She was lost in a cavern of diamonds from which she could not escape. The door behind her had disappeared and there was no way out. She was enveloped in cold blue fire, drowning in it.

When she fought her way back to consciousness, the flashing still seemed so intense that she could see it all around her. She sat up in bed, fighting the memory of the dream, lest it return and engulf her in further terror. But the conviction of reality remained. The blue fire had been real—she had seen it with her own eyes.

"What is it, darling?" Dirk spoke from the next bed.

She slipped from the warmth of blankets and flung herself across the space and into his bed, to be held close and comforted.

"I dreamed about diamonds," she said. "Everything around me was burning in a dreadful blue fire. Just as though I had really seen a fire like that."

He held her close, stilling her trembling, his lips against her ear. "Perhaps you have. Isn't it possible—"

But she would not accept that. "No, Dirk, no! Hold me—don't let me think, don't let me remember!"

He held her, at first tenderly and then more warmly, but though she went to sleep in his arms she could not free herself entirely of the subtle horror of the dream. Whenever she wakened it was there with only Dirk's arms between her and the fear that waited to possess her.

Not until morning did the nightmare begin to fade. Later she tried to explain it to herself. It had been caused by her mother's letter, of course, and Dirk's talk about the Kimberley Royal. These things had disturbed her and become a part of her dreaming. It was nothing more than that, she assured herself.

In the days that followed she was able to busy herself in a number of ways. Dirk took her downtown to visit her father's Cape Town store, where he had his office in the rear and kept an eye on things when he was not traveling to Johannesburg, or to some distant source of native art work in the far-flung reservations.

The shop enchanted her. There was no tourist clutter here. All was arranged with taste and an eye to subtly dramatic effect. Pieces of special worth were set apart against suitable backgrounds where they could be admired by the discerning. There was a corner for masks and fine wooden carvings, a current display of copperware from Northern Rhodesia, a glass case of delicate, carved ivory.

Dirk took her about, pointing out objects of interest—the painstaking beadwork, colorful blankets and woven mats—from the Transkei, Basutoland, Swaziland, Zululand. His knowledge was enormous, yet he displayed it in an offhand manner as if it were something that came naturally and which he did not particularly value.

"I can see where my father could hardly do without you," Susan told him proudly.

But Dirk disclaimed his own importance. "Hardly a day passes that Uncle Niklaas doesn't come down here," he assured her. "There's not much we handle that doesn't receive his attention before it goes on display. It's amazing the way he keeps a running plan of the store in his mind and knows just where everything is. Not a thing is changed unless he approves."

Susan could not share Dirk's feeling toward her father. Obviously there was much to admire about him, but remembering why he had brought her here, she had no desire to recapture old affection. She enjoyed the shop, but she did not look upon it as merely an expression of her father.

At the Aerie she went to work turning the house into a home for Dirk. He was willing to give her a free hand and she enjoyed being able to make her own plans. Her shopping list grew long and she began to learn about the stores of Cape Town.

Dirk had the rest of his own things brought up to the house and he and Susan had the fun of unpacking them together. One trunk still contained articles that had belonged to his father and mother, and this trunk he would not unpack. Susan had begun to sense that there were matters in his childhood that had left wounds he was reluctant to re-open. That his German father had been interned and that his mother had grieved herself into illness after his death—these things she knew. But he would not elaborate. There was a deep hurt in him that could be easily aroused and she learned not to tread upon quicksand.

One thing he sought for, however, in this family trunk, after he had it brought up to the bedroom. Though he would not unpack it, he reached along the sides and beneath the layers of clothing until he found what he had looked for. When he drew it out, Susan was startled.

The thing he held in his hands seemed to be a rounded, flexible black stick. It was over three feet long and perhaps an inch thick at one end, tapering to a point.

"It's a *sjambok*," he explained. "This one is made of rhino hide, cut wet, and then salted for preservation, rolled, and dried. It's the sort of whip the Boers used to drive oxen. Or it could be used for flogging, when necessary. In fact, the police still use *sjamboks* today. This one belonged to my father. See—he cut his initials into the thickened part that makes the handle."

He held the whip out to her, but she did not touch it. There was an ugly look about it that repelled her.

Dirk raised the *sjambok* and lashed it whistling through the air. Behind her Susan heard a soft sound of dismay. She turned to see Willi, her hands laden with fresh towels, standing in the doorway. Her eyes were upon the whip in something like horror.

Laughing at her expression, Dirk gave it another whack through the air, while Willi stood frozen, watching him.

"Don't do that again," Susan pleaded. "You've frightened Willi and you've frightened me. I don't like whips."

Dirk smiled at the colored girl. "This was just a practice session. I haven't had it in my hands since I was a boy."

Willi did not return his smile. Her gaze dropped and she went mutely away with her towels.

"You really did frighten her," Susan said. "It's a brutal-looking thing."

"She probably thought I was going to beat you with it," Dirk smiled.

"But why do you want it? Why did you get it out?"

He pulled the tough leather of the whip through his hands as if he enjoyed the feel of it. "Mainly because I thought it would make an interesting wall decoration. The voortrekkers used whips like this. They're part of our history."

She had no wish to oppose him, but she was not particularly happy when he fixed brackets on the living room wall and set the whip upon them. The pattern it made was far from decorative in Susan's eyes, and it lent a violent and disturbing note to their quiet living room.

7

Since Dirk preferred to avoid any social fanfare over their marriage and Niklaas van Pelt shunned publicity, no announcements were given to the papers. The news was allowed to spread gradually among Dirk's friends.

Susan was happy enough to postpone the day when she would have to take up the social role that might be expected of her as Dirk's wife. A life of leisure, of belonging to a club, of going in for tennis and watching cricket matches, was not entirely to her taste. In her mind she was still a working girl with a desire to earn a reputation by means of her pictures. Toward this attitude Dirk remained tolerant and encouraging, but she knew he did not take it seriously.

So far she had made no really constructive steps in the direction of furthering her work. Though she had a darkroom set up now, she had done no more than snap odd pictures like any sightseer. She must, she knew, determine upon some plan that would make her pictures marketable. Magazines were more interested in picture stories than in isolated shots. So she must work out such a story to photograph. There should be a good many possibilities in Cape Town.

One morning, ten days or so after her arrival, she awakened with a strong urge to get away from the house and wander on foot, tracking down a real story. She would set out, she decided, in the direction of the Public Gardens, which she still remembered affectionately from her childhood.

Learning her way about Cape Town had been an easy matter. The downtown streets crossed one another in the straight lines of a checkerboard, with Adderley Street running down to the bay as the main business thoroughfare, crossed near its foot by the Strand. Susan had already gone downtown on shopping trips and was learning to get about by bus and trolley.

But this morning she wanted to walk. When she set out soon after breakfast there was a brisk wind blowing and she was glad of the loose coat flung about her. Over one shoulder she carried by their straps both her camera and the big leather handbag in which she could put her light meter and extra rolls of film.

More than once she stopped for shots—of a sidewalk fruit stand, of a two-wheeled pony-drawn vegetable cart heaped high with bright orange carrots and green cabbages, of a house with the beautiful iron lacework that reminded her of New Orleans. She paused to watch boys on the way to school, dressed in the short pants and identical caps of the English schoolboy, and she caught a picture of them indulging in a bit of horseplay. Colored children were on their way to school as well, moving along with an air of independence, as though adult burdens had not yet descended upon them, and they too wore neat uniforms. It was notable, however, that the two groups of children ignored each other as if they did not exist.

The streets looked tranquil in the morning sunlight and, if this was South Africa, the screaming headlines seemed far away. Yet beneath the surface she knew the cancer of apartheid was at work. All was not as it seemed from this quiet

77

viewpoint. The hint of a picture story began to stir in her mind and she walked on, watching all she saw with a renewed interest.

She came at length to the upper end of what everyone in Cape Town called "the Avenue." Government Avenue had its history in Cape Town's beginnings, when the first vegetable garden had been planted by Jan van Riebeeck on the site of the present gardens.

The wide path of reddish earth was closed to vehicles and all day long pedestrians used it as a pleasant thoroughfare that led directly into Adderley Street. On either side oak trees had been planted and the day would come when their branches would arch overhead, but now they were still young trees, unable to rival the giants over in the Public Gardens at her left. This morning scores of gentle ring-necked doves were out and their bubbling coo was everywhere. If any sound was truly typical of Cape Town in spring and summer, it was the ubiquitous cu-cu-cooing of the doves as they walked and fluttered about the gardens and avenue.

When she came abreast of the noisy aviary, Susan left the walk to wander among flower beds aglow with everything from the conventional blossoms of England and America to South Africa's brilliant and exotic blooms. Paths wound beneath great trees that had been brought here from distant parts of the world. A belombraboom with huge uncovered roots caught her eye, and a clump of papyrus. Everywhere doves and pigeons paraded watchfully, their bright eyes ready for tossed peanuts. Squirrels came tamely down from their trees to feed from the hands of small children, out early with their English nannies. All this Susan had loved as a child and she took pictures purposefully of the quiet, peaceful scene.

Farther on, past a fountain where a boy clasped a dolphin in his arms, she came upon a statue of John Cecil Rhodes. His upraised arm pointed across the bay and there were words on a plaque in the stone: YOUR HINTERLAND IS THERE.

This she found puzzling. The bay opened to the ocean and there was no hinterland for South Africa off there to the west. She had walked around the statue twice, considering the matter, when she became aware of a man observing her. She saw him out of the corner of her eye, and when he continued to watch her, she threw him a quick look. It was John Cornish.

Her first instinct was to walk quickly away. This man had caused her enough trouble and it would be wiser not to speak to him at all. But he came toward her and she was caught.

"Good morning, Mrs. Hohenfield," he said.

She answered his greeting and turned to walk on, but he did not appear to see her movement away from him.

"I hope I didn't cause you any difficulty the other day," he went on. "I'm afraid your husband was displeased at finding me there."

This was something she had no intention of discussing, yet in spite of the disapproval she knew she might expect from Dirk she was still curious about this man. A few moments of casual talk could do no great harm. She glanced up at Cecil Rhodes for help.

"Why is he pointing out to sea?" she asked. "There's no hinterland out there."

Cornish gave her the grave, slow smile that had so little warmth in it. "Like most *uitlanders*, you've turned yourself around. The newcomer forgets that Cape Town, and the mountain too, face north. The Atlantic is really off to your left beyond the Lion's Head. Across the bay to the north lies Africa."

She felt like telling him that she was no *uitlander*, but remembered in time that he had no knowledge of her identity. Her curiosity about this man's determined purpose still held her from walking away.

"Have you managed to see Niklaas van Pelt?" she asked frankly.

He shook his head. "Not yet. But I've not given up. The chance will come."

Having committed herself thus far, she plunged on. "But why is it so important to you? Why can't you write about him out of the material that must already be available? And out of your own past knowledge of him?"

"Perhaps the past is the very thing I want to know more about firsthand," he said.

It came to her that here lay an opportunity to find out the things her father had forbidden Dirk to tell her and that she felt an increasing desire to know.

"Will you tell me what happened?" she asked. "These are things Dirk doesn't want to discuss. Understandably, since he works for Mr. van Pelt. But I would truly like to know."

He studied her from beneath craggy brows as if measuring her in some way. She sensed in him a deep intensity held well in check. He gestured toward a nearby bench where sunlight speckled through leaves overhead.

"Will you sit down for a moment? I'd like to tell you. Per-

79

haps if you know the story you won't think me quite such a blackguard as your husband believes."

She seated herself in a place of sunny warmth at one end of the bench. Doves cooed hopefully at her feet and a squirrel chattered his indignation when he found she had nothing for him. In the serenity of these gardens the rocky face of the mountain was hidden and she realized that sometimes its ever-present mass could be a little oppressive.

John Cornish clasped long, rather bony hands, interlacing the fingers loosely and staring off into the distance of Rhodes's hinterland. Susan waited for him to begin.

"Everything goes back to diamonds," he said at last. "Diamonds and their effect upon men. Niklaas van Pelt went to prison because he was convicted of stealing diamonds."

This seemed to be in contradiction to what Dirk had told her and she frowned. "Do you mean the big diamond that disappeared? The one they call the Kimberley Royal?"

"The bad luck stone?" he said. "No, not the Kimberley. That's another story, though I have my own idea of what may have happened to that particular stone. The cache found in the van Pelt house in Johannesburg was of much smaller diamonds—though still gem stones."

"Found in the van Pelt house?" Susan repeated, not quite believing.

"That's right. I'd been invalided out of the war." He patted his right leg, outstretched before him. "And I was working for a Johannesburg paper. I was given an assignment to do a piece about diamond smuggling. Always a popular subject in South Africa. I took it seriously and I was keen on doing a good job. In the course of my nosing about I came hot on a trail that I followed long enough to turn over to the authorities. The details are unimportant, but the search ended with Niklaas van Pelt."

A muscle had tightened in the rugged line of his jaw and she sensed how merciless this man might be as an enemy. In dismayed silence she waited for him to continue.

"My own father had died a few years before. Perhaps you don't know that Niklaas van Pelt was my father's close friend. My mother was American and she wanted to get home as soon as the war was over. I went with her when the time came, and stayed on in the States. But at this time I was fairly close to Mr. van Pelt. His son Paul had been my good friend and I was still broken up over his death in action. So you can see that I would not have unlocked this Pandora's box intentionally, knowing the van Pelts would be involved. Before I realized what might happen I'd cracked it wide open and the matter was out of my hands."

"Did they actually prove that Mr. van Pelt had taken the stones?" Susan asked, increasingly disturbed by what she was hearing.

"That wasn't necessary," Cornish said. "When he knew the jig was up he confessed the whole thing. He had been on the receiving end, though he would not name any accomplices. So the other, or others, got away free. He was given a three-year sentence and I found myself covering the story for my paper."

"But doesn't Niklaas van Pelt know this was something you couldn't help?" she asked. "Why should he still be angry with you and refuse to see you after all this time?"

"I suppose I could have quit my job. But I chose not to. I can't blame him for being resentful."

"Yet you don't believe he also took the Kimberley diamond? Why not?"

"While I don't believe he took it, I think it was a jolly good thing the big stone's disappearance was kept quiet at the time and the friend who had trusted him with it kept the whole thing under cover. His trust seems to have been justified because when Niklaas van Pelt got out of prison he made himself a poor man by paying back every cent of the market value of that stone. He had to build up a new life for himself on borrowed money."

Susan listened in increasing bewilderment. "But how could the same man who paid off the debt of that big stone have been guilty of stealing the other diamonds? The two things don't fit together."

"That," said John Cornish, "is exactly what has haunted me for all these years. That's the thing that has brought me to the writing of this book, brought me back to South Africa. But I can't clear it up unless old Niklaas himself is now willing to tell the story."

She was beginning to understand, and something of the animosity she had felt toward John Cornish was fading. Surely Dirk did not know all these things. He was protecting her father mistakenly.

"It must have taken a great deal of courage for Mr. van Pelt to begin all over again," she said. "He must have lost the trust of a great many people."

"But not all," Cornish told her. "There's a curious thing

about this matter of diamonds in South Africa. You have to remember that the country isn't very old. No older, really, than Manhattan, which the Dutch were settling at the same time they moved into the Cape. Even that three hundred years belongs more to Cape Town than to Johannesburg and Kimberley. Jo'burg was a sprawling mining town just seventy years ago, and Kimberley is only a few years older. In those early days there was a lot of smuggling going on and people got a bit casual about it. Even now there are some who regard it as a minor crime, not quite so reprehensible as stealing a man's ox. I suspect the color of romance hangs about the whole thing, a little like the romantic notions of America's lawless western days. The diamond people, naturally, take a dimmer view since too much leakage of diamonds out of the monopoly would send the world price down. Still, sentences are not so heavy as they once were, and a man may live them down. Niklaas van Pelt has done that to some extent. Though the stamp of disgrace is still there because of the high position he held, and never to be quite overlooked."

"But there's such a discrepancy between being honorbound over the big stone, and holding a cache of smaller stones in his own home. Haven't you any idea of the answer?"

The man beside her leaned over and picked up a pebble from the path, tossing it lightly in his palm as if he weighed the decision of whether or not to speak his thoughts. Then he dropped the stone and turned to her.

"There was a woman in the case. A pretty, rather frivolous American woman."

Susan stiffened. She folded her hands about the leather straps of camera and handbag to keep them quiet. She must say nothing, do nothing to stop him at this point, though something uneasy and fearful was wakening in her.

"Go on," she said softly.

"This woman was a good deal younger than Niklaas—she was his second wife. I believe she was stranded here after some sort of concert tour failed, and she went to work for De Beers."

"De Beers!" Susan could not help the exclamation. Claire had said she'd worked for some time in South Africa but she had never mentioned that it was for De Beers.

"Yes; that's where Niklaas met her. He was still connected with the company at that point, but he retired a bit later to give all his time to government matters. He wanted to run for Parliament and he became active in the government after his marriage. The woman—her name was Claire—had found herself a wealthy and distinguished husband. From then on she proceeded to ruin him."

"What do you mean?" Susan asked more sharply than she meant to.

John Cornish gave her a slow, searching look. "Perhaps I'm saying too much? For all I know, your husband may have thought very highly of the American woman who married Niklaas."

"I want to hear it all," Susan insisted, holding tightly to the leather straps.

"There's not much more. I suspect that it was Claire who had managed to smuggle out that little cache of diamonds into her own possession. Perhaps there were even more that she had disposed of from time to time. She must have held onto the remainder after her marriage."

"If this is true, why wouldn't she admit it when Niklaas was arrested? Why wouldn't she tell the truth and save her husband from going to jail?"

"So that she might go to jail in his stead?" Cornish raised a dark eyebrow quizzically. "It appears that she wasn't that sort of woman. It would also seem that Niklaas was a gentleman and would not betray her."

Susan let go of camera and handbag and faced him angrily. "I don't believe a word of what you're saying! It's all the wildest speculation! I should think it would be a horrible thing to release such a story after all these years and disgrace someone who can't speak for herself."

Cornish remained relaxed in the face of her indignation, though it must have puzzled him a little. "Oh, I intend to let her speak for herself. When I get as much of the story as possible out of Niklaas, I'll go back to the States and find her. I believe she's still living in Chicago. Of course she would be safe enough from prosecution by this time, even if she is guilty."

Susan had stood all she could. "At least she's safe from such a visit!" she cried. "You can't hurt her now—she's out of your reach."

He merely stared at her, and she rushed on, her words tumbling out almost incoherently.

"You might as well know the truth! Claire van Pelt was my mother. She died only a little while ago. And I won't let you touch her memory with your miserable, made-up suspicions!"

She was so angry she was close to tears and it was all she could manage to blink them back. John Cornish regarded her in dismay for a moment. Then the guard he had lowered a little seemed to slip coldly into place again.

"I'm sorry if I've shocked you by telling you things you didn't know. But you asked for this. After all, it was hardly fair to hide your identity at the same time that you were questioning me."

She had no interest in what he regarded as fair. "I can see now why neither my father nor Dirk wanted me to know about all this. They didn't want me to be hurt by such lies. It was better for me not to know."

He answered her without emotion. "If your mother was innocent, then that would be enough to protect her. She needn't have run away. In any event, it's better for you to know the truth. This isn't something you could hide from, or be protected from, forever. Not here in Cape Town."

She thrust back her anger as best she could. It was necessary to convince him that he was wrong—wickedly wrong.

"My mother was never a thief. She liked to be happy, and perhaps she was a little bit spoiled because everyone loved her and gave her what she wanted. Besides—what could she have done with illegal diamonds in her possession? How could she have disposed of them?"

"Sometime you might ask your husband to tell you about I.D.B.," Cornish said.

She knew there was no way of convincing him. Not now. And she could bear no more. Abruptly she stood up, scattering a flock of doves, but before she could turn away, he rose and caught her elbow firmly but lightly in his clasp.

"Wait," he said and there was a note of command in his voice that halted her in spite of her longing to get away. "You were right about one thing. I don't know the truth of this matter yet. I am only speculating. But neither can you be sure of the truth. It may be a painful choice either way. But less painful to the dead than to the living."

She saw his face through swimming tears, stern and merciless. "I don't care about the living!" she cried, and hated the way her voice choked. "My father means nothing to me. But I still love my mother. I was closer to her than anyone else was, and I know what she was like."

"Nevertheless," he said relentlessly, "the truth is something to be respected for itself, without regard to one's own emotional involvement or whether one believes this thing or that. If I'm wrong, why not prove me wrong?"

She drew her elbow from his grasp as if she found his touch repugnant. "What do you mean?"

"I think you know very well what I mean," he said, and his eyes held hers, though now he did not touch her.

This was a man who would never give up. She understood that clearly now and she began to feel a little frightened.

"What do you want me to do?" she demanded. "What do you expect of me?"

A smile touched his mouth and there was unexpected kindness in it. "I will leave that to you. Good morning, Mrs. Hohenfield." He touched the brim of his hat and walked away through the gardens.

She watched him go, noting the slight limp with which he moved, the erect carriage of his shoulders. And she detested him with all her heart. His very walking away so abruptly was an affront. It should have been Susan Hohenfield who had walked away and left him, spurning his ridiculous story. Still shaken, she turned in the opposite direction and began to walk toward home.

8

Not even the long brisk climb back to the Aerie assuaged her anger. She continued to feel keyed up and distraught, yet impatient with her own unreliable emotions.

Cornish, she reminded herself, was merely a journalist after a good story. His suspicions were not to be considered. He had not known Claire as she had. He could not realize how incapable of harm her mother had been.

In an attempt to quiet her thoughts, she went into the darkroom as soon as she reached home and shut herself in to develop the strip of pictures she had taken. Working in the quiet little room by the faint light of one red bulb had a calming effect upon her nerves. Here she could be busy with her hands, give her attention to the handling of her materials, and hold all thought in abeyance. It was a treatment she had used more than once in Chicago when things had gone badly at the paper.

By the time the film had been attached to a clip and hung up to dry she felt a little better, and was even able to eat the lunch that Willi served her. In the afternoon she returned to the darkroom to print the pictures from her strip of film trying to keep herself interested in the mechanical work before her. But now as her hands busied themselves she began to think of her father as she had seen him at the time of their interview. An old man who had never allowed himself to be swayed by emotion. An intelligent and thoughtful man, perhaps, but a cold one, who had lost all touch with the warmth and excitement of living.

Why had Claire run away? The question she was holding off flashed through her mind. Why had she not stayed to support her husband in his time of trouble?

Claire's story had always been that Niklaas had done some wicked thing for which he deserved imprisonment. She could never forgive him, she said, or ever again trust him. She had given all her efforts to getting her daughter away from South Africa so that she should not suffer for her father's sins. These, surely, were not the actions of a woman who was to blame for her husband's imprisonment.

Nevertheless, whether Susan liked it or not, John Cornish had set squarely in front of her a problem she must eventually face. The darkroom had given her a respite, only a postponement. When she finished with her prints, the problem was still there where he had placed it. Regardless of how Dirk might feel about this last encounter with Cornish, she would have to tell him about it, set the whole story before him, and ask his advice. She could not endure this turmoil and doubting alone.

Having come to a decision, she grew eager to talk to Dirk, and the afternoon passed slowly. She did not broach the subject immediately at dinner, however, but held to other topics through the meal. Dirk had spent the day in the store, where some difficulty had arisen, and he was tired and faintly absent-minded.

Not until they were in the living room after dinner, with a cheery coal fire in the grate, did she tell him of her meeting with John Cornish that morning. At her first words his attention was arrested but, though she saw his mouth tighten, she went on, straight through to the end, trying to make it as fair a story as possible, giving Cornish credit for the purpose he claimed—an attempt to learn the truth. But her voice broke a little when she came to the part about her mother.

Dirk's manner softened. "I'm sorry," he said. "You shouldn't have been told so cruelly. There were always rumors, of course. But I think you needn't worry about them. At least this should bring home to you the reasons why I've wanted nothing to do with Cornish. There's no reason for Uncle Niklaas to be tried twice. Cornish is a man bent on stirring up old troubles. Perhaps more trouble than you dream is possible."

"Trouble for whom?" she asked.

"Let me worry about that. Just let these sleeping dogs lie."

Puzzled though she was by his words, her thoughts turned back to Claire.

"*You* don't believe my mother was a thief, do you?" she asked directly.

Dirk came to sit beside her and took her left hand into his own, turning it so that light struck the pink diamond.

"Listen to me, Susan. Listen for once with your mind instead of your emotions. Perhaps the best thing for everyone concerned would be for you to recall whatever you can about the Kimberley Royal. If that mystery could be cleared up, it would help your father. It might even help to dispel any lingering suspicions against your mother. And, in part, it would answer John Cornish."

This persistent notion that she had something to remember was too much. Impatiently she pulled her hand from his grasp with a jerk that sent it backward against a heavy bronze bookend on the table beside her. The unintentional knock bruised her knuckles and the pink stone clinked against the bronze.

Dirk caught her hand and turned it so that he could examine the ring. "Take care," he warned, and ran his thumb over the diamond. "I'd hate to see you injure my lucky stone."

Her impatience, her bafflement increased. "Considering that diamonds are supposed to be the hardest of all stones, I'm not likely to hurt it with a tap like that," she said crossly.

He laughed at her indignation and let her hand go. "Don't be too sure. Diamonds are brittle stones. That's the way they shape them, you know—by tapping them along the lines of cleavage. Sometimes good stones are ruined in the process, though it's true it has to be a pretty sharp blow. Anyway, do remember that I've given my luck into your hands—so be careful with it."

There was an amused note in his voice as if he laughed at himself, but Susan's attention was still upon the issue that had irritated her.

"It's silly to expect me to remember something when there really isn't anything for me to remember."

"How can you be sure? What about the dream you had the other night?" he reminded her. "Have you ever thought there might be a reason behind it?"

"I know the reason," Susan told him. "There was talk about diamonds that day. It haunted me. So it was only natural that diamonds should get into my dreams."

"But why did you see a *blue* fire? Why was the flashing in your dream always a blue light?"

She stared at him. "What do you mean?"

"Has anyone ever described the Kimberley to you? It was a blue-white stone with a trick of flashing an intense blue light."

No, she thought, startled, no one had told her that, and his words frightened her a little.

"There's no accounting for dreams," she said quickly and turned from the subject. "Tell me what John Cornish meant when he said to ask about I.D.B.?"

"Anyone in the Union could tell you that," Dirk said. "The letters stand for Illicit Diamond Buying, the plague of the country. In other words, smuggling diamonds and selling them illicitly."

"But he surely couldn't have meant that my mother might have engaged in smuggling," Susan said.

Dirk's patience had clearly been exhausted. "Who knows what Cornish meant?" he said, and glanced at the watch on his wrist. "In any case, I've work to do at my desk tonight and I'd better be at it. You'll excuse me, darling?"

She sensed his disappointment in her and perhaps his exasperation. But at least he had not scolded her this time for speaking with John Cornish. He had been genuinely sorry that she had learned the truth of the situation in a sudden, shocking way. But still he had wanted more of her than she knew how to give.

When he had gone into the small room Mara had set up for him as an office, she sat staring at the whip that hung like a black exclamation mark against the wall. The *sjambok* stood for something more than voortrekker history, she felt sure, and she wished she could know exactly why Dirk had placed it there. In a way it was a symbol of the impenetrable side of his nature which she did not understand, yet longed to understand because it was a part of him and must be accepted.

The firelight no longer seemed cheery, and away from its immediate warmth the room was chill. She had no desire to sit here alone, so she went into the hall for her coat. Then she let herself quietly out the front door and walked about the quiet garden. The low sustaining wall again invited her, and she sat down on the stone.

An aching loneliness was once more upon her, and the familiar soreness of missing her mother that the talk about Claire had revived. Perhaps she was even a little homesick for the life she had led for the past few years in Chicago. Though there had been loneliness there too, and a sense of waiting for something important to happen that would give her days some depth of meaning. Until Dirk's coming she had felt shapeless and unformed. When he had put the pink diamond on her finger everything had begun to take shape, to make sense, and she had believed that she would never be lonely again.

Her own long sigh was the only sound in the evening hush that lay over Cape Town. The bubbling of the doves had quieted, the lowered murmur of traffic was distant. On the air was a scent that spoke of pines and the sea. Nearby a tall blue gum rustled its leaves and fell silent, as if it too had sighed. A bright full moon was rising, touching the great mass of the mountain, brightening the hillside below the wall. Leaning so she might look down, Susan could see that a narrow pathway wound through the grass, dropping away toward the black shadows of the ravine where the thick stand of pines stood guard. Just this side of the pines several tall objects shone with a dark gleam in the moonlight and she wondered what they were. If they were rocks, they were huge ones standing upright in monolithic fashion.

Outside the wall on which she sat the path ran uphill, appearing to end at the next street above. Sometime soon she must explore the downward plunge of the path and find out where it went.

The quiet of the night began to possess her, and to ease and still her unquiet spirit. The soreness and confusion were easing, leaving her relaxed, yet with her mind clear and free for once of stubborn resistance. Now she could begin to think quietly as she had not done before. Now she could face the question she had been thrusting so persistently from her mind.

Was it possible that some knowledge did lie hidden deep in her memory? A knowledge of something that had happened in her childhood and which she had long since forgotten? What if, instead of trying to resist Dirk's suggestion, which after all was a reasonable one, she tried to open her mind, tried to go backward through the years?

But *how* was she to do this? It would be necessary to retrace her steps, to recall incidents she had forgotten, to remember the days she had spent here in Cape Town. And this was not so easy. Happy memories came to mind readily but they were spotted here and there, without surrounding incident to give them continuity and complete a picture. All that was hurtful and unpleasant had been banished to some hiding place to which she had lost the key. That door would not open at will. Yet there must be a way to open it.

The cool, bracing night air seemed to shake away her cobwebby confusion and bring her to a state of clarity. She pulled her coat collar about her ears and swung her feet onto the wall, drawing her knees up so that she could rest her head against them and close her eyes.

Go back! she told herself intently. Try to remember what happened!

She could see the house again clearly—her father's house that she had visited a few days ago. But now for the first time since she had come here she could see it with a child's eyes, looking bigger than it really was, and with her father's study the focal point, the heart of the entire house. That was the room she had most liked—and most dreaded. It was connected in her mind with punishment and with lectures from her father, but such matters had not made her seriously unhappy for long. There was something more that brought the room into focus. Yet even as she struggled to remember a sense of dread began to possess her. It was subtly chilling and fearful, so that her impulse was to slam the door upon it and bring herself quickly back to the present. She managed to resist the impulse and let her memories come as they would in a bewildering rush.

There were angry voices now, clattering through her mind. A flashing glimpse of her mother weeping hysterically, of her father's face stern and cold as death. In the midst of all this crouched a child who sensed that something dreadful was happening, something no one would explain to her, something she could not understand. The adult Susan shrank as the child had done and the door closed swiftly upon all that was fearful, shutting it away from present consciousness.

She did not give up at once. Though she was shivering from more than the evening wind, she attempted once more to force the picture to come clear. But the voices had faded and all that was frightening had vanished. Instead, she could remember the sound of waves against a ship's side and long walks with Claire around and around a deck. Her mother's voice came to her clearly: "Forget what happened, dearest. We're going away from South Africa and we're never coming back. We're going to the place where I grew up and you'll never have to be frightened again."

She could hear her own voice questioning. "Will Father be

there too?" And her mother's answer: "No, dear. We must forget about everything connected with South Africa. We must—" But then her mother had burst into tears and would say no more. Soon the small Susan had found that Claire would cry whenever Niklaas was mentioned, so she learned not to bring up his name.

Even as they began to return, the pictures began to slip from her grasp. The power to go back faded like a mist as she reached out to hold it.

Somewhere on the hillside the voice she had heard before was singing in Afrikaans. She knew the words: "My heart is so sore, my heart is so sore . . ."

Swinging herself down from the wall, she turned back toward the house. She had met with defeat for the moment, but she had moved in the right direction. What better way was there both to please Dirk and prove to him that she had nothing important to remember than to recall all the details of that distant time?

The mournful words of the song followed her upstairs and possessed her spirit with their sense of time slipping too quickly away.

9

In the days that followed, Susan was unable to push remembrance any further or to solve the problem she had accepted that evening in the garden. Most of the time the door remained firmly shut and when she tried to think herself back into her father's house she could remember it only through adult eyes as she saw it now.

There were, too, new distractions in her life. Susan van Pelt's marriage to Dirk Hohenfield ceased to concern only themselves. The word had spread along the Cape Peninsula's grapevine and reporters from the *Cape Argus* and the *Cape Times* came up to the Aerie to interview her. The old story of Niklaas van Pelt was revived and reviewed and much was made of the fact that his daughter had returned to South Africa married to his ward. The stories were not unsympathetic, but Dirk said Niklaas was upset by them and had refused to see reporters. He had stated through Mara that his personal concerns were of no interest or concern to anyone in South Africa these days. He wished only to be left alone.

Once the word got about, a certain degree of social life reached out to include Dirk and Susan. People were socially minded here, though there was the clannishness too of old-established families. The Cape Peninsula boasted a genuine and gentle culture that was still unknown to that young and lusty upstart, Johannesburg.

One Sunday afternoon they drove with another couple in Dirk's car to the Kirstenbosch Gardens to see the breathtaking display of spring flowers that grew on the other side of Devil's Peak. On the way back they went through the grounds of Cape Town University, spread out handsomely below the jagged brow of the peak.

All this Susan enjoyed, yet she sensed that she and Dirk were somehow not a true part of Cape Town social life. They might be drawn to its perimeter, but they would never be deeply involved in its central activity. Perhaps because they did not wholly fit the pattern. Both, in their different ways, were outsiders—even Dirk. And there might be another reason. In spite of Cornish's claim that Niklaas van Pelt had pretty much lived down the blight of his disgrace, she wondered if the old scandal did not still linger in people's minds and reflect upon his ward and daughter.

Her own work with her camera offered a respite from uneasy thoughts, and her interest was growing as she developed the story picture she wanted to do. Sometimes it was necessary to take dozens of shots in order to get a few that would convey the impact of a story and so far the pictures she had taken were distinctly one-sided.

Her intention was to choose from many a few pictures that would show the peaceful everyday life of Cape Town, the easily visible surface life. Against these she would contrast a few penetrating shots of what lay beneath. But since the world of the dark people was not easily opened to her, this was hard to accomplish.

She had wanted to visit Langa, the native location where there had been so much trouble, but Dirk would not consider taking her there. Indeed, he warned her that under present circumstances she was liable to get herself arrested if she attempted to take pictures in certain localities.

Though blocked for the moment, she did not give up the

idea. There would be a way. In the meantime she contented herself with shots of the SLEGS VIR BLANKES signs that managed to convey the indignity they represented. Segregation in Cape Town took odd turns, she discovered. Benches in the parks were for anyone. In the libraries men and women of different races sat elbow to elbow. Yet the greater liberality of the English community was not permitted to extend to theaters or sports stadia. Bus lines run by the Union government were segregated. Those municipally owned by Cape Town were open to all. She also found that the colored citizen sometimes set himself above the black African and could be as prejudiced as anyone else.

It was Willi who told Susan about District Six. A half mile or so from the center of the business section, on a hill below Devil's Peak, was an area where many respectable colored people lived. But crowding in upon them, almost engulfing them, were the dregs of the colored group. The crime incident was high, young teen-age toughs known as skollies preyed upon the more respectable and fought with each other. The smoking and selling of dagga—a form of marijuana—was flagrant. Poverty and depravity were the lot of many. District Six belonged mainly to the coloreds and only a few black Africans lived or worked there as watchmen or caretakers in the schools.

This district, Susan decided, would be a place where she might get below the peaceful surface of white Cape Town. She had a strong suspicion that Dirk, if he knew, would forbid her to go there, so she kept her plans to herself. She had no reason to be afraid. After all, she had taken a good many pictures in Chicago's slums and tougher sections, and she had only sympathy for the underprivileged.

She chose a sunny early morning that would be good for picture taking, and before she left the house she told Willi where she was going. The girl looked both astonished and dismayed. Crimes were committed in District Six almost every day, Willi warned her with that flash of spirit that sometimes contradicted her usual gentleness of manner. Mr. Hohenfield would not approve of her going into that section alone.

"I won't tell him until after I have my pictures," Susan said cheerfully. "Don't worry. I'm not very reckless and I won't stay too long."

She set off dressed much as she had been that day when Dirk had found her taking pictures of the train accident in Chicago, in a beret, an engulfing trench coat, and low-heeled shoes.

A short distance from her goal she left the bus and set out on foot to penetrate the neighborhood she wanted to see. In many ways it was like the slums of Chicago's South Side, probably like those of any city. There was a teeming humanity on every hand, living in homes that had once been the elegant residences of prosperous white people, long since moved away. Now the houses were crumbling to ruin, undoubtedly rat-infested, vermin-ridden. Probably there were white slum landlords here, as elsewhere, who fattened on the misery of those who lacked the power to ensure better living conditions. Children swarmed on the stoops, in the streets, tumbling over the sidewalks, some screaming and shouting like children anywhere, others sitting in vacant-eyed apathy. For the most part their elders paid her little attention. She was aware of sidelong looks from a few, of resentful glances from others, but most of those she passed took the safest course by pretending she did not exist.

She was getting her pictures now, yet this sort of degradation existed in slums everywhere; it was not uniquely South African. It had probably existed before apartheid had come into being. Indeed, moving people out of such slums might give the government some justification for building new locations.

Then, as she was crossing an alleyway that opened off what seemed to be one of the main streets of the area, she saw something that made her stop to watch. An Afrikaner policeman was standing before a sort of shed. Its doors and windows had long since vanished and it stood open to the alley. A colored woman with a sleeping child in her arms sat on a tipped-up box, talking to a man who was clearly a black African. As Susan watched, the officer stepped up to the man, speaking curtly in Afrikaans, demanding what he was doing, why he was not at work.

Susan had recovered enough of the language she had known as a child so that she grasped most of the interchange. The policeman, not satisfied with the answer he was given, asked for the African's pass. The colored people, so far, were not required to carry passes, but without a pass none of the native population could move anywhere in South Africa, and passes must be presented on demand at any time. Not to have one was to invite arrest.

As she watched, Susan did not forget her camera. Unobtrusively, behind the policeman's back, she caught the picture. The African was gesturing toward a jacket, hung on a nail a few feet away. His pass was there, he said. But the officer would not give him a chance to get it. He had broken the law in not having it on his person, and that was that. Before Susan's eyes the unreasonable arrest was made, and her camera clicked through the entire incident, with pauses only for hurried film winding. What she had witnessed shocked her, and she was all the more eager to make a record that the outside world might see.

On the heels of her final picture, the policeman turned, prodding his captive ahead of him, and came toward her. There was no time for escape on her part. His first surprised reaction was due perhaps to her white skin. Then he saw the camera in her hands.

"Why are you in this place?" he asked in Afrikaans. "What are you doing with the camera?"

"I've been taking pictures around Cape Town," she told him in English. "There's no reason why I should not, is there?" Her attempted calm was a bluff. It was hard not to show her anger over what had happened, hard not to rush foolishly to the aid of the African, whose position she would only worsen.

The officer held his prisoner by one arm, ignoring the man's further effort to explain that his pass was in the jacket hanging not six feet away. He gave his attention coldly to Susan.

"You are English?" he asked, changing to that language.

Susan's position was not one she could quickly explain and he gave her no time. He looked as if he intended to arrest her too, and she had no idea what would have happened next if there had not been an interruption.

Behind her a car door slammed and feet came running. In a moment Mara Bellman was at her side, smiling at the policeman, speaking to him rapidly in fluent Afrikaans. She was saying in effect that the young lady from America did not know any better, that she was of course sorry if she had offended. She herself had been looking for the lady, fearing she might be lost. The officer would understand, of course.

What of the pictures the American had taken? the officer asked stolidly, not at all overwhelmed by Mara's charm.

The girl turned quickly to Susan. "Did you take any pictures? If you did, remove the film and give it to him."

Susan hesitated, not at all pleased by this rescue, even if it had saved her from temporary trouble. She was still indignant with the policeman. Indeed, with Mara here to help her out, she ought to speak her mind.

"You should have seen what just happened—" she began but Mara stopped her at once.

"Give him the film or I won't answer for the consequences. These are not ordinary times in South Africa."

They were both against her and there was nothing else to do. She opened the camera and took the film out without rolling it up, making sure that light reached her last few shots. At least there would be no evidence against her.

The policeman took the film and Mara thanked him graciously, giving Susan a little push toward Niklaas's car. She clearly meant to stand on no ceremony, and indignant though she was, Susan went. Mara started the Mercedes and drove down the street. She said nothing until they were out of District Six, and Susan sat beside her equally silent. She was furious at the policeman, furious over the loss of her pictures and with Mara for her highhanded rescue.

"It's fortunate that Willi phoned me after you set out this morning," Mara said when they had driven a few blocks. "I had some trouble finding you, or I might have stopped you more quickly."

"I didn't want to be stopped," Susan said. "If you hadn't rushed in, I might have been able to deal with the officer myself and saved my pictures in the bargain."

"You don't know our police," Mara told her dryly. "If it hadn't been for me, you might be in real trouble by now. They aren't fooling, you know, and they don't like such pictures being sent outside. I suppose that's what you intended?"

Susan had no wish to tell Mara what she intended. All her first instinctive distrust of the blond girl had swept to the fore.

"I'm a news photographer," she said a bit curtly. "I've been in difficult spots before and I've managed to get out of them. It was kind of you to interest yourself, but I'm quite capable of—"

"I didn't do it for you!" Mara broke in. "I did it for Dirk. I couldn't stand by and see you involve him in unpleasant publicity."

It was perfectly true that Dirk would not like what she had done, but Mara had no business assuming that publicity would necessarily have resulted if she had been allowed to handle the matter in her own way.

The car had been headed toward the Aerie, but suddenly Mara turned into a quiet side street of small white houses, drew the car to the curb, and switched off the engine.

"We might as well have this out," she said.

96

Susan, still lost in her own indignant thoughts, could only stare at her blankly. The other girl's cool poise had deserted her and she was breathing quickly, as if some long-simmering rage had suddenly boiled up in her and was out of restraint.

"You can't go on being fooled forever!" she said in a low, tense voice. "If it hadn't been for you, Dirk and I would be married by now."

Susan was as much appalled by the look in Mara's eyes as by her words. She said nothing at all.

Mara pushed back her heavy mass of blond hair as if the movement rid her of pent-up energy.

"I'm neither mad nor a fool," she went on. "I'm in love with Dirk and in the end I mean to have him back. So you might as well be warned."

Susan's amazement was growing. Somehow she could not take this outburst seriously. Mara was suffering from some dreadful delusion.

The blond girl had quieted a little, as if her first wild expending of emotion was over and she was groping her way back to her normal, guarded poise. Her tone was calmer when she spoke again, but there was still venom in the words.

"Don't you know why he married you?"

"Of course I do," Susan said promptly.

Mara went on as if she had not spoken. "It was because of the diamond. Because he wanted that fortune in his hands and if you could lead him to it, then you were worth whatever temporary sacrifices he might have to make."

"That's ridiculous," Susan said. "I suppose you're referring to the letter my mother wrote before she died. In the first place, that letter was a trick to gain me consideration from my father. Nothing else. In the second place, you surely can't believe that a man like Dirk would go so far as to marry simply because there might be a remote chance that his wife knew something about a diamond that disappeared years ago. The whole idea is silly."

Mara did not answer. She started the car and put it in gear.

"What do you think Dirk is going to say when I tell him about this?" Susan asked curiously. "Won't he be angry with *you* then?"

"You won't tell him," Mara said, and turned the car from the curb. "You won't take that risk. Because then everything would be out in the open and you wouldn't be able to pretend any more. Though if you do tell him it won't matter to me."

She sounded so angrily confident that Susan felt shaken for the first time in her own strong conviction. The evil of doubt

97

had crept subtly into her mind and now questions were there that had not existed before. She thought about them in silence as Mara drove her home. She remembered again Dirk's strangeness before their plane had landed in Cape Town, his stiffness at the airport, and the way she could not get through his guard that first day in the Aerie. That day when he had again been in touch with Mara Bellman. Yet later he had enveloped his wife with a love that she could not doubt and the uncertainties of their arrival had faded.

When the car drew up before the front gate, Susan quickly opened the door. She did not want to speak to Mara again, but the other woman reached across and caught her by the arm just as she would have stepped out.

"I pulled you out of trouble this time," she said. "And if you like we'll say nothing to Dirk about what you were up to. I jolly well don't want to talk to him about it. But next time I hope your troubles are a lot more serious. And if they are, I won't rescue you." Her eyes had narrowed and all the beauty was gone from her face. "In fact, I'd take great pleasure in helping them along."

Susan went into the house feeling a little sick. It was rather dreadful to see another woman rip away the guise of civilization and reveal what lay beneath. Could she be like that too? she wondered—and did not know the answer.

Willi met her in the hall, her manner one of quiet dignity, and Susan offered no reproach. Willi had acted upon the prompting of her own conscience and was not to be blamed for feeling that she must telephone Mara. Susan went upstairs and tried a little desperately to regain her composure before she had to face Dirk again. The cold look of the police officer's eyes, the limp jacket hanging on its hook, the helpless plight of the man arrested, mingled in her mind with the things Mara had said. The painful doubts she had planted began to take root.

Yet when Dirk came home that evening his mood was cheerful and her concealment successful. All went smoothly between them and a little of her fear subsided. No matter what had happened in the past, she told herself firmly, Dirk loved her now. Mara was simply a jealous woman who wanted to strike out and hurt the person who had hurt her. Seen in that light, she was more to be pitied than feared.

Yet it was necessary, Susan found, to tell herself this over and over.

10

The experience in District Six stopped Susan's picture taking for a time. If she could not catch the ugly side of Cape Town life as well as the pleasant, then there was no point in her trying the story she had in mind.

Her first sickness and shock over Mara's words faded and she made an effort to bolster her own confidence. She could not bring herself to broach the matter with Dirk, however, and evidently Mara had kept her word and said nothing herself.

As the days passed, she thought increasingly of the obligation John Cornish had placed upon her. More than ever she wanted to answer him, and to reassure Dirk. Once full remembrance had returned, there would be no more nonsense about a lost diamond. No more suspicions of Claire, and no more possibility that Mara's attack might have any truth in it. John Cornish would be stopped in his purpose and her marriage with Dirk would continue serenely with no threat of quicksand to betray her. It was a happy prospect and she dediced to further it without more delay.

She had not seen her father since her first visit to his house. No further summons had come from him. Nor had Dirk asked her to see him. But the conviction began to grow in her that the only way into the past was to seek him out again. Seek him out and ask that she be allowed to see the house she'd lived in as a child.

The morning she returned to Protea Hill was also the morning when she decided to explore the path that led downhill into the ravine. She told Willi she would be out for a while. Then she put on walking shoes and a sweater and went into the garden. The drop from wall to path was not great and she swung herself over the stone parapet and down into the grass on the far side. In bright sunlight the scent of pines was warm and spicy, and she took deep drafts of Cape Town's sparkling spring air.

The path dipped sharply beneath her feet as she followed it, and she saw that the upright objects she had glimpsed by moonlight the other night were indeed several rocks that stood upright like great monolithic shafts. They formed an irregular half circle away from the path and she looked behind them cautiously, a little fearful of snakes. There was something almost awesome about these rocks. Had some primeval force toppled them end over end to stand them at last in this position through all the ages since? The mountain above would remember that upheaval, she thought, gazing up at it. What she saw at the mountaintop brought her to a halt, watching in wonder as the phenomenon peculiar to Table Mountain happened before her eyes.

In an otherwise clear sky a fluffy cloud floated high above the mountain. Even as she looked, the Mountain exerted its attraction and the cloud dropped swiftly to its top. There it spread out in a layer of white over the entire table, drifting a little way down the sides so that it looked as if a tablecloth had been spread evenly over the flat top of the mountain. Above, the sky was still brightly blue.

Susan had seen this happen as a child, but she had forgotten until now what an astonishing sight it could be. Up there on the mountain, where all had been clear a moment before, the rocky top was now hidden by thick cloud.

Happy to have seen the mountain's performance, she followed the path down into the shadowy coolness of the grove where flat-topped pines clustered and then out into the open beyond. Here an amazing variety of tiny wildflowers spread over the fields. She stooped to pick a small flower with six widespread white petals, edged with black, its navy-blue heart touched with black and yellow stamens.

The path continued its downhill plunge to a place where a side path branched upward toward the houses on this opposite side of the ravine. Susan looked up to see her father's house a stone's throw away. The side path seemed to wind its way between houses to the street, with no wall to climb at this point. She followed it quickly and found herself outside the stone and iron fence of Protea Hill.

The yard boy saw her and came to open the gate. She went purposefully up the steps and stood before the familiar door with its long glass panels on either side. A maid answered her ring and invited her in just as Mara Bellman came down the stairs. Though she had prepared herself for this inevitable meeting, Susan winced inwardly at the sight of the other girl.

Today Mara wore a green suit that set off her fair skin and pale-blond hair and there was an aura of sophisticated perfume about her. Her eyes rested coolly upon Susan and she greeted her politely enough, without any of the letting down of her guard that she had displayed at their last meeting.

"If you're looking for Dirk," she said casually, "he's not here this morning."

"I'd like to see my father, if it's possible," Susan said.

"He has gone out in the car with Thomas," Mara told her. "I don't know when he'll be back."

She made no attempt to invite her in, and Susan knew that she would have to take matters into her own hands.

"I believe I'll wait for a little while in case Father should come home soon."

Mara hesitated, but Susan was Niklaas's daughter and she could hardly turn her away.

"Come in, if you like," she said grudgingly. "Though I can't promise that you won't have a long wait."

All she wanted was to get into the house, Susan thought. To be left alone with it. It didn't matter whether she saw her father or not. To reacquaint herself with one room would be a start. She could not very well ask Mara to show her through the entire house without her father's permission.

Mara led the way into a big, comfortable living room that had been changed considerably since Susan had last seen it. The furniture was set well back from the center of the room, arranged close to the walls. It was a room that had been made safe for a blind man, with no unexpected stumbling blocks.

Apparently Niklaas van Pelt had brought furniture here from his house in Johannesburg, for Susan recognized some of the pieces. She remembered particularly a great cabinet of stinkwood—that beautiful, ill-named wood of South Africa, odorous only in its freshly cut state. The grain had dark-colored markings that made a handsome, wavelike pattern, and the drawers were set with Cape silver key plates and handles. Over the fireplace hung a long copper warming pan, clearly Dutch in character. These old things suited the room and somehow suited Niklaas van Pelt.

"There are magazines on the table." Mara was curt. "If you want anything, just ring the bell near the door."

"Thank you," Susan said and sat down on a long couch, wanting only to be left here alone.

But Mara stood in the doorway, reluctant to go. "Have you thought over what we talked about the other day?" she asked.

Her audacity was surprising. Susan hesitated for a moment, once more taken aback. Then she spoke quietly:

"What was there to think about? Whatever may have happened in the past has no bearing on the present. I haven't been brooding about it."

Open dislike was alive in Mara's eyes. "You're wise not to put the matter to a test. As long as you don't lead Dirk to the diamond, you're safe enough. For a time at least."

Susan said nothing, refusing to be drawn into an open quarrel. Mara shrugged and went out of the room.

Now all hope of regaining contact with the house was gone. The necessary mood had been destroyed and Susan knew it would not return. When the maid came in with the inevitable eleven o'clock morning tea, Susan drank a cupful, trying to still the quivering resentment that Mara had aroused in her. Did the woman mean to bait her every time they met? The prospect was unthinkable, but for the moment she knew of no way to stop her. She was not yet ready to turn to Dirk about the matter. Was it fear of the truth that held her back? she wondered. Surely what had happened before she married Dirk need not concern her now. If she told Dirk, he would reassure her, but he would also think her foolish. There was no need to speak.

The sound of a car in the driveway indicated that her father had come home. Mara did not appear again, but the maid came to tell her that Mr. van Pelt awaited her in his study.

Again her father sat behind the great desk upon which every object had been placed with meticulous care so that there might be a minimum of groping for what he wanted. The heavy, polished cane with the silver head leaned against his red-leather chair, ready when he wanted it. As he took Susan's hand and drew her into the chair beside him, she felt again the cool, dry clasp of his fingers. She did not wait for him to ask the reason for her visit, but plunged at once into what she had to say. At her first mention of John Cornish's name, she sensed a stiffening in him. But his dark glasses gave nothing away and his face was expressionless as he listened.

She told him of her meeting with Cornish in the Public Gardens and of the story he had unwittingly told her, before he knew she was Claire van Pelt's daughter. She went on to speak frankly of Cornish's suspicions concerning Claire, and her father heard her through without interruption.

"So you see," she ended a little breathlessly, "I want to remember. I want to find my way back. Perhaps you can help me."

He was still for a long moment and there was a tightness

about his mouth. "I will not help you," he said at length. "Remembering is pointless. I know all that happened, and the only thing that is important to me now is to forget. I am sorry, indeed, that John Cornish has returned to Cape Town."

"But what if there really is something to that letter from my mother?" she persisted. "What if it's true that I may have known something as a child that I could bring back to mind if I really worked at it?"

"You mean concerning the diamond?" he asked. "Forget about that. I don't want to know what happened to it. The man who owned it is dead. And he was paid in full long before he died. The stone has caused nothing but misery in its history."

If he spoke the truth, then he had not been impressed by her mother's ruse, after all. He had not sent for her because of the diamond. In this realization might lie an assuaging of pain, but something else was more important now. She had no time to think of her own hurt.

"Do you think my mother took it?" she demanded. "Because that's that's what John Cornish believes and it's what he means to write about in his book."

"He will not do that," Niklaas said. "I will not permit it."

Remorselessly Susan went on. "He thinks she took the small diamonds too. He thinks she stole them when she worked for De Beers. He means to bring all this into the open in his book whether he has a chance to talk to you or not."

"Then I shall talk to him first." Her father's blue-veined hand slapped the desk before him and for an instant she saw him as she remembered him from her childhood—a physically powerful, forceful man, of whom many were afraid. Including, sometimes, herself and her mother.

Without intending to, she had favored Cornish's cause. She had changed her father's mind about seeing him. And perhaps this was for the best. There was no one in a better position than Niklaas van Pelt himself to stop Cornish and prevent these fabrications about her mother from being published.

"When will you see him?" Susan asked.

His fingers uncurled and rested limp upon the desk. The moment of force had drained from him. "There is no hurry. This will take some thinking about. I do not rush into things."

"But his book—" Susan began.

"This book will not be written overnight. There is time."

She knew there was no time. If John Cornish was to be stopped, then it must be done at once. The further he carried his plans the more determined he might be to complete them. And Niklaas was not the man he had once been.

"I think you ought to see him very soon," she urged.

He smiled at her unexpectedly. It was not a warm smile, but one that seemed coldly amused. It did not reassure her.

"You will have to leave this matter to me, my dear. But enough of Cornish for now. I wonder if you would care to come with me for a drive this afternoon? The day is comfortably warm and I'd like to get out into the sun. There's a spot in Cape Town that I often visit—the Rhodes Memorial. From it I can promise you an unsurpassed view of Cape Town. If you agree, I will pick you up this afternoon."

The sudden invitation surprised her. Perhaps he was merely offering her a distraction as adults sometimes did with a child. At any rate, she would go. Whatever small advantage she might have with him she meant to press.

"Thank you, Father. I'll be ready whenever you say," she told him and rose to leave.

The crack of the twelve-o'clock gun from Signal Hill reached her just as she started home. A plan was stirring in her mind and, even though she knew Dirk would not approve, she felt impelled to follow her instinct. After all, it was because she wanted to answer Dirk and set his doubts at rest that she must do this very thing.

The moment she reached the Aerie she went to the phone and called John Cornish.

11

The van Pelt car, with Thomas at the wheel, followed the curving drive around the base of Devil's Peak. Here the table was no longer visible and there were only great crags like the back of a dragon, with steep rock sides, encroached upon to some degree by determined stands of pine. In the clear thin sunshine of spring the Hottentots Holland Mountains were visible, their sharply notched peaks showing beyond False Bay.

Susan remembered the story of their naming from her

childhood. The Dutch settlers had known that the Hottentots looked upon their mountains with the same homesick longing with which the Dutch remembered Holland, so the name of Hottentots Holland had been given to the mountains. "Hottentot" itself meant "stammerer," and was what the Dutch had called the Bushmen because of their odd language.

There were tall blue gum trees along the drive, and carpeting the woodsy areas of the hillside were hundreds of arum lilies, growing wild. Once, when the trees opened and she could look upward, Susan caught a glimpse of white columns set splendidly apart on the crest of a small hill, with the dark peaks rising behind.

Thomas turned his head. "There is the monument now, madam," he said.

Her heart quickened, not because of the beauty but because of her own uneasiness over what she had done—the result of which must now be faced.

Niklaas van Pelt sat back in the seat beside Susan, his thin hands clasped upon the silver head of his cane. There was an air of alertness about him this afternoon as though all his senses except that of sight were sentient and open to every impression that touched them.

This is my father, she thought—and felt nothing. Perhaps it was too late for any feeling between them, even though he claimed it was not her mother's words about the diamond that had caused him to send for her.

"Rhodes is not buried here, you know," Niklaas said. "He chose his own burial place in Southern Rhodesia—a wild mountainous spot near Bulawayo. Not a place where many go. I visited it once as a young man."

The car turned onto a side road that climbed upward, and now the monument was hidden until the road turned again and came upon it in profile. Susan could see the tall white columns at the top, the broad flight of stone steps mounting toward them between a guard of eight bronze lions. At the foot of the steps a bronze figure rode a prancing horse high on a pedestal of its own. On either side were green lawns and terraces and the parasol-topped pines. Close above, as always, were the craggy peaks.

Thomas parked the car and came around to open the door. Gently he helped Niklaas out and the old man stood leaning upon his cane until Susan stepped out to join him.

"Go along on your errand, Thomas," Niklaas said. "My daughter will give me her arm. And you'll find us here when you return."

The colored man touched his cap and went back to the car. Slowly father and daughter walked toward the parapet before the monument. Niklaas's left hand rested lightly on Susan's arm, the other used the cane as he moved easily and without hesitation.

"I'm troubled about Thomas," he said as they reached the cobbled expanse before a low semicircle of wall.

Susan was only half listening. Uneasily she glanced up and down the steps, searched the shadows of the colonnade above with a swift glance. John Cornish was nowhere in sight and she could not help feeling a certain relief. Perhaps he would not come after all. He had not been certain that this was the right approach.

Her father was still talking about Thomas when she began to listen again.

"He should be a teacher by now. It's in him to do splendid work along that line. But this chauffeuring and acting as a blind man's eyes is achieving little for him. His bitterness is our own doing, I'm afraid."

"He seems to be in the same position that Willimina is in—the girl who works for us as a maid," Susan said.

"Willimina Kock?" her father repeated, sounding surprised.

"Yes. Miss Bellman brought her to work for us on our second day here."

"That's strange," Niklaas said. "Mara never mentioned the fact to me. Willi is more or less engaged to Thomas, you know. Though marriage hasn't seemed possible for them. Mainly, I gather, because of a certain obstinacy on Willi's part. Or so Thomas says. Another reason for his state of resentment."

Susan recalled the flashes of spirit she had seen in Willimina. Gentle though she was, it was possible that she could be obstinate if she chose. Then, too, there was at times about the girl an evasiveness that Susan had been forced to recognize. Certainly she had not revealed the fact that she knew Thomas. But, then, there had been no reason for her to do so.

Her father drew his hand from Susan's arm and moved with certainty across the cobblestones until his cane touched the low parapet. In this open space the wind blew strongly upon them, and the great panorama of Cape Town and its suburbs lay fanned out below around the curve of the bay. Wind sighed in the pines, and somewhere there was the dripping sound of water. Niklaas turned toward the wind and it was as if he saw all that lay before him, as if he savored the grandeur of the view.

At length he moved away from the wall. "Let's climb to the top," he said. "I want you to meet Mr. Rhodes."

They climbed the flight of granite steps, past the figure of "Energy" on the prancing horse, and started up the several levels toward the colonnade at the top. On either side the reclining lions guarded the way. Two small boys had climbed upon the back of one beast and sat astride, their young voices breaking the silence of the secluded place. At the top of the wide steps, enclosed by roofed columns, was the heart of the memorial: a bust of the man who had so loved and served South Africa, and himself as well. The man who had dreamed an empire into being. Rhodes's head rested upon his hand and there was a distant brooding in his face.

Softly Niklaas van Pelt began to recite, as if he read the words engraved below:

> THE IMMENSE AND
> BROODING
> SPIRIT STILL
> SHALL QUICKEN
> AND CONTROL
> LIVING HE WAS THE
> LAND AND DEAD
> HIS SOUL SHALL BE
> HER SOUL

With a vividness that startled Susan, the words came ringing back to her over the years. All this was remembered, familiar. She had heard these words before. That other time she had stood here as a small girl, with her hand in her father's. She had felt only love and trust and confidence in him that day. His eyes had been able to see the engraved words and his voice had been the voice of a younger man. Yet still the words rang as he spoke them and there was a love for this precious and beautiful land in his very forming of the words.

"You knew him, didn't you?" she asked softly.

"Only to see him from a distance. I was a very young man at the time of his death, and I had been fighting on the other side with the Boers. I knew Paul Kruger better—I had at least spoken to him. Both men were giants. Who is to say which was the greater of the two. This one loved the land almost too possessively."

"You are no longer in sympathy with the Boers—the Afrikaners—are you?"

"They are my people." The ringing note had faded from his

voice. "Far more so than the Englishman is, when it comes to blood, though I married an English woman."

He paused, listening. He had caught the sound of footsteps on the cobbles below and he turned to her inquiringly.

"Someone is coming?"

"Yes," Susan said, "someone is coming."

John Cornish stood on the lower steps looking up at them. Susan made no move, caught up in her own sudden dread. Slowly he started up the great blocks of granite that made the steps. The two small boys climbed from their lion and ran downward past him, hurrying off to new explorations.

She must warn her father. She must tell him that it was John Cornish coming up the steps toward him. But before she could manage her voice, Cornish himself spoke. His words were in Afrikaans and Susan recognized the "Oom Niklaas" by which he addressed her father. The old man beside her tensed and she saw his hand tighten on his cane. He stood where he was without moving, the mask of his face betraying nothing, though he spoke to her in a low voice.

"You should have warned me," he murmured.

It was clear that he had not been deceived into thinking this a chance meeting.

He waited as the other man climbed the steps below him, and he did not hold out his hand in greeting.

"You were the friend of my son," he said in English. "You were the one he trusted."

"Paul was my friend and I loved him," Cornish said. "I loved his father as well. I would like you to know how it was. May I tell you?"

Niklaas made a gesture of indifference and used his cane to guide himself along the level of a step until he reached the side of the monument. There he sat down on the high step above and waited, while Cornish came to stand just below him. Susan withdrew a little, gazing out across the wide vista of Cape Town.

Cornish told his story simply. He explained how he had been caught in spite of himself in a trap from which there was no escape. He had not, he said, ever believed in Niklaas's confession. It was his conviction that Niklaas van Pelt had been protecting someone. Now it was time for the truth to be known. There was no one left who could be hurt.

"There is the girl," Niklaas said.

For the first time Susan broke in upon their talk. "I'm not important in this. The truth is important. I want to see my mother's name cleared."

108

Her father nodded gravely. "There is no hurry. These are things I must think about. A book takes time to write—we cannot hasten this."

"I mean to hasten it," Cornish said. "Since you would not answer my letters or agree to see me, I've been pushing the writing ahead."

The old man broke in abruptly. "What letters, John? I have received no letters."

There was sudden anger in the younger man's eyes, but it was not directed at Niklaas. "I wrote you several. They were sent to you at Protea Hill. I have written you at least three times."

This was Dirk's doing, Susan thought unhappily. Dirk's orders to Mara, undoubtedly. But he had gone too far this time in protecting Niklaas. No matter how Dirk felt about John Cornish, it was for her father to decide whether or not to see him—not Dirk.

"Had I received your letters, I would have paid you the courtesy of an answer," Niklaas said. "I shall look into the matter. But tell me now why there is such need for haste."

"I want to leave South Africa as soon as I can," John said. "I've no wish to stay here and see my country destroy itself by this insane course it's taking. If you won't help me, then I must go ahead on my own."

"You sound like a man filled with bitterness," Niklaas said. "Yet you have known many Afrikaners in your lifetime. You know their worth."

John Cornish turned toward the colonnade above with a quick angry gesture. "This is one monument built by South Africa. But there is another. One that stands near Pretoria in the Transvaal—the Voortrekker Monument."

"I know it," Niklaas said.

Cornish went on, a ragged note in his voice as he described the great stone building crowning a hilltop in the rolling Pretoria country. So vivid and compelling were his words that Susan could almost see the vast structure standing foursquare and sturdy as the men who had built it. The huge square tower was surrounded by a circular outer wall of concrete set in the form of a *laager* of wagons guarding it as the voortrekkers had guarded themselves from attack behind real wagons. Inside on the walls of the ground floor were stone bas-reliefs, John said. All around the great circular room they ran, depicting the history of South Africa, showing graphically the sufferings of the settlers, the massacres, the battles, the triumphs.

"A great history," Niklaas said gravely. "A brave history."

Cornish went on relentlessly. "From a railing in the center of the floor you look down through a wide opening to a quiet, empty room below. Empty except for the marble tomb enshrined there engraved with the words 'Ons vir Jou Suide Afrika'—'We for you, South Africa.' Down there too in that quiet room there's a niche in the wall where an everlasting lamp burns—a torch that signifies the light of civilization that was carried forth by the voortrekker movement."

Again Niklaas nodded. "A worthy memorial to history."

"These were brave men, and if it were only that I wouldn't quarrel with it," Cornish said. "But the monument has been used to turn a knife in the wounds of memory. It says in effect, 'These cruelties were done to your fathers—never forget them. The black man is your enemy—never forgive him. The Englishman is your enemy—hate him.' These are the meanings being urged on descendants of the voortrekkers today. The lamp has been buried in that pile of concrete. For South Africa the light is going out."

Niklaas van Pelt sat with his hands clasped upon the head of his cane, his sightless eyes behind their glasses fixed as if on some inner vision and he made the younger man no answer.

With an exclamation of impatience, Cornish walked along the level of one step and back again. Then he bent toward Niklaas as if he wanted to reach past the guard of those dark glasses and make him see the truth.

"All Africa is on the move. Do you think a handful of white men can stop the tide?"

"This country belongs to white men," Niklaas said calmly. "White men settled it and built it into what it is now. It is our only homeland."

"I suppose that's true enough. Nevertheless, the only way the white man can continue to live here is to accept the fact that we're all, black and white alike, natives of South Africa. Not Afrikaner or English. Not white. Not colored, or Malay or Indian, or black—but South Africans together. Don't you see that you no longer have any choice? It is this or chaos."

"You are almost an American now," Niklaas said. "You live in a glass house. How can you point a finger at others?"

Forgetting herself, Susan broke in. "Why shouldn't we point our fingers wherever we see prejudice? Lots of us point quickly enough at what exists in our own country—in the North as well as in the South. Racial discrimination ought to be condemned anywhere it exists, no matter by whom!"

Cornish smiled gravely. "I agree. America may move slow

110

ly, but at least it moves ahead. The national law is on the side of the angels. Here the movement is only backward."

Susan drew closer on the stone steps, absorbed by the argument. Her father seemed to be baiting the other man almost coldly as if he tried deliberately to anger him.

"There's the matter of education," Niklaas pointed out. "You can't expect the black man from the reservation to stand beside the educated white man or understand the white man's world."

"Whose fault is that?" Cornish demanded. "Lack of education is always the excuse given by those who've not made enough effort to educate. Time catches up with them. The education must come *now*. Don't think I'm unaware of the complexities of the situation, but I can't help remembering something I heard Rebecca West say not so long ago: that it would be to the glory and honor of South Africa for its people to work together and solve the problem, however difficult. But I see no evidence around me that South Africans mean to rise to the challenge."

"While it may be our own fault and the fault of a good deal of historic hostility," Niklaas said, "we nevertheless have a tiger by the tail. How do you propose that we let it go without being devoured?"

Cornish did not answer, but stood looking up at the bust of Rhodes above them.

Niklaas turned his blind face toward the other man and there was unexpected sadness in his voice. "You speak of a challenge, yet you, who are a young man, will run away from it."

John looked startled. "I've no wish to see the night close in when there's nothing I can do that will hold it off. I'm getting out. I came here to right a personal wrong that I helped to perpetrate years ago. So, whether you like it or not, I will get on with my book. There will be a chapter about Niklaas van Pelt. I know the story well enough. Those early days of yours in the diamond mines. The later days when you worked for your country in Parliament. The courage with which you met disgrace and took the blame for someone else's guilt. There are a good many friends of Niklaas van Pelt to be found in South Africa today. They'll give me the story. I'll write it and go away."

"You are a determined young man and a foolish one," Niklaas said. "What you plan is ridiculous, of course, and completely wrong." He sat for a little while in silence, lost in thought.

111

"There's nothing more to be said." Cornish looked about for Susan and his eyes thanked her without betraying her with words. His silence made no difference, she knew. Her father was clearly aware of how this meeting had come about. She would have to face him on this score when Cornish had gone.

"Wait a moment, John," Niklaas said. "Since you are both determined and stubborn, it will be necessary to change your mind. Will you come to stay in my house for a time? There are empty rooms—we can make you comfortable. Then you and I can speak at length of all these matters and cover them at our leisure. When you understand fully, you will change your course about this book."

For an instant John Cornish seemed astonished. Then he accepted with eager alacrity. "Thank you, Oom Niklaas. It would be good to visit with you again, even if there were no book to discuss. You won't change my mind, but I accept the invitation gratefully."

"Good," Niklaas said. "Pack up your things and come over at once. We'll expect you tonight for dinner. There's Thomas now—I know his step. May we give you a lift back to your hotel?"

Thomas had appeared and stood waiting at the foot of the monument.

"Thanks, no," Cornish said. "I've a cab coming to pick me up. But I'll be with you this evening, if you'll have me. *Tot siens.*"

He gave Susan a smile that was less cool than usual and ran down the steps. At the bottom she saw him stop and speak to Thomas, as if he knew the colored man. A sudden recollection returned to her mind. On their first day in Cape Town someone had told Cornish where Dirk was making his home. Had it, she wondered, been Thomas? In which case, was he as wholly loyal to Niklaas van Pelt as her father believed?

"Mr. Cornish seems to know Thomas," she said in a low voice.

"Of course," her father said. "Thomas Scott's parents worked for my family on their farm. John knew him as a boy." The old man stood up and held out his hand to Susan. "Give me your arm, please. I'm not as sure on these steps as I used to be."

He leaned upon the arm she crooked for him and they went down slowly. At the foot of the steps Thomas offered his own arm and they moved toward the grove of trees near which the car was parked. John's cab had apparently come and gone.

"Do you think you can convince John Cornish?" Susan asked, when she and her father were settled in the car.

Niklaas sighed as if the encounter had wearied him. "I shall try. There will surely be a way."

She was silent as the car turned toward home, expecting him to reproach her for precipitating this meeting, but he said nothing further, lost in his own thoughts.

She was not satisfied with his uncertainty. She had brought these two together for the purpose of preventing John Cornish from writing about her mother as he intended. But now it began to seem that it was Cornish who might convince her father. The thought was far from reassuring.

12

The day had been a disturbing one and she waited uneasily for Dirk to come home to dinner. She knew she must tell him about the drive to the Rhodes Memorial and of the meeting there with John Cornish. She would have to confess her own part in what had happened and the probability of his displeasure, coming on the heels of Mara's hints and outrageous behavior, left her increasingly apprehensive. The calm counseling she had given herself during the past few days suddenly crumbled and left her without confidence or defense. Her mind could follow only one disturbing course.

Mara had been in love with Dirk. She had spoken of getting him back. She had said they would have married if Dirk had not left South Africa. If this was true, it would mean that Dirk had once been in love with Mara Bellman. And Mara would not be willing to allow whatever had been between them to remain in the past. Nor would she stop at anything to gain her ends. There was a promise of conflict in the days to come and Susan hated the thought. She wanted no game of combat with anyone, and least of all with Mara. More than anything else she longed for complete security in Dirk's love for her. All her life she had been waiting for him. If she lost him now there would be nothing left to hold to, to believe in. The thought was devastating and she knew that she could rid herself of it only in the reassurance of Dirk's arms, of Dirk's love. And so there was impatience in her for his coming that evening.

When the telephone rang, and Willi came to tell her that Dirk was on the line, she hurried to take the call, feeling that she could not bear it if he did not come home to dinner tonight. It was *now* that she needed him. But he said merely that he would be delayed by a half hour or so and asked her to have Cookie hold the meal. She hung up the phone, both disappointed and relieved. At least the postponement would be a brief one.

After she had passed the word along to the kitchen she went outside. The sun was dipping behind the tawny head of the Lion and the softness of dusk lay over Cape Town. A walk before Dirk came home might quiet this feeling of urgency that would not allow her to sit down and wait.

Knowing the way now, she went easily over the wall and down the path. She would walk only as far as the pine grove and back. By that time Dirk would be at home and she could talk to him.

The sky was still partly light, with the night haze encroaching gradually from the east. Only the tall rocks and the pines in the ravine below were hidden in darkness. She walked briskly, meaning to turn back before she reached those black recesses. Not until she neared the half circle of monolithic rocks did she hear the sudden sound of voices from the direction of the grove beyond.

An uneasy awareness of the solitude of this spot came over her. There had been so much trouble of late in Cape Town that she had been warned not to go out alone in deserted places after dark. But it wasn't truly dark yet, and this was so close to home that she had given no thought to the matter of her safety. Now she paused to listen and heard the voices cease, heard the sound of footsteps coming toward her up the path.

Swiftly she stepped around the base of one tall stone, and let the shadows take her. It was wiser not to meet whoever was coming up the path. When he had gone she would leave her hiding place and hurry back to the house. Tensely now, she leaned forward against the base of the stone to blend herself into its shadow and felt its rough cold texture beneath her hands, against her cheek. It was to be hoped that she would stir up no snakes' nest in this hidden place.

Footsteps went past her and she peered warily through a

crevice of stone in time to see Dirk striding hurriedly uphill toward home. The fact in itself would not have surprised her. She knew there were times when he did not take the car and used the short cut of this path between the Aerie and Protea Hill. But tonight someone had been with him. She checked her first impulse to run after him, turning instead toward the grove. She had to know. She had to see for herself.

Careful to make no sound, she entered the darkness of the pines where the path turned and curved between the trees. Around the first turn Mara Bellman's light-green suit was visible, her figure silhouetted against the paler dusk beyond the trees. Her face was in her hands and she was weeping soundlessly.

Unheard, unseen, Susan stole away, running now as she hurried toward home. In spite of this meeting she had nearly been witness to, she felt more relieved than disturbed. For the moment she had no pity for Mara's tears. If the woman was crying, it was a good sign for Susan Hohenfield. One must be hurt for the other to be happy, and if it were Mara, then it would not be Susan. Her reasoning was primitive and direct.

Nevertheless, she did not want to meet Dirk before she was over the wall. She did not want him to know what she had seen. She slowed her steps a little, to give him time to go inside the house, meaning to steal into the garden before he knew of her absence.

But when the path turned upward to the wall, she saw that she was trapped. Dirk was in the garden, standing beside the wall, watching the path up which he had so recently come. Perhaps he was merely composing himself before he went into the house. In any event, he saw her before there was time for retreat and waited for her in silence as she came up to the low place in the stone. She felt a little frightened as she put her toe in a crevice and pulled herself up and over. He made no move to help her, but stood motionless and silent until she was beside him in the garden.

"You should know better than to go out alone after dark," he said. "There are always ruffians about ready for mischief."

Perhaps he was hoping that she had seen nothing, but such evasion she could not accept. Her own sense of caution had suddenly vanished.

"Mara had to go home alone in the dark," she said a little sharply.

Even as she spoke she knew the words were ill-chosen and impulsive. He stared at her for a long moment. Then he turned away without waiting for her further response. Follow-

115

ing him slowly into the house, feeling shaken and sick, she heard him tell Willi that he would soon be ready for dinner.

The very thought of food was distasteful. She ran upstairs and into the bedroom. If she had not chosen her words so clumsily, he might have taken her into his arms and comforted her. Probably he would have made nothing of the meeting with Mara. He would have explained that whatever might have been between them was long in the past and that he loved only Susan. But she had antagonized him instead, and she could not blame him for turning away from her.

When Willi came to call her, she wanted no dinner. She had a headache, she said, and would lie down. Willi went softly away, and Susan slipped into a quilted robe and flung herself down on her bed. The tears came easily now and she did not try to stop them. The figure of Mara Bellman stood openly between herself and Dirk and she did not know how to fight a past that might imminently become the present.

She could see Mara now, not as a woman who had lost the man she loved, but as one who had never given him up. She could see her as Dirk must see her—beautiful and confident and poised. So many things that Susan was not. How important had Mara been to him? How important was she now? Over and over the same tormenting questions turned in her mind.

From the dining room downstairs she heard the sounds of a meal being served. In spite of herself, she followed them through each course to the end and then an aching hope began to rise in her. Perhaps he would come upstairs to her now that he had eaten. His anger would have abated. Surely he would recognize her hurt and come to comfort her.

But when the meal was done, she heard him go into the living room where they had their coffee after dinner. She heard Willi bring in the silver service and then return to the kitchen. Dirk was having his coffee alone, still remote, still angry.

She turned her cheek against the pillow and wept again, as miserably as a child. When someone tapped on the bedroom door, her heart gave a foolish, hopeful thump and she opened her eyes to see that it was only Willi. But the colored girl's appearance was something to draw her from her mood of self-pity and despair, and she recognized the need to brace herself and make an effort toward outward recovery at least.

Willi came in carrying a tray that she set down on the bedside table.

"I've brought you some good tomato *bredie*," she said. "Le me fix your pillow so that you can sit up and eat."

116

The savory South African stew gave off an appetizing steam and Susan considered the girl who had brought it to her, wanting now to keep her here as a distraction against her own misery.

"Stay and talk to me, Willi," she said.

"I'll stay if you wish, Mrs. Hohenfield," Willi agreed.

She plumped up Susan's pillow, set the tray upon her knees, then stood beside the bed, waiting.

"Do sit down," Susan said. "How can we talk if you stand up like that?"

A guarded look came into the girl's face and she made no move toward a chair. Susan took a spoonful of the *bredie* and found it delicious. An impatience with her own weakness was beginning to hearten her.

"Listen to me," she said, finding herself more impatient with South Africa than with Willi. "You're a woman and I'm a woman. Please sit down and talk to me."

Still a little wary, and with an instinctive distrust of someone who wore a white skin, Willi seated herself on the edge of a chair and waited.

"Why must you make a difference between us?" Susan asked.

"I am working for you in this house," Willi said gravely. "It isn't considered suitable—"

Susan broke in quickly. "I've never had anyone work for me before. I feel uncomfortable being a mistress. I've had no training at all in running a household."

Willi's dark lashes swept her cheeks and she said nothing.

Susan tried a new approach, tantalized by her inability to break down the girl's careful guard, her mistrust. "My father told me today that you're engaged to Thomas Scott." She ate another spoonful of stew, watching her the while. "Are you planning to be married before long?"

This time Willi answered with an air of quiet reserve. "I am not engaged to Thomas. I don't intend to marry him."

There was a spark of reproof in her words and Susan found herself flushing. "I'm sorry. I shouldn't have asked you. This is my day for being clumsy."

With an effort Willi attempted to overcome her own reserve. "I don't mind your asking. Marriage for people like Thomas and me isn't easy. We have to think of the future. What of our children? That frightens me. I don't want the responsibility of bringing children into the world we know today in South Africa."

Susan was silent, unable to offer any reassurance. She re-

117

membered John Cornish's words at the Rhodes Memorial that afternoon and of his own wish to get away from the ugly promise of violence in South Africa. But people like this girl could not leave the country even if they wanted to.

"There is another thing," Willi went on, as though something of Susan's sincerity had reached her and she had begun to relax a little. "Thomas has a university education. And he is lighter-skinned than I am. There are doors open to him that might be closed to me. Why should I handicap him with a dark-skinned wife? You don't know how hard it is to have a dark skin in South Africa."

She was beginning to know, Susan thought. She was beginning to feel this thing strongly within the safety of her own white skin. In the face of Willi's problem her own worries had receded a little. But at the sound of Dirk's voice speaking suddenly from the open doorway, everything swept back in a returning sea of misery.

"May I come in?" he asked.

Willi sprang to her feet and Dirk spoke to her curtly in Afrikaans, in reproof and dismissal.

"Thank you, Willi, for bringing me the stew," Susan said as the girl took the tray and went off.

"You mustn't encourage her like that," Dirk said. "You Americans spoil your servants. Part of the trouble we're having in South Africa these days grows out of just such people as Willi and Thomas. Too much education, too much ambition, and nothing to do with it. It's foolish to give it to them in the first place."

She did not want to oppose him in some new way, yet she could not live with herself if she let his words pass.

"You can't deny education to anyone who wants it," she said hotly. "Or the opportunity to use it either."

"No one wants to deny it to them." Dirk was clearly impatient. "Let them have it in their own schools and their own way. That's what apartheid is all about."

Aparthate, Susan thought. That was the way it was pronounced and it could hardly have been a more graphic word. It hurt her deeply to see this attitude in Dirk, yet she knew that it was something he had grown up with, just as certain Americans grew up taking racial prejudice for granted. Eventually they must talk about these things, but this was not the time.

He came to sit beside her on the bed. "Let's not quarrel about Willi. She's a good girl in her way. But I don't want to talk about her now."

Susan made no move toward him. She felt miserably torn between love and indignation and hurt. He put out a hand and pushed back the bright hair from her forehead. "I do believe it's beginning to grow a little," he said. "You're not snipping it off any more?"

She shook her head, sensing that he would come in his own way to the point if she gave him time.

"I wonder," he went on, "whether you can understand if I try to tell you something? Sometimes you're so capable and independent that you alarm me. And sometimes I wonder if I've married a child instead of a grown woman."

Still she waited, her heart thumping raggedly.

"You mustn't think I don't understand how you feel about Mara," he said. "I'd have preferred not to have you know. But since you've stumbled on something that you may build up out of its proper proportions, I think you must look at this realistically."

"Look at what?" Susan asked in a low voice.

"At the way it was before you came into the picture. Mara is an attractive girl. We were both unattached. Why shouldn't we console and amuse each other for the space of time that we were free? There was never any intention of marriage on my part. She knew I didn't consider myself the marrying kind. Perhaps she hoped to change that. I suppose women always do. Perhaps she isn't yet reconciled, though I didn't expect her to mind as much as she apparently has. I wrote her from the States as soon as I knew we were going to be married. But I haven't seen her alone more than once or twice since I've returned. When she asked me to meet her this evening I felt I owed her that—I couldn't refuse."

Susan leaned against her pillow and closed her eyes. The important thing was the fact that Dirk wanted to tell her all this, that he wanted everything in the open between them. She must accept the past realistically, as he wished. Nevertheless, there was a question she had to ask. She opened her eyes and looked at him.

"Why does Mara continue to work for my father? Will she leave now, do you suppose?"

"I doubt it," Dirk said frankly. "Uncle Niklaas would be hard put to train someone to his ways as thoroughly as Mara has been trained. She's necessary to him. Can't the three of us be adult enough to accept that?"

She was not sure she could ever accept such a situation and she was positive that Mara could not. But there was a softening toward her in Dirk's manner and that was all that mattered. She raised her head from the pillow and in a moment she was in his arms, her cheek in the comforting hollow of his shoulder. He held her to him, murmuring assurances of his love in her ear. This was what she had wanted and needed. Mara could not touch her here.

But long before she was ready to leave the safety of his arms, he took her by the shoulders and held her away so that he could look into her face.

"There's something else we must talk about, Susan. I've just learned that there was a meeting between Cornish and your father this afternoon. It's hard to believe it was an accident. Can you tell me how it came about?"

So he knew, and there was no help for it.

"I arranged it," she admitted. "I telephoned Mr. Cornish and let him know where Father would be this afternoon."

The moment of tenderness was past. Dirk let her go and rose, moving about the room as if to restrain himself. When he turned back to the bed, she watched him miserably.

"Cornish is actually moving into Protea Hill," Dirk said, "and what will come of it I don't know. He's a troublemaker, as I've warned you, and he can harm us all. Particularly your father. Now it will be harder than ever to save Uncle Niklaas from harm."

Here it was again—that threat of something hidden in their lives, and further evidence of a devotion to Niklaas that had grown from past gratitude into a near obsession.

"Father knows you kept the letters from him that John Cornish wrote," she said, trying to speak coolly herself. "Has he told you that?"

"Yes! And he wasn't pleased. Couldn't you see that I was acting out of concern for Uncle Niklaas? What am I to do about a wife who betrays me at every turn?"

The shock of his words was like ice water in her face. She put up her hands as if she might ward them off physically.

"I would never betray you!" she cried. "Never, never! That's not fair. You haven't tried to understand my feelings in this. How could I stand by and let John Cornish write lies about my mother? That must be stopped and Father is the only one who can stop it."

"Your father is an old man—he will stop nothing. But now you've offered him innocently into the lion's paws. How can you be sure that what Cornish might say about your mother is a lie? How do you know you haven't made everything worse by getting your father and John Cornish together in such headlong haste?"

"Claire was my mother," Susan protested. "I know how silly it is to think she might be guilty of what Cornish suggests."

"Is it silly?" Once more Dirk sat beside her on the bed. He took her hands into his own strong clasp. "I wonder how I can make you understand what your father has been through. Even what he's going through now, with your return to South Africa and the opening of old wounds. Even the publicity our marriage has been given in the papers lately has focused attention on him. Do you think he's a man to carry disgrace lightly? And what of our children, darling—growing up here? The grandchildren of an important and well-respected man who broke his country's laws and went to prison as a thief!"

She was silent, a little frightened by his vehemence. Somehow she had been divorcing her father and all that concerned him from her own life and Dirk's, as if the past could not touch them in any way. But it was true that she wanted children—Dirk's children. She had not considered this aspect of the future.

"I'm sorry," she said more humbly. "Perhaps I'm the one who hasn't tried to understand your viewpoint, or my father's. What do you want me to do to help?"

"Have you tried what I've suggested?" he asked. "Have you really tried to remember the things that happened to you just before you left South Africa?"

"I have tried," she told him in a low voice. "But nothing comes clear. I can remember a few things, and then everything disappears in a fog. Sometimes I think I'm afraid to remember."

"I've suspected that was true," Dirk said. "But if you understand the reasons behind what I'm asking of you—if you somehow force this thing through—"

"Through to what? I don't even know what it is that I'm trying to remember."

"Through to the Kimberley Royal," Dirk said.

There was a moment of silence in the room and Mara's words concerning her marriage swept sharply through Susan's mind. But that was the very thing Mara wanted. It was her purpose to rouse suspicion in Dirk's wife. And Susan would have none of that.

Dirk was speaking again and she listened. "Even your mother seemed to think you knew something," he reminded her, "that you might have witnessed something. If you don't remember, it will always look as though she took the diamond herself when she left South Africa. If she really did, then we

121

ought to know because it may lead us to the truth about the other diamonds."

"It wasn't my mother," Susan whispered, the strength of her denial fading a little. "We never had much money and Mother worked hard all the time I was growing up. If we'd owned a fortune, don't you suppose things might have been different?"

"Perhaps she was afraid to sell it."

"If she had it, then I'd have found it in her possessions after she died. And surely she would have given me some warning about it."

"The warning she sent was to your father," Dirk said. "Now the rest is up to you."

Susan sat up on the bed and slid her feet to the floor. She had a feeling of being hopelessly cornered, so that whichever way she turned disaster faced her. But she no longer felt sick and sad. Dirk was right. The time for action was upon her.

"All right then—I'll try in every way I know to remember," she promised. "I'll do my best to find the truth, whatever it is."

He cupped her face with his two hands and kissed her warmly. "There's my girl. Between us, we'll clear old Niklaas yet."

She was not at all sure that would be the final result, but she knew now that she must move ahead in some positive way.

"First of all you'll have to get me into Father's house," she said. "I want to go upstairs. I want to see my old room. How else can I begin to remember?"

"That's easily arranged. Let's give your father a few days' time to get Cornish settled, and then I'll talk to him about your seeing the house. But we mustn't say it's because you want to recall something about the diamond. There are times when I think your father doesn't want to know what became of it. He hasn't that much liking for diamonds. In fact, he's almost superstitious about the Kimberley."

"Perhaps he's right to be," Susan murmured.

Dirk laughed and drew her into his arms. "At least we've cleared up the doldrums. You're all right again, aren't you, darling? You won't worry any more about Mara?"

"Not if you say I needn't," she told him. The bliss of being safe again, of having his love close about her, was the only thing that mattered. She would do everything she could to please him.

13

A few mornings later, with time on her hands once more, Susan went down to the library at the end of the Avenue, where Adderley Street began, to look up some books on photography. When she had what she wanted, she came out the door to discover Thomas Scott standing on the library steps with a book in his hands. He was leafing through the pages with such absorption that he did not see her, and she was struck by the change in him.

The usual guard he seemed to hold against everyone had lifted. He had lost himself completely in the book he held and it occurred to her that a shot of him here on the steps might fit into the series she was planning.

If he saw her, the picture would be spoiled, so she focused her camera quickly and set the stops. As the shutter clicked, Thomas looked up from his page and saw her. With a quick, almost secretive movement, he closed the book and thrust it under one arm.

"I hope you don't mind," Susan said, abashed a little too late by this invasion of his privacy. "You—you made such a good picture there on the steps and . . ." Her words died lamely away at his lack of response.

For an instant she saw hostility flare in his eyes. Then his guard was in place again as he came down the steps toward her.

"Good morning, madam," he said correctly and made no reference to the picture she had taken.

"How is my father?" she asked, wanting to hold him there a moment and perhaps find a way to soften her action, to apologize, if that would help.

Thomas gestured toward the gardens. "Mr. van Pelt is just over there, madam, if you wish to see him." He touched his cap and walked away, the book still under his arm. For all his courtesy, she felt that she had been reproved, and with justification. But the change she had seen so briefly in his face held her interest, and she wondered what book might have given him that different look.

She stood on the sidewalk for a moment longer, watching passers-by and the hurrying traffic. The usual assorted crowd thronged Adderley Street. There were Malay women with veils across their foreheads and under their chins, colored messenger boys wearing white pith helmets, now and then a "blanket native," barefoot and wearing wrapped about him the blanket that distinguished him from those who had left the reservation long behind. There were many white people, of course, and many of the colored people of the Cape.

When she turned toward the gardens she did not move quickly, not being entirely sure that she wanted to see her father. None of her meetings with him had been very happy ones, and perhaps he took no more joy in her company than she had found in his. However, since Thomas might report having seen her, it seemed only courteous to stop and speak to him.

She followed a path into this unexplored corner of the garden, past the marble statue of Sir George Grey, a gentleman in a long coat and tight trousers who had once been governor here. Then around an ancient and enormous holly oak where a colored man and woman sat together on a bench, speaking earnestly. There were no "Europeans Only" designations here.

The path led her toward a quiet and secluded corner and she saw the sign at once—this was a garden set apart for the blind. On a green bench in the sunlight sat her father, his hands resting in characteristic fashion on the head of his cane, and a look so dreaming and gentle upon his face that she hardly knew him.

"Good morning, Father," she said hesitantly. "I met Thomas just now on the library steps and he said you were here."

He accepted her presence without surprise, and motioned to the bench beside him. "Won't you join me? I've been sitting here thinking about your mother."

Always before when Claire's name had been mentioned there had been a coldness in his tone. But now there was a tenderness she had not heard before. She sat beside him in silence, not wanting to break this gentle spell that lay upon him.

"Do you remember how much your mother loved flowers?" he asked.

"I remember," she said. "That was the thing she liked best about South Africa—the flowers."

For a little while he was silent. When he spoke again his memories of Claire still claimed him.

"She used to love this little garden. She loved the small, scented flowers—the little English flowers that were so different from her South African favorites. Do you remember what she used to do when we came here?"

Susan did not remember. She could not recall ever having been in this place—except perhaps for Sir George Grey, who had looked vaguely familiar. Strange the things a child's memory retained or rejected.

Her father went on. "In those days we both had our vision. But Claire liked to play a game when we came here. She would cling to my arm and pretend she was blind. I would lead her about and she'd bend her pretty head toward the flowers to catch their fragrance. Then she would identify the scent, and nearly always she was right."

There was a tightness in Susan's throat, and she could not speak.

Her father went on, recalling a younger Claire than Susan could remember, and the note of affection in his voice was surprising. Always Susan had thought of Claire as running away from a man who had hurt her and did not love her.

"Why did she leave South Africa?" she asked. "What was she escaping from?"

He answered her indirectly. "We must remember that your mother was a fragile person. Her wings were easily bruised and she could never bear unhappiness. She would have crumpled under the strain of what happened to me."

"But you must have needed her then," Susan said impulsively. "How could she bear to leave you at a time like that?"

He turned the blank surface of his dark glasses toward her as if in inquiry, as if her words surprised him. But he said nothing and she knew he would give her no answer. With his cane he began to draw blind patterns in the earth at his feet and the silver knob shone in the sunlight, catching Susan's eye.

"I've noticed your cane," she said. "It's very beautiful."

He held the head of it toward her. "It was given me by friends some years ago. Do you see the enamel embossing on the silver?"

She took the cane from him and studied the raised symbols on the head and saw that they represented the three flags of South Africa. One the Union Jack of the British Commonwealth, one the flag of the Orange Free State, the third the *vierkleur,* the old flag of the Boer Republic. When she gave the cane back to him he traced the embossing with a forefinger.

125

"Three flags are not one flag," he said enigmatically, and she wondered which he favored.

He leaned upon the cane to rise from the bench and she stood up beside him.

"I mean to walk over to the flower market—would you care to come with me?" he asked.

"I'd like to," she said. "But before we go, may I take a picture of you here?"

He did not mind and she asked him to move about as he would if he were alone. For the first time she had seen in him something to which she could respond, and she sought for it in her picture. When it was taken, she went to walk beside him and drew his hand gently through the crook of her arm as they moved together toward the street.

"Would you have gone to the market alone, if I hadn't come by?" she asked.

He nodded. "I come here two or three times a week. First I visit the shop, and then Thomas leaves me for a while in the garden if the weather is fine. When I've sat in the sun long enough, I walk over to Adderley and there is always someone to help me through traffic. I prefer to get about by myself as much as possible."

When they reached the curb he felt for it with his cane and stepped down without hesitation. His sense of hearing had been intensified by his loss of sight and he seemed aware of the nearness of any person or moving object in an astonishingly sure way. As they crossed to the right side and followed the old-fashioned street with its elderly buildings and busy modern traffic, Susan asked him about the visitor in his house.

"Has Mr. Cornish moved in? Have you had any talks with him yet?"

"He has moved in," Niklaas said. "And I'm glad to have him under my roof and within easy reach. At the moment I'm afraid we're sparring and wary of each other. We've not been able to come together on the matter that interests us most. However, I've filled him in a bit on my early life—when my first wife and your half-brother Paul, who was his friend, were alive. On all this past history we are in accord."

It seemed strange to hear about these people whom she had never known—Paul, who was in school in England much of the time when she was small, and later in the war, never to come home. She listened with interest as they approached the arcade opening off Adderley Street, where the flower market occupied the center of an alley a block long.

Down the length of this arcade a double row of tubs and containers were set high on stands, revealing an almost solid bank of brilliant blooms. There were irises and poppies, tulips and jonquils. There were carnations and roses and cornflowers. And of course the exotic blooms of South Africa as well —flowers Susan had no name for. Along the outside aisles moved housewives and tourists, old gentlemen and young girls, all making purchases. Brown-skinned women stood amid the riotous color, urging their wares upon the customer, each calling attention to her own more superior blooms.

Niklaas van Pelt stood still for a moment at the entrance, breathing deeply of the fragrance. A nearby colored woman called him by name and began to speak to him in Afrikaans. He smiled and shook his head.

"We always play this game," he said to Susan. "They know very well that I will make a circuit of the entire market before I select what I want, but they always try to coax me to buy before I am ready. Come, let's see what they have for me today."

As he moved along the row with Susan at his side, a middle-aged woman, whose waistline bulged above her checked apron, spoke to him in greeting and reached out her hand for his cane. As she touched it, Niklaas gave it readily into her keeping. Apparently he wanted both hands free now and had no need for the cane in this restricted area. The woman placed it out of the way beneath her flower stand, and as they moved on down the row the flower buckets themselves seemed to guide her along.

Once he put out his hands and held them above a great basin of marigolds, not quite touching them. It was as if he sensed the mass itself and would do the delicacy of a flower no harm by touching so much as a petal. Often he bent closer to breathe an individual fragrance and there was a quiet enjoyment in him that Susan found moving to see.

When they had circled the market, with the flower sellers greeting him and sometimes thrusting a bouquet beneath his nose, Niklaas began to make his selections. He seemed to remember exactly where the flowers were that he wanted, and he chose lavishly and with evident pleasure, often calling the market women by name.

Susan stepped back toward the street and took out her light

meter. Only color film would truly do justice to this display, and she had none in her camera at the moment. Nevertheless, she was interested in the central figure of her father, the smiling flower sellers nearby, the expression on the face of the fat old woman who was returning his cane. She snapped the last two shots on the roll and began to turn the film on its spool. When she looked up again, she saw Thomas Scott waiting near the entrance to the market.

Niklaas raised a finger, as if he knew he would be there, and Thomas came to gather up the flowers the girls had wrapped into cornucopias with paper and string.

Susan bought a few roses and a bunch of green chinker-ichees for herself. She had loved these South African "chinks" as a child, with their green buds that climbed a long stalk and would open later into long-lasting white flowers.

When she walked back to the car with her father, he offered her a lift home, but she thanked him and refused. The car drove away and she returned to the scented garden for the blind and sat on the bench which she and Niklaas had shared. There was much that she wanted to think about here in this quiet place.

One thing she had learned this morning and it was something she had never believed in before. Niklaas van Pelt had loved his wife deeply. He still retained for her a tenderness that he succeeded in hiding most of the time. Apparently he had reached a state of acceptance and understanding, so that he did not blame her for running away. Yet, in spite of this, Claire had raised her daughter with the belief that Niklaas had cared for neither of them, had not wanted them, had somehow betrayed them. For the first time a faint doubt about her mother began to rise in Susan's mind.

More than ever now she felt a reluctance about delving deliberately into the past. Whatever she found was sure to injure one or the other—her father or her mother. Yet she knew she must take the action she had promised Dirk. One way or another, she must have the answer.

14

When she reached home Susan was eager to see how her new pictures had turned out. She went directly to her little dark-room to develop the roll of film. Since her enlarger had not yet arrived, she could not complete her work as perfectly as she wished, but she could at least develop the film and make the first contact prints.

Just before lunch she finished her work and took the roll out to hold it up to the light. The shots of her father looked as if they had come out well. She hung the strip up to dry and was ready when Willi came to call her to lunch.

The thoughtful, shutaway time in the darkroom had in-creased her feeling that she must wait no longer to take the first step back into the past. She would not wait for Dirk to make the arrangement for her to visit her father's house. She would go there this afternoon on the very heels of Niklaas's kindness to her this morning and would hope that he might hear her request receptively.

After lunch she set off for Protea Hill. The colored maid admitted her and showed her into the living room, where French doors stood open. Afternoon sun shone into the room and she walked to the doors and looked out. On the terrace John Cornish sat before a table on which rested a portable typewriter. He looked up at once and saw her.

"Do come and talk to me," he said, as though he expected nothing but friendliness from her. "I'm getting nowhere today. Cape Town distracts me and so does the feeling of spring."

She crossed the flagstones to the low wall of the terrace. From here Devil's Peak was behind her, and she could see the full sweep of the Lion, from its tawny stone head to the flanks that reached toward the sky.

"I've had no chance to thank you for arranging a meeting with your father the other day," Cornish said. "Considering the rather brutal way I'd blurted out the story to you, it was kind of you to help me."

"I didn't do it for your sake," Susan told him frankly. "I wanted to see my father stop you from writing whatever you had planned. I had no idea that it would wind up with you here in his house."

John Cornish continued to study her with his oddly intent gaze until she began to feel uncomfortable beneath the scrutiny. There was never any knowing what he thought, or what plots this man might be hatching. There was still something in his purpose with her father that she did not understand and that made Dirk feel that he was dangerous. Was it, she wondered, because there was even more to what Niklaas van Pelt had done in the past than John Cornish had originally brought to light? Since her encounter with her father this morning, she disliked such a suspicion. But what else could Dirk mean?

Idly Cornish tapped the space bar on his typewriter. "How is your photography coming?" he asked.

This was a safe enough topic and she told him about the picture story she was planning and her efforts to get beneath the placid surface of Cape Town life. Before she was through, her father came to the door of his study and stepped out upon the terrace.

"Susan?" he said and waited for her response.

The softer mood of the morning was gone and he was distant again, even a little forbidding. She rose to greet him, but before she could state the reason for her visit, he drew a ring of keys from his pocket and began to detach one of them.

"Dirk tells me you want to explore the house," he said. "You're welcome to do so now if you like. You may go into any room you please—even Mara's and John's, with their permission. And of course my own. There's only one door you'll find locked. This is the key for it."

Her problem was solved more easily than she had expected. Relieved, she thanked him and returned to the house with the key in her hand. In the downstairs hallway she stood looking about for a moment. The great Chinese vase, filled now with African poppies her father had bought this morning, stood on the hall chest, a glowing splash of color in gloom that sunlight did not penetrate. But now she had no desire to look through the downstairs rooms.

Quickly she mounted the stairs, following the right-angle turn to the floor above. Near the top was the open door to a room she remembered as her father's. She merely glanced in and went on. It was not her father whom she sought up here. Across the hall a second door stood open and she saw that this was the guest room John Cornish must be occupying. She glimpsed a desk with manuscript pages spread out upon it, and on a tall dresser the framed picture of a pretty, smiling woman.

Hastily she moved away, not wanting to pry. Somehow the picture surprised her. In her mind John Cornish had come to be more a symbol than a man. He was the well-known author, and more recently a rather sinister figure who had stepped threateningly into her own life. She had no idea who the woman in the picture could be—wife, fiancée, sister? No one had ever mentioned a woman in connection with him.

She crossed back to the room next to her father's. This had been her mother's room, as she knew very well. Was it here that she would need the key? But the knob turned under her hand and the door opened at her touch. It was strange to have her returning memory of the room erased in a flash. Everything had been changed. There remained not a stick of furniture that her mother had used, though this was clearly a feminine room. A pale-blue negligee lay across the bed and there were jars of cream and bottles of perfume upon the dressing table.

For an instant a queer vertigo possessed her. It was as if the world about her whirled and fell into angry sound and she felt with compelling conviction that something dreadful was about to happen. She steadied herself and closed the door upon the wave of fragrance that she recognized as Mara's French perfume. She had been half afraid that she might see a picture of Dirk upon the dressing table, but there was nothing save those bottles and jars and boxes. Yet it was not her sense of Mara's occupancy that had caused this sudden dizziness. For a moment it had been as though something had reached out of the past to smother her in nightmare fear. But as she stepped back from the threshold her head cleared and the oddly threatening impression was gone.

Shaken, she moved on toward the rear of this upstairs hall. It was her own room that she was now approaching. There was no fear in her now, no sadness. She had loved this room as a child, and had always looked forward to returning to it for the summer months that the family spent in Cape Town. There was no need to try the door. She knew it would be locked, knew the key she held would open it. The key slipped easily into place, but before she turned it she closed her eyes and rested her forehead for a moment against the darkly varnished wood. This time she did not want memory to be suddenly dispelled, and she called back a clear vision of the room in detail, impressed it upon her consciousness so that it might be recalled even if everything in the room was different. Then she pushed the door open and stepped across the sill.

Her first impression was of a place that was dark and dusty and long unused. There was a stuffy odor and the very opening of the door roused a stirring of dust. As her eyes grew accustomed to the gloom, she saw that all was the same as it had been when she was a child. There was a small bed and a low bookcase still filled with rows of books. A worn leather hassock stood before the bookshelves as if it had been used only yesterday by a little girl who loved to read. There was a small desk, and a chair too, and a full-sized chest along one wall.

Softly Susan crossed the room, hesitant to disturb whatever was left here of her childhood. She opened the casement window and unhooked green shutters to push them outward. In the frame of the open window the full sight of the mountain, gray and rocky and massive, caught away her breath. This was the view she best remembered, and it was the one she had both loved and feared. Sometimes the mountain had seemed her friend and guardian. Its strength and eternal presence had seen her through many a childhood problem. Yet at other times that mass of rock could seem relentless in its judgment of her. There had never been any way to hide from the mountain. It knew everything.

The block of the lower cable-car house made a spot of white at the place where the slope began to steepen. As she watched, a tiny car started upward, rising like a bead upon an invisible thread. Up, up, slowly—and there was its counterpart coming down. The cars passed like the figures in a formal dance and each disappeared into its own white cubicle at the foot and at the top. The mountain remained unmoved, untouched by this display of human engineering. In spite of the continuous assault made upon it, no human figures could be seen along that vast expanse of the table. The mountain would have dwarfed them, made them invisible. Only when one came close could an occasional climber be seen, finding his precarious way up that great face. The easier paths were hidden in ravines, or lay out of sight on the other side. Every year the mountain took its toll in human sacrifice. Its strength and immobility affected all Cape Town, set a stamp upon it, but sometimes its influence and import were less than benign. Yet every child who grew up in the Cape, both colored and white, loved to go climbing. Last Sunday, on her day off, Willi had gone up the mountain on a date with Thomas, and Susan knew that if she had stayed here as a child she would sooner or later have gone up the mountain herself.

She turned her back now on its stern face and looked at the room. She found it both touching and disturbing to realize that her father had kept her room exactly as it had been in the days of her childhood. Had he expected that she would someday return? Had he kept it waiting for her, even though he had wiped the memory of his wife's room from existence?

There was a tightness in Susan's throat as she went to the chest that stretched along one wall. It was a fine old *kist* made of beautifully grained stinkwood and it had been given to her by her father to keep her treasures in. She did not question now what she would find inside. If all else had not been changed, this, surely, would remain the same.

She pulled over the leather hassock and sat down before the chest, pushing the heavy lid back against the wall. Sure enough, an all-too-familiar jumble of toys lay within. Not all her toys, it was true, but only those she had brought to the Cape Town house the last time she had journeyed here from Johannesburg. She pulled out a stuffed toy rabbit with one pink glass eye and grayish fur. There was a small box camera with a broken lens, a china doll with a missing arm—how she had loved that vacant-eyed doll. And then—at the bottom of the chest among other odds and ends she discovered a treasure. It was the album of old snapshots she had taken before she had broken the camera.

This was a find. Perhaps these pictures would be something to jog her memory. She took the big book with its woven grass cover out of the chest and was about to close the lid when she heard a sound from the doorway. Looking up quickly she found Mara Bellman watching her.

"Your father sent me to see if you were all right," Mara said. "You've been quiet for quite a while and he began to worry."

"I'm fine," Susan said curtly and waited for her to leave.

Mara, however, came into the room with unconcealed interest.

"Bluebeard's closet!" she said. "I always expect to find a body hidden in here, or at least evidence of some crime."

Susan said nothing, merely waiting. This was an intrusion she heartily resented and she was not deceived by the other girl's suddenly affable manner. Mara remained insensitive to her wish to be alone. She strolled idly to the window and looked out at the mountain.

"We're allowed in here only once a year, for spring cleaning, you know. The rest of the time your father keeps it locked. I understand he had the room closed when he came down here to live after he was released from prison. Not that he ever saw it again himself. I suppose you know that his blindness came on while he was in prison."

"I didn't know," Susan said in a low tone. There was pain for her in the sudden revelation. It seemed doubly tragic that he should have gone into prison, never to see the bright free world again. It was as if the prison sentence still lay upon him and always would.

"How dusty everything is," Mara said. "I'll have to get the key away from him soon so the servants can clean up." Looking about, she noticed the chest beside which Susan knelt. "That, of course, is a treasure," she added. "A beautiful old piece. It's odd that it should have been given to a child to use for toys."

Restraining her irritation, Susan answered evenly, "When he gave it to me, Father said I was to take care of it. He always believed that children should learn very young to take good care of their possessions. He said this was to be my wedding chest when I grew up. I didn't dare let it get scratched or dented because he would have been angry."

Perhaps Mara did not care for the reference to a wedding chest. She moved on about the room, revealing her impatience now, opening a drawer here, touching a chair there. Ignoring her, Susan reached into the chest again. This time she drew out a faded pink candy box with a heavy content that rattled in her hands.

At once she remembered what it was and opened it delightedly, to reveal what had been her prized rock collection. She dumped the entire contents out upon the floor and began to identify bits of rock and shell that she had not thought of in years. This bit of shell with the mother-of-pearl colors had come from Camp's Bay, where her parents had friends and where she had often gone swimming. This piece of black porous rock had come from the top of Table Mountain. Dirk had brought it down after a climb, especially for her collection. Something with a bright gleam to it caught her eye and she held up a piece of quartz.

Mara had come to stand beside her, watching. "What's that?" she asked.

Susan's resentment at this continued intrusion brimmed over. "The one thing it is not," she told Mara, "is the Kimberley Royal," and she looked up at the other girl angrily.

For once Mara's poise failed her. A flash of dislike so intense flared in her eyes that Susan was startled. Without another word Mara went out of the room. Thoughtfully Susan began to put the bits of rock back into the box. She wondered if Dirk had any conception of how much Mara Bellman detested her.

When everything except the photograph album had been returned to the chest, Susan closed the lid and came out of the room, locking the door behind her. Then she took the key back to the terrace where Niklaas sat talking to John Cornish.

15

"Keep the key if you like," her father told Susan when she would have put it into his hand. "I have a duplicate. You're welcome to visit the room whenever you like. Everything in it is yours."

His manner had not softened and the offer was made almost indifferently. Yet so close was she at that moment to her childhood that the impulse to touch him in a remembered caress was hard to resist. She made no move toward him, however, and only thanked him softly.

He did not let her go at once. "I've been thinking about inviting a few people in for tea to meet you before long," he said surprisingly. "It's been a good many years since I've entertained in this house, but I believe there are some who would come. There are a few people I would like you to know. Would you have any objection? I've already mentioned it to Dirk."

"Why, no, of course not," she told him. "It would be very kind of you."

He nodded. "I'll set the wheels to turning then."

She said good-by and nodded to John Cornish, who had risen when she had come out on the terrace and stood watching them both with that look of his that was somehow different, Susan thought, from the way other people looked at you. Always there was an intensity in his gaze, a lively awareness of all that went on around him. Yet there was no knowing what his conclusions were or how he was summing you up.

"I believe I'll take a bit of a walk," John said. "I've sat at an unresponsive typewriter long enough for one day. Do you mind if I come a way with you?"

She did mind, but as always there seemed no way to escape him.

"If you like," she said carelessly and they left the house together, following the street and the longer way home.

"I've wanted a chance to talk to you," he said when they were away from the house. "Yesterday your father showed me the letter your mother sent him shortly before her death."

So now, Susan thought, John Cornish too meant to sound her out about that letter. She was silent, ready to resist whatever he might urge.

"It opens all sorts of strange possibilities, doesn't it?" he went on. "If your mother didn't take the diamond out of the country herself, it may long since be in other hands."

"Of course," she agreed a bit dryly. "I've thought so all along. Though I've wondered how such a famous stone could be disposed of. Wouldn't it be identified if it appeared on the market?"

"It would be, providing it reached a legitimate dealer's hands before anyone tampered with it. But an expert cutter can change any stone, disguise it, as it were, so that it wouldn't be recognized. Though if it went into black market channels, that might not be necessary. There are world powers eager for diamonds. And private collectors and dealers who are unscrupulous."

His words were taking an unexpected turn. He was not urging remembrance upon her, as others had done, but seemed to be deliberately opening another door, a door of escape from some of her worry.

"By a world power I suppose you mean Russia?" she asked. "But I thought Russia possessed treasures of cut stones herself."

"You're thinking of Czarist Russia. After the revolution diamonds poured out of the country in the hands of escaping nobility and were sold in a flood that dropped the price of diamonds everywhere until the outpouring ended and the price could be brought under De Beers control again. Now Russia occasionally sends out stones for sale, but for the most part she seems to be snapping them up in the illicit markets. Especially in the field of industrial diamonds."

Susan glanced at him hopefully. "If you think this is what may have happened to the Kimberley, then you won't have to write about my mother at all in your book."

"There are still the other diamonds," he said, not ungently. "Those found in your father's house—the ones that sent him to prison."

She did not want to think about those stones at the moment and returned quickly to the safer subject of the big stone. If one side of the problem could be cleared up, then she would face the other side.

"One thing I've never understood about the Kimberley is why one man would give it so casually into the keeping of a friend to take from one city to another. You'd think something that valuable would be sent with an armed guard."

Cornish smiled. "You don't know South Africans. I've seen fortunes carried about wrapped in bits of paper. After all, that's the safest way to carry diamonds—unobtrusively. At any rate, your father had the big diamond in his possession. He brought it to Cape Town and after that what happened to it is anybody's guess. Though the letter from your mother opens a new possibility."

This was what he was leading up to, of course. Now he would do as the others had done. He would put the weight of remembering upon her shoulders and urge her to start thinking back into the past. Her resistance against him stiffened.

"You needn't ask me what I remember. I don't remember anything. And I hate to have everyone prodding me. Just now Mara Bellman came up to the room I had as a child and stood watching me as though she expected me to produce the Kimberley diamond at any minute."

"If I were you, I'd pay no attention," he said quietly.

"To Mara, you mean?"

"To anyone who tries to push you into remembering," he said. There was a sudden grave urgency in his voice that surprised her. "Don't try to remember, Susan. Don't let anyone force you back into the past."

His words astonished her. John Cornish had been the truth seeker, the one who had told her that she must face the truth, whatever it might be. She stole a look at him as he walked along beside her, and noted the craggy look of his head in profile, the stern set of his chin, the unsmiling mouth.

"That day in the Public Gardens you were the one who said that truth was to be respected for itself," she reminded him. "You said I ought to seek it out, no matter how involved I was emotionally."

"I've changed my mind," he said.

Somehow this unexpected reversal left her puzzled and disturbed. "But why? What has happened to make you change your course?"

They had reached a corner that brought the Aerie into sight a block or so away and John took her arm, drawing her to a halt on the sidewalk.

"Not my course—yours. This is difficult to put into words, and that's unlike me." He smiled ruefully. "There's a feeling about that house—Protea Hill—that I don't like and can't quite put my finger on."

"But what has that to do with me? What has it to do with whether or not I remember what might have happened years ago?"

"Perhaps nothing," he said. "But I have a strong feeling that it's wiser to let the matter rest. Perhaps, like a good many journalists, I play my hunches. Take care of yourself, Susan. Be very careful, won't you?"

Startled, she looked into his eyes, trying to read there the things he had not told her. "I—I don't know what you mean."

"I'm putting it badly. But will you promise me one thing. If you remember something, if you find the road back, will you make one move before any other?"

She could only stare at him blankly.

He spoke more gently, as if he wanted to soften the effect of his words, and there was a kindness of manner that she had seen in him before only in the presence of her father.

"If you remember anything that seems to be significant, go first of all to someone you can trust. And I mean someone you trust wholeheartedly. If there's no one near enough, then take what you know to the police." He touched her lightly on the shoulder, perhaps in admonishment. "I won't take you clear home and embarrass you with Dirk. I've done enough of that. Rather blindly, I'm afraid. Good-by, Susan. And think about what I've said."

This time he waited for no answer but went off, moving rapidly in spite of his limp. Both disturbed and astonished, she watched him out of sight before she turned toward home.

She did not understand any of this. Someone she could trust? Dirk? Her father? John Cornish himself? It was a chilling thing that she could give no confident assent to any of these.

Cornish she had trusted least of all. For the most part she had disliked and resented him, and yet as she walked the last block toward home the reluctant feeling of having found someone to depend on began to possess her. It was as if she had come up against a rock wall that was cold to the touch and would lacerate her flesh if she brushed against it, yet which stood there, unalterable, for her to lean against if she were at bay.

At bay? What a strange thought to cross her mind. Nothing threatened her—this was nonsense.

How strange too that he had urged her not to remember even if she could. This was no longer advice she could take. Dirk was her husband. It was he who must guide her. It was he who was trying to save her father from further pain. Besides, once the door of memory had started to open, it was unlikely that one could ever again keep it shut. This afternoon memories had begun to stir vaguely in the background of her mind. There had been that moment when she had stood, shaken, on the threshold of her mother's room, on the verge, it seemed, of some knowledge. The snapshot album that she had brought home with her might well open the door completely.

Nevertheless, when she reached the house she put the album down in the living room and left it there without turning so much as a page. John's words had made her hesitate.

She went next to the darkroom to see if the strip of film was dry. There was still time to make prints before dinner and she wanted to be busy. The film, however, was not where she usually hung it, and she looked around to see whether she could have put it absent-mindedly in some different place.

She even went into the dining room and the living room to see if she could have laid it down somewhere, having been called from what she was doing. But no amount of searching revealed the strip of film downstairs. She was about to go upstairs to look for it when she noticed a basket of sewing she had left on the coffee table. Her sewing scissors lay beside the work. As she picked up the scissors and basket to carry them upstairs something on the carpet caught her eye. She bent and picked up a stiff, transparent sliver with shadings of light and dark in it. When she held the sliver up to the light, it was easily recognized as a tiny strip that might have been snipped from a piece of film.

Increasingly puzzled, she put the sewing things down and looked into a wastebasket, finding nothing of any significance. Then she went out to the kitchen and searched the garbage container, much to the cook's astonishment. No, missus, Cookie said, she had not seen any picture-taking materials.

There was a large outdoor container in the yard and Susan,

139

possessed now by a hunch, hurried out to it. Hidden beneath a heap of damp potato peelings she found what she was looking for. Someone had deliberately cut her strip of film into tiny slivers and hidden them in this waste from the kitchen. More puzzled and shocked then angry, she fished out the mess of cut-up bits and wrapped them in a sheet of newspaper. Then she went into the house and rang for Willi.

The girl came from her room looking a little sleepy as though she had been taking a nap. In the living room Susan gestured toward the scraps of film on the paper.

"Do you know how this happened, Willi?" she asked.

The girl stared at the slivers with eyes that were expressionless.

"What is it?" she asked.

Susan told her of looking for the length of film she had hung up to dry, of finding the clue of a bit of film not far from scissors that might have been used to cut it off, and of hunting down the rest.

Willi shook her head. She had seen nothing, heard nothing, knew nothing.

"Why would anyone do such a thing?" Susan cried. "I'd taken some really good pictures of my father and I was anxious for them to turn out well. Are you sure, Willi, that no one might have come into the house while you were in your room?"

"Not unless someone entered through a window, Mrs. Hohenfield," Willi said. "The front door is locked, and the cook has been out in the kitchen all the time. The only person who has entered the house is Mr. Hohenfield."

"You mean he came home early?" Susan asked in surprise.

Willi nodded. "He said he wasn't feeling well, and he went upstairs to lie down. I don't believe he has left."

She thanked the girl and let her go. Then she went upstairs to the bedroom door. Dirk must have heard her step for he called out to her.

"Come in, darling. I'm awake."

She opened the door to find him lying on his bed, wrapped in a maroon robe, his shoes off.

"Is anything the matter?" she asked quickly.

He shook his head. "Nothing to worry about. I had a rugged day and felt a bit seedy, so I chucked it and came home early. What's happened to you? You look as though you'd met a ghost."

Susan carried the newspaper over to his bedside and set it down. The paper curled open, revealing its soggy contents.

"What on earth?" Dirk said, and there seemed to be genuine surprise in his voice.

"I finished a roll of pictures this morning," she said, "and developed them before lunch. Then I went out for a while this afternoon. When I came home, my film was missing and I found it cut to bits and hidden under rubbish in the yard."

Dirk lay silent, his eyes closed for a moment as if he fought the return of a headache. "I suppose I'll have to give Willi and the cook a talking-to," he said.

"I've already questioned them. Neither one knows anything about it."

"Of course they'd lie if they did know," Dirk said. "These people always lie when they're trying to save their own skins."

Always before when Dirk had made derogatory remarks about the dark races she had either argued with him gently or tried to make allowances for his very different upbringing. There was always the hope that she could gradually get him to see these matters with a less prejudiced eye. But now outrage sprang up in her at his words and she made no effort to check it.

"That's a dreadful thing to say! There isn't any such thing as 'these people.' We're only considering Willi and the cook and I expect they are as honest as we are."

Dirk looked at her with an air of pained distaste and sat up on the edge of the bed. "Listen to me, Susan. This entire racial situation is dynamite. I've hoped you would stay out of it. You haven't lived in South Africa since you were a child and you don't know one thing about it. The romantic idea of equality between black and white, or even colored and white, is a dangerous one. If we give them too much, we are the ones who'll be thrown out. Look at the Congo. Leave Willi and the cook to me. What sort of picture did you take on that strip of film?"

She could see the futility of arguing with him further now, but the resentment his words had aroused did not die out. She was beginning to be sorry that she had told him what had happened. But there was nothing to do except try to remember the pictures she had taken.

"Nothing of any consequence, I'm sure," she said limply. "A few shots around Cape Town. A picture of the van Riebeeck statue at the foot of Adderley Street. Several pictures of my father."

"You've seen him today?"

"I saw him this morning in that little garden for the blind, just off the Avenue. I took a picture of him there and then one or two more in the flower market."

He seemed to consider her words as he moved slowly toward the door, tying the cord of his robe around his waist. "And that was all?"

It didn't seem quite all. There were some scenes she couldn't recall, but nothing surely that was significant. Anyway, she no longer cared. She was too upset about Dirk to care.

"This sounds like malicious mischief," he said. "I'll have a talk with the servants now."

She did not go with him, but remained upstairs where she would not hear what he said. Restlessly she moved about the room, fighting the turmoil within herself. Dirk was set wholly in opposition to something she believed in with spirited conviction—and this diverging of viewpoints could hardly be ignored in South Africa. His own attitude hurt and grieved her and it promised continued friction between them unless some compromise could be reached. Yet this was a subject on which she could not compromise and still retain a sense of self-respect.

Idly she picked up the little carved impala she had brought from Chicago and smoothed the satiny wood, searching out the whorls of the carving. The diamond on her finger blinked as she moved her hand and she stared at it unhappily. The ring stood for happiness, marriage, the security of the love that she had believed existed between herself and Dirk. The impala seemed to stand in contrast to all this. It represented Africa and the dark strong heartbeat of its rising peoples. It stood for what was right—for the idea of freedom in which she believed so strongly.

She put the impala down and turned toward the window beside her. Must a choice between the two be necessary? Perhaps she could find a way. No man and woman were ever in agreement on every aspect of their lives in a marriage. Divergent viewpoints, even though fundamental, did not always destroy love and loyalty.

Thinking of compromise, of giving somewhere in her own stand, she began to consider Willi.

The girl had been brought here by Mara Bellman. Not even Niklaas had known that she was coming here to work. Might that mean that Mara held her under some obligation which Willi could not escape? Was it possible that Willi would feel bound to let Mara into the house and would keep the secret of her entry? Mara was fully capable of malicious mischief, especially if it might disturb Dirk's wife.

This afternoon at Niklaas's house Mara had not appeared until that moment upstairs when the toy chest had been opened. Could she have come to the Aerie during that earlier interval? Or perhaps by the short cut while Susan and John Cornish were walking slowly the long way home?

Dirk's step sounded on the stair and she stiffened as he came into the room, offering him no inquiry, continuing to stare out the window.

He came up behind her and put his hands on her shoulders. "You can relax, darling. I gave them a very small talking-to and made no accusations at all. You'd have been pleased with me."

Relief flooded through her and she turned to him quickly. He was trying too; she didn't have to bridge this gulf alone after all. And if only he would try, she would make all the more effort to understand his viewpoint, even if she could not accept it for herself.

By nighttime the troublesome happenings of the day had receded to some extent. When she went to bed the load on her shoulders felt considerably lighter. Yet when her conscious mind slept, what lay beneath could roam as it pleased. During the early-morning hours she awakened once more with the sweat of terror upon her body and the flash of blue fire all about her. A cold fire that cut through her flesh with an icy thrust that seemed about to destroy her. She awoke struggling, fighting against something utterly fearful and shattering, to find Dirk holding her, gently shaking her awake, his voice coaxing her back to consciousness.

"You're all right, darling. It was that beastly nightmare again. It's over now. You're safe and I won't let anything come near to hurt you."

She clung to him, the terror still upon her, and it was a long time before she would let him go. The dream seemed a fore-warning of the door that was slowly pushing open somewhere in her consciousness. A door with all the force of long-suppressed memories behind it. And there were no means by which she could prevent its opening. Nor did she really want to. Whatever was fearful and hidden must be faced, exorcised. Only then would she be free of it. Only then would the nightmare cease to recur.

16

Dirk stayed at home the next day. He was not ill, but there seemed in him a nervous dissatisfaction that worried Susan. How much was this mood a reaction to her own emotional vagaries of yesterday and last night?

When she told him of her father's plan for inviting a few people in for tea some afternoon, hoping the idea might please him, he grimaced.

"I know. Uncle Niklaas has mentioned it to me. If it gives him pleasure, let him go ahead. We can see it through, I suppose."

They were sitting together in the living room and Susan was waiting for Dirk to make some decision as to what they would do with this free day. Once she would have been full of suggestions, but now she hesitated, leaving it up to him.

"I thought it was kind of Father to suggest such a party," she said mildly.

Dirk shrugged and stretched, yawning. "I can warn you that the people he invites will be a bore. But he's unlikely to take our suggestions."

Idly he reached out and picked up a book from the coffee table. It was the snapshot album from her childhood.

"What's this?" he asked, and smiled as he opened the cover. The handwriting was her father's and Dirk read the words aloud: " 'The picture life of Miss Susan van Pelt, aged six and a half.' " He glanced at her teasingly. "I remember you when you were the very young Miss van Pelt. Where on earth did you find this?"

"In my room at Protea Hill," she said. Was this the road back? Did the answer lie in these pages?

He turned the leaves and, drawn by her own uneasy fascination, she found herself looking at the pictures with him.

So young a photographer had been haphazard in her approach. Some of the pictures were blurred because the camera had moved. Some were crooked because it had been tipped. There was one of the Lion's Head that looked as though it

144

was toppling away from the observer because the camera had been tilted directly up in snapping it. The better pictures had clearly been taken by adults.

"There I am," Dirk said, amused, tapping a picture with one finger. "There in my climbing outfit."

She looked at the page. How bright and shining a person he had seemed in those days; how wonderful to a little girl's eyes. In this picture he wore shorts and a jacket, cleated shoes, and a rope slung in a coil over one shoulder.

"You went up Table Mountain that day," she said. "You brought a black rock down for my collection."

He laughed. "So I did. I'd forgotten the existence of that collection. How important you felt about it."

He turned a page. "There you are with your collection. Isn't that what's spread out on that board in the garden?"

It was indeed. She could remember her pride in the labeling. Grownups had helped her to spell the words, though she had been able to make the letters herself. She had been seven by then and reading rather well. The pictures were too small to reveal the wording on the labels, but she could recall some of the details as she studied them. Invisible hands were pushing at the door again, widening the crack a little, and she shivered, suddenly afraid. This was too soon. She was not ready. She took the book out of his hands and closed it.

"What is it?" Dirk said. "What's the matter?"

But she could not tell him. "Let's not sit here looking at old pictures when a free day is waiting for us. Let's go outside and do something."

"What would you like to do?" he asked.

She suggested the first thing that came to mind, wanting only to get out of the house, to leave the album and all its crowding memories behind. Later she would face it, but not yet.

"Let's go up Table Mountain. It looks like a good bright day, with no wind." She knew the cable cars did not operate if the wind was high.

Dirk was willing. He seemed gayer now and more affectionate than he had been in a long while. When they were dressed in warm sweaters and Susan had put new film into her camera, they went out to the car and Dirk drove up the Kloof Nek Road, where a pass opened between the Lion's Head and Table Mountain.

On the way up Susan watched the little white cable house at the foot, but no cars seemed to be moving, in spite of the perfect weather. When they reached the Kloof and turned left to follow the road along the side of the mountain, they lost sight of the house for for a time. But when at last the road curved beneath it and Dirk got out of the car to investigate they discovered that there were no cars running. A cable was being repaired and the cars would be out of service for a day or two.

"Let's get out anyway," Susan said.

Dirk drove the car off to the side of the road and they got out and climbed a little way up the rock-strewn lower slope of the mountain. The houses of Cape Town stopped well below this level and all about them great boulders jutted from the hillside with tiny wildflowers emerging from the stubby mountain growth. At their feet lay the town spread out between Devil's Peak and the Lion's Head, and behind rose the precipitous rock sides of the mountain, the table a straight black line against the sky. From the town below the ever-present cooing of the doves reached them.

Susan raised her face to the sun, clasping her arms about drawn-up knees. Dirk lounged lazily beside her, plucking at a scrubby clump of heather. A question she had been wanting to ask came to her mind and she put it into words.

"Yesterday when I visited my father's house and went through it upstairs, I looked into a room that must be the one John Cornish is occupying. I saw a picture on his dresser—of a woman. Does he have a wife?"

"Cornish again? The fellow's becoming an obsession with you." Dirk sounded annoyed. "He did have a wife. She was an English girl who died five years or more ago. He's been a lone wolf ever since, I gather. Anything more you want to know?"

She shook her head, wondering at herself for asking the question. The thought of John's odd warning had come back to her more than once, though she had been unable to puzzle out his meaning. But she had not expected to be curious about him personally.

It was pleasant here on the mountainside and she fell to dreaming a little as they sat in silence. A further remembrance of her visit to Protea Hill yesterday returned to mind: that moment when she had found her childhood rock collection. She stared up at the top of Table Mountain, from which Dirk had long ago brought her a piece of black stone. Above the mountain the sky was a bright warm blue—almost the blue of an alcohol flame. She closed her eyes to shut away the sight, but now the flash of blue fire seemed all around her, as it had been in her dream. Without warning, the thing was there in her mind—established in full detail. The door had blown open on a great gust of memory and she knew quite clearly what had happened.

Dirk must have seen the change in her face and sensed the tensing of her body. He left the rock on which he had been sitting and took her by the shoulders. He shook her gently so that her head fell back and her eyes looked widely up into his.

"Tell me what you've remembered," he said urgently.

She sensed by the grip of his fingers that he would shake her far less gently if she did not reply. Now that the thing had come through so clearly there was no way to keep it from him. In words that sometimes halted and sometimes rushed ahead, she told him exactly what had happened that long-ago day in Cape Town.

She had been playing with her rock collection out on the terrace behind Protea Hill one afternoon. The day was hot— the burning heat of their January summer. As a child she had always had an affinity for the heat of Africa, and she had set up her collection in the sparse shade of a blue gum, just as it had been arranged in those childhood snapshots.

That day she was admiring a new stone she had added to her collection. She could not remember when or how she had come upon it, but she had liked it better than any of the other stones. True, it was not as big as the shiny lump of quartz, but it had sparkled with a most amazing fire. A blue-white stone it had been, flashing blue fire when she turned it in the light. Her mother had come out of the house and seen her playing there. Even now Susan could remember her distraught and worried expression.

"Susan dear, I wonder if you've seen—" she began. And then her eyes fell upon the stone in her daughter's hands. She flew across the terrace and snatched it out of the child's fingers. It had been an alarming thing to Susan to see her mother, who was always gentle and loving, grow almost hysterically angry. She had slapped her daughter and scolded her thoroughly. What she said, Susan could not remember, but she could still recall how puzzled and wounded she had been by the outburst.

When Claire ran back inside and up the stairs, taking the stone with her, Susan, hurt and bewildered, crept after her. Not in order to spy, but wanting desperately to understand what she had done that was wrong, to understand why adult anger had struck out at her so unexpectedly, like lightning across a clear sky—when always before she had been praised and encouraged for her rock collection.

She went softly to the door of her mother's room. It had

been closed, but the latch had not caught and she pushed it open without a sound. That was how she came to see exactly what happened. Her mother stood for a few seconds staring rather wildly about the room, her back to the door and the flashing stone in her hands. She looked as if the very touch of it burned her flesh. Then she went to her dressing table.

On its surface sat a glass powder bowl with a silver top that had always fascinated Susan. It was a Chinese piece with silver dragons entwined around the lid so that their raised heads made a knob in the center. Claire lifted the cover from the bowl, dropped the stone into the flesh-pink powder, and thrust it well out of sight with her fingers. Then she wiped off the powder with a handkerchief, wiped up a sifting of it from the dressing table, its delicate fragrance reaching the child who watched around the corner of the door. Claire's face was visible in the mirror, but she did not see the door ajar or Susan watching behind her. She looked only at her own pretty face and gradually the anxiety faded out of it. She began to look pleased as a kitten, as if she thought herself a very clever person.

The hidden Susan lingered a moment more, shaken as much by what she had seen as by her mother's anger. Her teeth had begun to chatter and she knew with frightening certainty that her mother would be even more angry if she discovered her here. Tiptoeing as if the very house watched her, she had returned to her rocks. But all her pleasure in the collection had vanished and the remaining rocks seemed dull and unmagical compared with the beautiful, shining stone it had been so wicked of her to possess.

"The Kimberley!" Dirk said tensely.

Susan came back from the sharply etched past to see his face. There was something almost avid in his expression. It was a face she did not recognize, had never seen before.

"So you did find it!" he went on. "You did know what happened to it. Go on with your story. Tell me the rest."

She stared at him blankly. So thoroughly had she been caught up in the illusion of the past that her feelings were those of the young Susan, and her eyes still watched her mother with a rising fear that was beyond her years. Why had she been so frightened? Why had so vivid an experience been thrust out of her mind, for so long buried and forgotten?

"Do go on," Dirk prompted impatiently.

She could only shake her head. "That's all I know. That's all I can remember."

Clearly he did not believe her. "That isn't possible. You

must have been curious. You must have wanted to know why your mother hid the diamond in the powder and what became of it afterwards."

"I didn't even know it was a diamond," Susan said in a low voice.

"What does that matter? You thought the stone pretty, didn't you? You wanted it for your collection." Excitement had risen in him, and an urgency she hated to see.

Again she shook her head. "I don't know. Truly I don't know any more than I've told you."

The door had blown open on a wave of vivid memory. And as surely it had blown shut again. There was nothing left except a sickness at the pit of her stomach and a feeling that the threat of utter disaster hung over her head. New questions were crowding her thoughts. Was this something she had felt as a child or was it her reaction now—this foreboding and dread? What had really happened that day?

In any event, the moment had been spoiled. Dirk would not forgive her now. She stood up limply. "Let's go home," she said.

For a moment she thought he meant to urge her further. Then, without a word, he started down to the car, striding impatiently, and she went with him. But when they had driven to the Kloof, where the roads branched, he took the downhill highway that led through the gap and south along the Peninsula. He drove recklessly, wildly, and his speed on the turning road frightened her.

To their left lay the wine valleys and Groot Constancia, with all its history, but Dirk turned sharply onto the coast road and mountains shut away the calm, sunny valleys as the car sped toward the ocean level. Here they were beyond the flanks of the Lion and this was no longer Table Bay, but the cold South Atlantic.

Below the clustering houses, pink and yellow and creamy white, gay with red roofs, curved a crescent of white sand. The car plunged down a zigzagging road that led to Camp's Bay. Above them the sharp leaning peaks of the Twelve Apostles stood out against the sky.

Dirk braked to a jarring halt beside the palm-lined drive and came around to pull open the door on her side. He said nothing, but merely held out his hand. There was no gentleness in his fingers as he drew her from the car. Together they walked down a bank and out upon the warm sand. Susan stepped lightly, carefully, so that her shoes would not fill with fine white sand, but all her movements were automatic and she was shaken by a sickness of despair. Now she had truly angered him, and in a way she could not help. There was an ugliness in his anger that she had never seen before and she winced away from it as though he had lashed at her physically.

A roaring of surf sounded where the rolling line of breakers pounded in. The water was still too cold for swimming and no one else walked the beach. They had the sand and the creaming surf, the breeze from the ocean, to themselves.

She did not move quickly enough for him and he caught her hand again to pull her along. Bits of broken shell strewed the rim of the high-water mark, and there were dry brown coils of seaweed like snakes upon the sand. Ahead a great mass of smooth, rounded rocks encroached upon the beach from shoreline to ocean, looking like huge animals with their wet brown heads in the sea. Dirk sprang ahead of her upon the nearest rock and held out his hand to pull her up. They moved from rock to rock and Susan saw the green marbling of the water where the surf roared in, saw it break high in the air over the farthermost point.

The calming effect of sea and sky, the physical effort, was quieting Dirk's anger and when he said, "Let's sit here for a bit," his tone was gentler than before. She took her place beside him on the warm smooth stone, but she could find no comfort in his change of tone. She sat staring mutely at the scene about her.

Toward the land golden lichen grew upon the rocks, and between them clung small purple flowers. On the water side seaweed hung like strands of long dark hair, drifting and lifting with the movement of the waves. Far out across the water was a small island where cormorants gathered on the beaches. And always, all about them, was the roar of the waves, rising and falling endlessly.

She knew why he had brought her here and there was only bitterness and sorrow in her at the thought.

"This is where we said good-by before I went away to America," she said, musing aloud. "I tried to take a picture of you that last day, but it never came out because I had broken my camera. Father never knew I'd broken it. It was a special gift from him and he was always angry when I broke anything. I was afraid to tell him. So I have no picture of you the way you looked that day. But I can still remember."

She did not know why she related these things, when obviously he did not care and they were not the memories he wanted. He was looking away from her toward the land, toward the familiar tipping peaks that numbered twelve and had been named for the Apostles. The strangeness had gone from his face, but there was no true relenting in him.

She brushed the warm surface of rock with her hands and saw the greenish shine of mica in the sun. Beneath her feet was a sandy crevice and she bent to peer into it—a flat cave large enough for a child to crawl through. On every hand was nostalgic memory. She leaned over to pick up a handful of sparkling sand from a crevice and let it sift through her fingers. Was this sifting away what was happening to her marriage? The boy she had said good-by to on these rocks was not the man she had married. Or was there perhaps less difference than she supposed? Had the promise of the man been there in the boy and she too young and adoring to sense in him the things she shrank from now?

Softly Dirk began to whistle and her heart caught in pain as she heard the tune, remembered the words. "I'll see my darling when the sun goes down . . . down, down below the mountain . . ." Sadly she turned the ring palmward on her finger so that the pink diamond would not glow so brightly in the sun.

He saw her gesture and it must have told him he would get nothing more from her. This time it was he who said, "Let's go home," and there was a coolness in his eyes.

They clambered across the rocks and returned to the car. Dirk chose the lower road into Cape Town, below the flank of the Lion that made Signal Hill, and around Sea Point to the shores of Table Bay. Ahead the table was in view again and suddenly Susan felt oppressed and hemmed in by the mass of gray stone with its flanking, guardian hills. As she had always known, she could never escape the mountain. It knew everything.

17

The tea party Niklaas van Pelt gave for Susan and Dirk proved a mixed success. The afternoon, to begin with, was gray, cold and drizzling. Mara, acting as hostess, looked beautiful but distant, so that her presence did little to warm the atmosphere.

It was clear to Susan that she detested the task that had been assigned her. When Mara's eyes met hers there was a fierce burning in them that was close to hatred. Susan, who had never found herself so intensely disliked before, recoiled inwardly and did her best to avoid the girl. Dirk seemed to notice nothing out of the ordinary and Susan could hardly appeal to him for protection against hostile glances.

In any event, it was impossible for her to give herself wholeheartedly to this affair when the aching soreness that had possessed her since that day on the mountain had never lessened for a moment. Dirk had not been unkind, but the breach between them had widened wordlessly. She knew he was blaming her for something she could not help. Memory would give her only so much and no more. There was no forcing it.

The matter of the destroyed film had gone unexplained. Dirk had not mentioned it again, nor had Susan. Indeed, it had begun to seem of little importance when set against the estrangement that had developed between herself and Dirk.

So Niklaas's tea came at an inopportune time, and Susan's heart was scarcely in it.

South Africans were a friendly people and pleasant to know, but even the guests who came did not make it a complete success. It had been so long since Niklaas had entertained that there was a curiosity behind the polite façade of his visitors. And there was, as well, the usual undercurrent of uneasiness that so often presented itself in South Africa these days, so frequently possessed the conversation. Niklaas had many Afrikaner friends and their viewpoint was in political opposition to that of the English South Africans present.

One gray-haired English Capetonian spoke fervently to Susan on the subject. "I suppose you Americans are puzzled by what's going on down here. The majority vote is out of English hands—our own fault, too, since we practically gave away our birthright. And there's no way to save our necks down the beastly course we're being driven. Afrikanerdom wears blinders."

In opposition to this view, an old friend of her father's told Susan indignantly that the outside world did not understand the purpose of the great experiment of apartheid and should mind its own business.

"We want only to help the black man," he said with a fervor surpassing that of the Englishman. "When we separate the

152

races completely, each can grow at his own pace and the black man will return to the tribal life that best suits him and govern himself as he wishes."

John Cornish had paused beside Susan to listen. "I know—I've been in the Transkei. But the white man still calls the tune there and makes the rules."

"We merely guide them wisely," the other man said and turned away.

John shook his head despairingly. "There's no ground on which we can get together. It's an Alice-in-Wonderland world when it comes to logic. The only thing that's sure is that everyone is badly scared and waiting for the next explosion. I hope I'll get my book done before it comes."

"How is it going?" Susan asked.

"Not very well. Your father manages to block me on all except obvious roads. We're still talking and at least I'm getting a clearer picture of the past."

Dirk joined them, nodding coolly to John, and after a few words the writer moved away, leaving Susan with her husband.

"How are you bearing up?" Dirk asked. "It's an odd lot Uncle Niklaas has invited here today. Oil and water. The trouble is that your father hasn't stirred himself to get out among people for so long that he doesn't know how fierce the issues are."

Someone spoke Dirk's name nearby and before he moved to answer he murmured a few words under his breath for Susan alone. "When we get home, darling, remind me to tell you how pretty you look."

His words surprised her and she tried to feel pleased and reassured, but everything had gone flat. She went over to where her father sat in an armchair, alone for a moment.

He spoke to her as she reached him. "Tell me about the gathering, Susan. Make me see it."

"I'll try," she said. "But, first, how did you know it was I?"

"Your scent, of course," he told her. "It's light and flowery, yet not too sweet. I could pick it out anywhere. I noticed it the first day you came to visit me."

"Appleblossom?" She must remember not to change, she thought to herself, touched that he had found this means of identifying her.

She took the liberty of painting the tea party in slightly more cheerful colors than were warranted as she told him about it. He listened attentively, but with a slightly disbelieving air.

"You describe everything with a photographer's thoroughness," he told her when she paused, "but I doubt if everything is going as smoothly as you say."

It was clear that he was not so ignorant of what was happening as Dirk thought.

A woman came up to speak to him and she could not answer. Later, after she had gone into the hall with someone who was leaving, she returned to the dining room to stand hesitantly near the door, looking about for Dirk, half concealed by a great jar of flowers on the sideboard. These days she was often at a loss when he was with her, yet when she was away from him she wanted unreasonably to be at his side again. As she stood there the voices of two women, hidden by the flowers, reached her.

"My husband says there's still a good bit of it going on, in spite of I.D.S.O., the security organization. There's always a leakage out of Cape Town."

The second woman's words were lightly mocking. "Perhaps Niklaas van Pelt is up to his old tricks?"

"That's unkind and unworthy of you," the first one said sharply.

The second woman laughed and they moved off together to have their teacups filled.

Susan went quickly away to find an empty corner of the living room where she could stand looking out at the gray day. The surge of angry emotion that swept through her was surprising. She had not known that anything could stir her to such anger in connection with her father. For just an instant she had needed to keep a restraint upon herself, lest she spring indignantly to his defense. It would do no good to involve herself and make a scene.

When the party at last drew to a close and guests began to leave, her one reaction was of relief because an ordeal was over. After the last visitor had gone, Dirk came to tell her that a question had arisen concerning the new stock of silver jewelry and he must remain for a little while with her father. He would be at home for dinner, and in the meantime Thomas could drive her home. But Susan said the drizzle seemed to have let up, and she would enjoy the walk.

Dirk joined her father in his study, and she went into the hall to put on the mackintosh she had worn against the rain. As she was buttoning it up, the doorbell rang and the maid appeared to accept a package from a man at the door.

"Mr. van Pelt's cigars," the maid said. She put the package

on the hall table beside the Chinese vase and went back to her work of cleaning up after the party.

Susan considered the box of cigars for a moment. Why not take them to the study herself? Dirk had bustled her off rather hurriedly and she'd had no satisfactory opportunity to thank her father or to say more than a perfunctory good-by. The words of gossip she had overheard still left a bitter taste and she had the feeling that some small gesture toward him might help to erase them.

She reached out to pick up the package, but somehow the table runner of Indian brocade caught beneath it as she lifted the box. The big Chinese vase filled with proteas tilted forward at an alarming angle. Seized by her old horror of breaking anything, Susan dropped the cigars and reached for the vase, catching it just as it tipped toward her. Water splashed over her hands and the box she had dropped struck the corner of the table, bounced off to the floor with a crash and broke open, scattering its contents about. She had saved the vase at the cost of the cigars, but the latter mattered less.

With hands that were shaking she set the vase upright and searched her purse for a handkerchief to dry her hands. Then she knelt to put the cigars back in the box. She knew this trembling over nothing was ridiculous. Nevertheless, she fumbled clumsily as she picked them up. One had broken free from its cellophane wrapping, strewing tobacco on the floor. She snatched up the broken cigar, gathered up the shreds of tobacco and thrust the lot into the pocket of her mackintosh as guiltily as though she had been a child trying to hide some wrongdoing. Now she would have to tell her father what had happened, she thought in unreasonable dread. Perhaps he would let her buy him another box . . .

She was suddenly aware that someone was watching her and she looked up to see that Thomas had stepped into the hall. He came to help her and she was murmuring to him apologetically about what had happened when Mara came down the stairs.

Mara saw at once what had happened. "Don't trouble yourself," she said to Susan, sounding impatient over such clumsiness. "Do run along. We can take care of this. Thomas, fetch a brush, will you? That is, if you're sure, Mrs. Hohenfield, that you don't want him to drive you home." The spite in her eyes was barely veiled.

"No; it's not raining. I'll take the short cut," Susan said hastily. "But if you don't mind, I'll tell Father what happened first. It was entirely my fault."

"It's not necessary, but do as you like," Mara said curtly and began to rearrange the cigars in the box.

The moment Susan stepped into the study she knew she had interrupted some grave discussion her father was having with Dirk. Niklaas seemed a bit absent-minded as she explained about dropping the box of cigars, and Dirk looked distinctly displeased with her intrusion. She had half expected her father to reproach her for carelessness, as he used to do when she was a child, but he said merely that it did not matter, and dismissed her rather quickly.

When she returned to the hall Mara and Thomas were gone and so was the box of cigars. She let herself out the door and went through the dripping garden, feeling more disturbed and uneasy than ever. She had sensed some sort of cross-purpose between her father and Dirk and wondered what it was.

In the street she stood undecided for a moment. Overhead the sky looked threatening, as if it might pour at any minute. Should she go back and accept the offer of the car? But she did not want to return to the house. It would be better to chance the rain by way of the short cut and get home on foot.

The path was wet and muddy in spots, and she walked in the grass along the sides wherever possible. When she started the climb down the ravine she moved more slowly than usual because of high heels, instead of walking shoes. The clouds overhead were scurrying before a wind that set the pine trees shivering and tugged the hood of her mackintosh back from her head. She had been letting her hair grow to please Dirk and she could feel the longer ends blow loose from their restraining pins.

On one hand the mountain stood black and wet, with silver falls of water down its face. The pine grove in the ravine was awhisper with raindrops falling from branches onto the brown, needle-strewn earth. Ahead, where the uphill climb toward home began, the tall rocks glistened like black marble, a little eerie in the gray light. The ravine was deserted, and it was foolish to be afraid of passing a mere huddle of rocks. Perhaps it was their shape that always vaguely disturbed her, as if they had been raised into position by some antique force that had left a malignant spell upon the place.

She thrust her hands deep into the pockets of the mackintosh, feeling the crumbled cigar beneath the fingers of her right hand. She had been foolish once today and once was enough. As she started up the hill toward the rocks she did not permit herself to hurry in the panic of her own imaginings.

There was no sound at all save the dripping of moisture from bushes and trees, and the movement of her own feet on the steepening path. The odor of wet pine was heavy on the moisture-laden air. She was safely past the rocks now and her fears had proved childish, as always. Soon she would be at the house and out of this cold wind. The crack of a twig on the path behind her sounded at the same instant that something struck her full in the back. She was flung forward to her knees, the breath knocked out of her, and something rough was thrust over her head and pulled down, smothering her cry, blinding her. A rude hand snatched the purse from her grasp and she heard the thud of someone running.

Kneeling on the wet stony path that bruised her knees, she fought the coarse sack from her face and struggled free of its stifling odor of earth and potatoes. When she had pulled it from her head she stumbled to her feet, the taste of earth in her mouth. For an instant she glanced back at the black, silent rocks, the dark cluster of pine trees and deepening shrubbery in the ravine. There was no one in sight. Nothing moved, no footfall thudded. Yet her assailant might be hiding there watching her. She turned and ran toward home as quickly as her high heels would take her.

Willi met her at the door and saw her disheveled hair and the mud on her mackintosh. Sensibly she asked no questions, but picked up Susan's muddy shoes as she kicked them off.

"Someone was hiding in the ravine," Susan said. "Someone snatched my purse. Willi, please call Mr. Hohenfield at my father's and tell him what has happened. Ask him to come home right away."

Willi went at once to telephone. Susan ran upstairs in her stocking feet and began to walk nervously about the bedroom, heedless of her wet mackintosh. She felt increasingly shaken by what had happened, even though it might have been worse. At least she had come out of the experience without serious physical injury.

There was a sore place in the center of her back where the push had come and her hands were scratched and bruised where she had fallen on them. She wished they would stop their trembling reaction and she thrust them into her pockets to steady them. Again her fingers found the broken cigar and she drew it out, aware of the not-unpleasant odor associated with her father, and dropped it into a wastebasket.

Her mind was still going over what had happened to her—the suddenness, the unexpectedness of the attack. Someone must have been waiting in the shadow of those rocks, though that usually empty path seemed an unlikely place to wait for a victim to rob.

She busied herself absently by taking off her coat and turning the pocket inside out to rid it of tobacco shreds. Several bits of a harder material fell out upon the carpet and she knelt to pick them up. Four or five tiny hard pellets lay upon her palm. They were dull in color—yellow, black, dark green. Bits of stone, they seemed to be, smaller than a pea. Her attention caught, she retrieved the cigar from the wastebasket and crumbled the tobacco over a piece of tissue. When the cigar had been reduced to powder, she had collected a number of the tiny stones. They lay inert in her hand. Inert and possessed of terrifying implications.

Hearing Willi on the stairs, she wrapped the tissue quickly about her find and put it back in her mackintosh pocket. Willi reported that Mr. Hohenfield would be here at once, and remained in the doorway, her eyes questioning.

"I'll be all right," Susan assured her. "I was pushed down on the path with sacking over my head, but I wasn't really hurt."

When the girl had gone, Susan looked quickly about the room for a suitable hiding place. Then she tucked the packet of crumbled tobacco and tiny stones into the toe of a shoe in the armoire and set a shoe tree in against it. The cigars had been sent to her father and the knowledge left her alarmed. She did not want to tell Dirk or anyone else of her discovery until she had time to think about it.

Dirk came home a few moments later. He made her go over her story several times, explaining exactly what had happened. Then he phoned for the police. He was clearly concerned and did not remind her that he had advised against her use of the ravine path.

When the police came there was further questioning, though she could be of no help in identifying the person who had made the attack. The Afrikaner officer shook his head in grim disapproval over her walking about at dusk in the lonely ravine.

A search was made of the path she had followed and the potato bag was found as well as her discarded purse, with the money missing. Sacking of the sort used might come from anywhere, and there were no other clues to be discovered. The path was used just enough so that there were footprints in muddy places of the few who had followed it. On the other hand, a man running in the grass along the side might leave hardly a trace of his passing. The officer concluded that it had been the act of some "Kaffir" who was interested only in the money she carried. She was fortunate not to have been seriously injured. Let this be a lesson to her.

Susan thought of the crumbled tobacco tucked away in the toe of a shoe in her wardrobe and said nothing. She could only hope there was no connection. No casual assailant could have known she had the cigar.

When the police had gone and the long-delayed dinner was served, she found it difficult to eat. The shock of what had happened had worn off a little, but she could not relax. The thought of those tiny significant pellets hidden away upstairs haunted her. She did not want to talk to Dirk about them. It was her father she must go to first. Tonight—immediately. But when she suggested seeing her father right after dinner, on the thin excuse of telling him what had happened to her, Dirk would not hear of her leaving the house.

He was gentler than he had been in a long while, but he was firm about the fact that she was to go up to bed right after dinner.

"There's a delayed reaction about this sort of thing," he warned. "I've already phoned the doctor to come in this evening and have a look at you."

Frustration made her all the more nervous but, though she fretted over Dirk's ministrations, there was nothing to do but give in.

When he had tucked the covers around her and gone downstairs, she lay awake with sleep the farthest thing from her mind. She could think only of the cigar and the tiny stones that had been hidden in it. Though she had never seen anything like them before, she could not doubt their importance. She knew very well what they must be. And her first hope that there had been no connection between what had happened to her on the path and her possession of that cigar was growing dimmer as she examined the possibilities.

Someone at Protea Hill was involved. Someone who knew she had dropped the box of cigars and broken it open, someone who suspected that she might have picked up a cigar from the contents and put it in her purse. There were just four people who knew what had happened, and there would have been time for one of them to cut ahead of her down the path and lie in waiting.

Thomas had found her in the hallway first, and then Mara. Leaving them, she had gone into the study and told Dirk and her father what had happened. A blind man could hardly

159

have gone down the path to waylay her, even if he had been so inclined. But he might have sent someone else. She hated to believe that and turned her mind quickly to a readier suspicion. What of Mara? She knew perfectly well that Mara was capable of vindictive action against her. That rough thrust in her back might have carried the added strength of Mara's hatred.

Or had it been Thomas? She closed her eyes, shutting out the light from a dressing-table lamp and thought about Thomas. Because he was a colored man she had a special reluctance to suspect him. That sort of thing was too easy, too much the obvious course to be taken by a person whose skin was white. Then, without warning, a vivid memory returned to her. She could see the man clearly as she had glimpsed him that day on the steps of the library, his rapt attention upon a book he had quickly hidden when he saw her. That day she had taken a picture of him. A picture that was on the strip of film that had been destroyed. A picture she had not remembered until now. She was beginning, all too reluctantly, to see where this might lead.

The doctor was long in arriving and Willi came upstairs with a cup of hot tea and an offer of encouraging sympathy. Susan watched as she moved quietly about the room, drawing the draperies across each window against the darkness.

"Willi," Susan said, her voice so low that it could be heard only in this room, "was it you who destroyed that strip of film?"

The girl was turning back the covers of Dirk's bed and her hands were suddenly still upon the satin coverlet.

"I don't want to hurt you, Willimina," Susan said, "but I need to know the truth."

The colored girl left her work and came to stand beside Susan's bed.

"Yes, Mrs. Hohenfield," she said. "I destroyed it."

"And it was Thomas who told you to get rid of it?"

For a moment longer the girl held to her outward calm. Then words began to spill out. They were spoken with spirit, revealing the often-hidden essence of independence in Willi. While she expressed regret, there was about her a dignity that was appealing. She had hated to do such a thing, she said, when she had been treated well in this house. Now she must leave, of course. She should have left before this. It was no right to stay on after what she had done.

"But why would Thomas tell you to destroy that strip of film? Was it because of the picture I took of him on the li brary steps? If he disliked my taking a picture of him, why couldn't he simply ask me not to print it or ask me to give him the negative? Why should the entire roll have been destroyed?"

Willi was quiet again. The moment of lost control was past. Her eyes met Susan's without fear but she stood silent, saying nothing. She might admit her own action, but it was clear that she would not further incriminate Thomas.

The bell rang downstairs and Willi turned toward the bedroom door. Suddenly Susan knew that she did not want to lose her, no matter what had happened.

"Wait a moment," Susan called, and the girl paused. "Don't leave us for good, Willi. Please stay."

There was surprise and sudden warmth in Willi's eyes. She nodded gravely, said, "Thank you," and went to answer the door.

Dirk came upstairs with the doctor and remained while he examined Susan's back and concluded that little damage had been done.

The sedative the doctor gave her did not take effect at once and when she was alone Susan lay thinking about what she must do. She must talk to someone, and very soon. John Cornish's words, so puzzling at the time, came back to her. He had warned her to be careful, though he had not told her of what. "Talk to someone you can trust," he'd said. Someone she could trust wholeheartedly. But who was there? She still shrank from going to Dirk though she did not want to examine the reasons for her reluctance too closely. And she was beginning to see that she could not go to her father either. She did not know how seriously he was involved. She did not want to judge him, but she could turn to him least of all.

No, it was John she must talk to. She could remember the odd sense of confidence that had come over her that day he had brought her home. There had been a feeling of strength about him, of a solidity which might serve her well if her need was great. Tomorrow she must find a way to see him without anyone else's knowledge. See him and show him those strange pellets she had found.

The sedative began to have its way and she dropped into a heavy sleep in which there were no dreams.

18

When she wakened late the next morning, Susan felt a little groggy. Dirk's bed was empty, the covers thrown back. She had not heard him get up or heard him leave the house. Sleepily she touched the bell that would summon Willi and the morning cup of tea with which every proper South African began the day.

On the tray Willi brought to her was propped a note from Dirk. Susan sat up, sipping the hot, strong tea and reading Dirk's words as Willi flung open the draperies to a bright morning.

Regretfully, considering Susan's recent experience, Dirk was off to Johannesburg. Something had come up in her father's store there that needed his attention. Niklaas had told him yesterday, but he had not wanted to disturb her with the news after what had happened. He would be gone overnight and would fly home tomorrow on the afternoon plane.

"I hate to leave you at a time like this," he concluded. "But the doctor said there was nothing to worry about. Do be careful, darling. And miss me a little."

She folded the paper into its envelope with a sense of lassitude. Only a little while ago she would have been desolate at the thought of being parted from Dirk for a day. This was the first time he had been away from her overnight, and she did not care. Perhaps it was the drug the doctor had given her that had left this limp indifference. Except that it was laced with something like relief as well. She did not want to believe that she would not miss Dirk and yet, suddenly, that seemed to be the truth. It was a distinct relief to know that she need not see him today.

The telephone rang downstairs as Willi turned toward the door.

"Perhaps that is Mr. Cornish," she said. "He rang up earlier, Mrs. Hohenfield, and I said you were still sleeping."

She went down to answer the phone and Susan slipped out

of bed and put on a dressing gown. She followed Willi downstairs and took the phone from her.

"Susan?" It was John's voice. "I've been concerned about what happened to you last night."

"I'm fine now," she told him, and the sense of relief she had felt over Dirk's absence increased. She was free now to talk to John. Willi had gone out to the kitchen and she lowered her voice. "I'd like to see you sometime today, if you can make it. Not here or at Protea Hill. There's something I want to consult you about. Dirk has gone to Jo'burg and won't be home till tomorrow, so I can get away at any time."

"Then what about dinner?" he said. "What time shall I pick you up?"

She glanced over her shoulder, but the hallway was empty, the door to the rear of the house closed.

"Let me meet you away from the house. And please don't say anything there about having dinner with me."

He named a small restaurant where she might meet him. She hung up with the certainty that John Cornish would know what everything meant. He would take the pieces out of her hands and tell her what to do. It did not even seem strange that she should be willing to place herself in his hands, when only a little while ago she had been bitterly set against him. Now she was only sorry that she must get through an entire day before she could be rid of her burden of worry and bewilderment.

When she had bathed and dressed and had breakfast alone in the dining room she tried to think of something to do with her day. Perhaps she would read awhile, sit in the garden with some sewing—anything to make the time pass. Twice she opened her wardrobe and checked the presence of the wrapped-up tissue thrust into the toe of a shoe.

It was nearly noon when the doorbell rang and Willi came to say that Mr. van Pelt was here to see her. Surprised, Susan hurried downstairs and found her father standing in the middle of the living room, one hand on his cane, the other upon the arm of Thomas Scott.

"Good morning, Father," she said, and gave the colored man a quick look. "Good morning, Thomas."

Thomas returned her greeting without meeting her eyes, and there was nothing to be read in his light-skinned, good-looking face.

"How are you feeling?" Niklaas asked, holding out his hand to Susan. "I want you to tell me exactly what happened."

"I'm perfectly all right," she said. "A little stiff, perhaps, nothing more. Thomas, will you bring a chair for my father, please."

Thomas drew forward an armchair, but he did not help Niklaas into it. The old man felt for it with his cane and sat down without undue groping.

"Don't go away, Thomas," he said. "We won't be long and I'll need you shortly."

Thomas said, "Yes, sir," and went to stand near the doorway to the hall. He faced the room, but he did not look at either of them.

"Now then," Niklaas said to Susan, "tell me what happened. From the beginning. When did you leave my house?"

She told him how she had hesitated over the weather and then started home by way of the short cut.

"And you saw no one along the way? Heard nothing?"

"Nothing at all," she said. "Nothing until I heard someone on the path just before I was knocked down. A rough bag that smelled of potatoes was pulled over my head and by the time I was able to struggle out of it and get to my feet whoever it was had snatched my purse and run away. I dashed for home and asked Willi to telephone Dirk. That's all that happened."

Again she glanced at Thomas and saw that he was staring at something on the opposite wall of the room with a fixed gaze that made her curious. When she turned her head she saw that the object which held his attention was the whip, the *sjambok* Dirk had fastened against the wall. But there was no telling from his face whether he really saw the whip or what his reaction was to her story.

Her father seemed lost in grave thought over what she had told him.

"Was there anything in your purse that someone might have wanted?" he asked at length.

She could answer that readily. "Only a little money, which was taken," she said. But her thoughts were upon those strange small stones hidden away in the bedroom upstairs. Did he know? Was that what he meant? Did he know perfectly well that what was sought had not been retrieved?

The dark glasses were like a guard upon his thoughts. Nothing was revealed behind them.

"You must avoid the short cut from now on," he said. "These are uneasy days in South Africa. Take care, my dear."

Was there a warning in his tone? She could not be sure.

He smiled at her suddenly, lightening the mood of the interview, changing the subject deliberately. "As soon as you feel yourself again, I'd like you to join me on a small trip. Every spring I take a morning's drive around the Cape. We'll make a little party of it this year. Perhaps a picnic at Cape Point. If Dirk agrees to drive the car, I'll give Thomas a day off. Eh, Thomas?"

"Thank you, sir," Thomas said and continued to stare at the wall.

"I must learn to get on without Thomas before long," Niklaas went on. "There's a school post coming up for him shortly in one of the new locations. I shall miss him, but I'll be glad to see him get what he wants. Perhaps you can talk Willimina into marrying you now, my boy."

Thomas said nothing, but for a moment the familiar bitterness showed in his eyes.

Susan saw it and spoke to him across the room. "Thomas, do you remember the time I photographed you on the steps of the library? What was the book you were reading that day?"

For the first time he looked at her directly. "It was a book by Mr. Cornish, madam."

"The one on Ghana?" Niklaas put in. "You read me several passages from it and I thought it very good."

Thomas offered no opinion and Susan felt increasingly puzzled. There would seem to be little reason why Thomas should be disturbed because she had seen him reading a book by John Cornish. Or why he should later have asked Willi to destroy the film.

"It is a book about freedom," her father mused. "About the difficulties and the price and responsibility freedom brings with it. Democracy has to be both learned and earned. Wouldn't you say so, Thomas?"

For once the colored man stepped out of his careful role. "At least, sir, they are stewing in their own juices in Ghana. Which is better than being stewed by someone else."

Niklaas nodded. "There's something to that, of course." He seemed oddly amused by his own words. Once more he changed the subject, turning to the personal as it concerned his daughter. "Tell me what you've done with this room, Susan. I knew the house years ago when a friend lived in it long before I became its owner. Tell me so that I can picture you in a setting."

She did her best to describe the room for him, explaining how the furniture was arranged, telling him of her own touches of small bright pillows that were not frilly and pink like Claire's. And of her framed photographs on the wall. When she had finished, she looked again at Thomas.

"Have I forgotten anything?"

"Yes, madam," he said and nodded toward the wall. "That." He did not name it, but left it for her to do so.

It was the whip he had indicated and Susan mentioned it reluctantly.

"Dirk has put a South African *sjambok* on the wall," she said. "A whip that once belonged to his father."

For an instance the room was as still as it sometimes was at night when Dirk was away from the house and the darkness seemed so quiet and ominous.

Abruptly Niklaas held out his hand. "Bring it to me, Thomas."

The colored man was tall. His long arms reached up to the brackets which held the black whip; he took it down and brought it to her father without a word.

The old man ran his fingers along the thickening of the handle. His sensitive, seeing fingers came to the initials that had been cut into the leather. He weighed the whip in his hand for a moment as though he were satisfied.

"It is the one," he said and gave it back to Thomas.

The colored man replaced it on the wall while Susan watched in bewilderment.

"What do you mean, Father?" she asked. "Have you seen that before?"

"I have. You might ask Dirk about it sometime." He stood up, tall and straight, and as cold as she had often seen him as a child. "If you please, Thomas," he said.

Thomas came at once to offer his arm. They crossed the unfamiliar room and Susan went with them to the door.

"Thank you for coming, Father," she said. "And you needn't be concerned—I'm quite all right."

He went down the steps on Thomas's arm and seemed to remember their number, so that he did not hesitate when he reached the walk, but followed it quite surely to the gate. Susan ran ahead to open it for them and her father paused before he went out to the car.

"On second thought, my dear, it might be wiser to say nothing at all to Dirk about that whip. Old angers are best left buried. Eh, Thomas?"

"Yes, sir," Thomas said, and there was no inflection of any kind in the words. He helped the old man into the car and they drove away.

When they had gone Susan returned to the living room and stared at the whip on the wall. What an ugly thing it was. And why, if there were angry memories bound up in it, had Dirk wanted to display it upon the wall of his living room?

She turned from it impatiently. How weary she was growing of secrets, of hidden threats, of knowledge withheld. What a relief it would be to talk to John Cornish tonight, to tell him everything and see what he could make of the odd pieces.

Once more she ran upstairs and checked the hiding place of the small stones. It was nonsense to worry about them, of course. No one was likely to steal them from under her watchful eyes. And this evening she would take them with her to show John.

Late in the afternoon, when she was dressing to meet him, she decided, half grimly, half in amusement at her own action, to set a few small traps. Here and there about the bedroom she made small preparations. Here a drawer left open an eighth of an inch, there a tracing of face powder upon a knob, a bedroom slipper set at an exact angle on the floor of the wardrobe, the hangers just so on the rod. And, as a last touch, the little carved impala put in an exact spot on the gold tooling of the jewel case on her dressing table. Then she took a last look at herself in the mirror and approved the simple black dress with its scoop neck and wide satin collar that set off to good effect her necklace and earrings of American Indian turquoise.

She put on a coat and a decorative veil over her hair. She had already told Willi and the cook that she would be out for dinner tonight and when the time came she phoned for a cab.

When they drew up before the small Swiss restaurant John had named, she recognized the van Pelt Mercedes at the curb. John Cornish was waiting for her inside.

"Your father generously offered me his car for the evening," John said as the hostess placed them at a corner table.

They were early for the regular dinner hour and for the moment had the small room to themselves. It was a bright, simple room, with scenes of Switzerland on the wall, a cuckoo clock in the form of a chalet, and yellow primroses set in small blue vases on all the tables.

He had dined here before, John told her, and the food was good. They ordered fondue and when the waitress had gone John poured wine for her from the bottle he had brought with him. One of the delectable wines of the Cape. Susan took the small packet of stones from her handbag and poured them into an ashtray on the table.

167

Four students came into the restaurant and took the next table—two girls and two young men. They too had brought their own wine, as was apparently the custom in an unlicensed place, and were laughing and talking, paying no attention to anyone else.

Susan pushed the ash tray toward John. "Are these what I think they are?"

He picked up a green stone and rolled it about on his palm, then dropped it back in the tray.

"Better put them out of sight before anyone sees them."

"Then I'm right?" She wrapped the stones in the tissue. "They're industrial diamonds, aren't they?"

"Bort," he said softly. "Diamond residue that won't make gem stones but is used for industrials and diamond dust. How on earth did you get the stuff?"

She told him about the cigars which had come to Protea Hill for her father, of her own carelessness in dropping the box, and of the way she had nervously picked up the broken cigar and put it into her pocket.

He heard her through, his expression grave. "Where do you think this leads to?" he asked, more as if he were curious about her conclusions than that he had any doubt about his own.

"Isn't it possible," she said, "that whoever snatched my purse yesterday was trying to retrieve the cigar with the stones hidden in it? If that's true, then someone in my father's house . . ." She paused, not willing to mention names.

John Cornish nodded a bit grimly. "It's not only possible. It is, I'm afraid, quite likely."

A waitress brought the steaming hot tureen of fondue and a green salad served at the table from a big wooden bowl. The students at the next table were lively and their voices filled the little room.

Susan speared a cube of bread on a fork and dipped it into the fragrant mixture of cheese, eggs and wine. Her attention, however, was scarcely on the food she was eating.

"I still don't understand. Why would anyone smuggle this —this residue from diamonds? If it is smuggling. How could it be worth-while?"

"Illicit Diamond Buying—I.D.B., as they call it here— doesn't restrict itself to gem stones," John said. "The market for industrial diamonds is enormous. The demand is always greater than the supply allowed upon the market. In the past decade or so hundreds of new uses have been found for industrials and the United States, as well as Russia, has been stockpiling them. They're harder than gem stones and suited for the pressures of high-precision tools. Their value in the making of armaments is especially important. The West hasn't been willing to sell industrials to Russia, so she gets them on the black market and pays a good price."

"Then these are valuable?"

"Not when compared to gem stones. It takes a lot of carats of this stuff to add up to real money. But there are grades of value even here. What they call bort is really poor-grade stones. But up from that there are degrees of hardness, of quality, that raise the value. If I remember my figures—and I've done some research on this—industrials account for eighty per cent of the diamond business in bulk and perhaps twenty-five per cent in profit. Not to be sneezed at. Especially if a gem stone is smuggled into the lot occasionally, as is likely to be the case."

He was silent, dipping thoughtfully into the fondue. Frightening possibilities rose in Susan's mind. No wonder someone who knew she had picked up the cigar might be desperate to regain possession of it. Desperate enough, indeed, to make an attack upon her in order to search her purse. Who? Which one in Niklaas van Pelt's house?

She spoke the thought aloud. "John, who could it be?"

"I don't know," John said evenly. "There's not much use in speculating, is there? We can go in circles that way. Besides, there's something else that troubles me."

"What do you mean?"

"The cigars. Why would anyone try to smuggle diamonds by hiding them in a box of cigars?"

"Why not?" she asked. "I should think that would be a very good way to conceal them."

He quirked an eyebrow at her. "Exactly. And one of the oldest tricks there is. Cigars are always suspect when sent or carried across boundaries where inspection takes place. How did this package come to the house?"

"I think it was by special messenger," Susan said. "It must have been sent inside the country."

"Then a fairly obvious means of concealment wouldn't matter. Though I wonder why it should be used in the first place."

"They would have to go out of the country sometime," Susan said. "Perhaps they were intended to go from Protea Hill by means of another step."

"But why *cigars*? Why the most obvious means possible? There's something here I don't understand."

"I don't understand any of it," Susan said. And added forlornly, "Perhaps I'm afraid to understand."

The charm of the little restaurant and the excellent food were wasted that evening, and briefly Susan regretted the fact. Perhaps John Cornish would bring her back another time, on a happier occasion. Though that was unlikely. She would not be out with John again. As it was, this was one more thing she could never tell Dirk.

When they had finished the meal with fruit and coffee, Susan sat on at the table, reluctant to leave, feeling that the puzzle had deepened instead of being dispelled.

John sensed her concern. "We've a bit more talking to do, and since we have the car, why not go for a drive and discuss these matters further?"

She was relieved not to go home in her present unsettled state of mind. When they were in the car he turned toward the Kloof Nek Road and followed its winding length up the hill. She wondered if he was going out along Table Mountain, but when he reached the place where the roads branched he made a sharp turn right onto the road that ran the length of the Lion.

A cool wind blew past the car and Susan turned up her coat collar, though she liked the feel of its freshness on her face through the open window. The road climbed in a straight line toward Signal Hill, and Cape Town lay below them, a bright carpet of light. When they had made a final circle around the hill and come out on top, the entire coast was visible, with the lights of sea towns beading the edge of the dark Atlantic.

They sat in the car for a few moments, held by the tremendous view. Then, pausing now and then, stumbling a little, Susan began to tell him of the way she had remembered having once held the Kimberley Royal in her hands as a child. And of her mother's taking it from her and hiding it in a silver-topped powder bowl. It no longer mattered that she had once regarded John Cornish with distrust or that his purpose had been to expose her mother to an accusation she could not defend.

"She had the diamond in her possession," Susan concluded. "Yet I still find it hard to believe that she actually meant to steal it. She was more like a little girl that day, playing a trick to amuse herself and fool someone. When she thought she had lost the stone she was frightened, but as soon as she had it again she seemed to be enjoying herself."

"What if I use what you've told me in my book?" John asked, studying her curiously in the dashboard light.

She returned his look, meeting his eyes without hesitation, liking what she saw. At the moment he reminded her of that badly lighted picture she had seen of him on a book jacket. His eyes were steady and deep-set, his mouth surprisingly sensitive in so strong a face. He no longer seemed a cold person to her, though he hid his feelings behind a reserve that broke down only when he was angry.

"If it's necessary to you, then you'll have to use it," she said. "Whatever you use will be the truth. I know that now."

"I don't want to hurt you, Susan," he said, "but sometimes the truth can be a shattering thing."

"I know," she agreed.

He looked away from her. "I'm sure now that there's something hidden going on in your father's house. My room's over the terrace and once or twice visitors have come at odd hours. I don't quite like it, but I don't know what to think."

Susan took the little wad of green and yellow stones from her purse. "To do with this, do you suppose?"

"What else am I to believe, now that I've seen these?" He took the tissue from her and opened it so that the dull stones were spread out upon the paper. "Some of these may be of good quality as industrials. And here's one that might even be a small gem stone. Some diamonds have a sort of greenish skin over them, you know, and there's no telling their worth till the skin is removed and the expert can look into the heart of the stone."

"Where do you think they come from?" Susan asked.

He shrugged. "There are many places. It's not too hard to smuggle diamonds in small quantity out of Sierra Leone these days. Or they might come from South-West Africa, or the Congo."

"But then they would have to be smuggled into South Africa, as well as out. Why would anyone go to that trouble?"

"Smuggling them in isn't nearly as big a problem as getting them out. Of course the more direct way would be through Beirut. In these days of planes Cape Town is a back door, yet it's still a good port for diamond smuggling. Ships stop here from every country. And there are deep-water coves along the coastline that can't be watched all the time. Of course it's even possible that this stuff is coming out of the Kimberley area or from around Pretoria."

"But aren't the big mines guarded?"

"No absolute way has ever been found to guard them. Trained dogs are used and high electric fences. Africans are let off the premises only at intervals and they are carefully searched. X ray has done away with some of the former indignities. But there are always white men who have to be trusted and who come and go without much interference. You can't X ray a man every time he leaves the mine—you'd kill him. So there are still leaks. This may be one of them." He folded the tissue carefully around the small stones. "Will you let me keep these for the time being?"

"I want you to keep them," she said. "I don't want them in my possession, now that I know what they are. Will you—" she hesitated—"will you go to the police about this?"

"I'd rather wait awhile," he said. "Once before I acted too hastily. I want to be sure this time. Have you told Dirk about these stones?"

"No!" she cried, and was astonished at the strength of her own denial.

John gave her a quick, sidelong glance as if her tone surprised him too. But he said nothing, and she was relieved when he switched on the engine and turned the car back along the road by which they had come. There were questions she had not asked, suspicions she had not put into words, a fear that she had not expressed. Now she did not want to. Any direction her thoughts might take seemed frightening and she could not choose their course safely.

John drove her downtown where the Cape Town streets were growing quiet, unlike Johannesburg after dark. At her request he put her into a taxi and she went home alone.

In the bedroom upstairs at the Aerie a lamp burned against her return and her night things were laid out upon the bed, her slippers on the floor. She had forgotten that of course Willi would be doing these things for her. So her little traps were foolish and no test at all. In the wardrobe her clothes had been slid a little way along the rod, her shoes moved on the floor when the slippers were taken out. The drawer that had been left a fraction of an inch open was neatly closed. And it all proved nothing.

Except—there was still one thing. There would be no reason why her small jewel box should be touched in any way, yet when she looked closely she saw that the little impala no longer sat upon the gold tooling where she had left it.

The discovery galvanized her into action. She ran downstairs and out the back door. The yard was hushed and still, with the nearness of the mountain somehow adding to the quiet. Light shone along the sill of Willi's door and Susan tapped upon the panel.

19

Willi came at once to open the door, a book in her hands. She stepped aside to admit her visitor and Susan saw other books on a table and scattered on the bed. They were schoolbooks, so Willi was apparently studying by herself.

Susan went directly to the point. "Willi, did anyone come to the house while I was out this evening?"

For an instant the girl's eyes wavered. "I've been out here reading, Mrs. Hohenfield," she said.

"Did you go upstairs and search the bedroom?" Susan asked.

"Oh, no!" Willi cried, and her distress was evident. "I put your things out for the night, Mrs. Hohenfield, and then I came straight out here to study."

"And after that? Who came to the house tonight, Willi?"

The girl clasped her hands tightly about the book she held and then released her grip with a helpless gesture and dropped it on a table. "Miss Bellman came," she said. "I let her in and waited downstairs while she went up to your room."

"Was she there very long?"

Willi sighed. "I didn't look at a clock. It seemed a long while. Perhaps half an hour."

Enough time for a rather careful search of a single room.

"What excuse did she give you?" Susan asked.

"She didn't give any." Willi threw further caution aside and spoke frankly. "When I came here, she warned me that it might be necessary to protect Mr. van Pelt in certain ways. She told me that because you were the daughter of the wife who left him, we could not wholly trust you, even if Mr. Hohenfield chose to shut his eyes to the danger. She said there might be times when we must watch what you did."

A nice little plot on Mara's part. With more reasons behind it than Willi knew. Mara, hating Dirk's wife, would be anxious to know all she could about her.

"Yet you're telling me all this now," Susan said.

Willi spoke without hesitation. "Because I don't believe you
173

would ever try to harm your father, Mrs. Hohenfield. Because
—" suddenly she discarded the maid's guise she wore in this
house and became what she was, a young woman of courage
and intelligence—"because I like you. And because I trust
you more than I do Miss Bellman."

Impulsively Susan held out her hand. "I want to trust you,
Willi. Thank you for telling me."

Willi took her hand in a firm clasp, but her dark eyes were
troubled and Susan sensed torn loyalties in the girl. Not so
much to Mara Bellman, but to Thomas, perhaps, and to Niklaas van Pelt.

"You can count on one thing," Susan assured her. "I would
never willingly injure my father. We all know he has suffered
enough."

"Thomas's parents worked on the farm the van Pelts used
to have in the veld," Willi said. "So Thomas has known him
all his life. He knew him at the time of his trouble, though he
wasn't working for him then. Thomas would do *anything* for
your father, Mrs. Hohenfield. I think there's no other white
man he wholly trusts."

Her emphasis on the word "anything" was almost a warning, though Susan did not know what she was being warned
against. She turned toward the door, then paused.

"I understand Thomas is to receive a teaching post," she
said. "Will this make matters easier for you?"

"I'm not sure," Willi said. "I just don't know."

Susan then said good night and returned to the house.
Twice now Willi had failed her, yet Susan's instinctive trust of
the girl and liking for her remained. If Willi would only realize it, she and Susan were on the same side in their desire to
protect Niklaas van Pelt from further harm. Might this be, in
the long run, a difficult thing to do? An impossible thing—
since John Cornish now held that little cache of stones?

Lately something of her old feeling for her father had risen
in her again, and added to it were new respect and admiration
for his courage in these trouble-inflicted years. She found it
difficult to believe any wrong of him and she did not want to
see him needlessly injured. There had been diamonds in the
cigars sent to him, but that did not necessarily make him an
accessory.

The emptiness, the quiet of the house was oppressive tonight. She could not endure the living room with that whip
making an ugly black slash across the wall. The bedroom at
least was brighter, but the loneliness here seemed even
greater. It was almost a palpable thing that hung upon the air,

something she drew in with every breath. She was shut away from everyone tonight—not only in her physical presence in this house but in her mind and spirit as well, through her own dread of looming calamity. Yet in her longing to stave off disaster she could turn to no one. Not to her father or Dirk, not even now to John Cornish, whom she trusted yet who might himself spell danger. Nor to Willi, who was coming to be her friend, but who had a prior loyalty.

She lay restless upon her bed, trying to think, trying to find an answer. Someone in her father's house was engaged in smuggling industrial diamonds. This much at least was clear. Mara Bellman had handled the cigars and knew that Susan must have picked up the missing cigar with its hidden stones. Mara had come to this house tonight and searched through Susan's things in this very bedroom. She had counted on Willi not to betray her.

But Mara might be no more than an instrument, just as Willi had been an instrument and perhaps Thomas as well. Whose was the brain and will behind all this? There were only two people from whom to choose. Her father and her husband. Perhaps both together?

She remembered the words John Cornish had spoken that time in the Public Gardens when he had made her so angry. Wasn't it better, he had said, to hurt the dead than the living? Her mother had held the Kimberley Royal in her hands. She had hidden it—whether playfully or cunningly, her daughter had no idea. The truth might reveal that Niklaas had been bitterly betrayed by a woman who had sought only to save herself. Painful though the choice between them might be, Susan no longer wanted to protect Claire's reputation blindly. Her father mattered more.

Yet now something else had come into the picture. There was a present-day connection with diamonds with which her mother had nothing to do. Had the gossip at the tea party been true? Could it be possible that her father, having the name, had decided that he would have the game as well? What was the meaning of those nighttime visits to the house John Cornish had mentioned? Who was coming to see him and why?

Then, as John had pointed out, there was the curious matter of the cigars. Why *cigars* if such a means was too shop-worn to use?

She sat up in bed and wrapped her arms about her knees, rocking back and forth in bewilderment and worry. The house was so empty, so lonely. Yet this was nothing new. It was always lonely, she admitted in sudden honesty, even when Dirk was home. Falling in love had been an exciting thing, a rapturous, hasty, reckless thing, an unhoped-for gift of all she had ever longed for. Or so she had believed at the time. But growing in love was something else and a marriage that involved no growth was empty of meaning. Love had to be lived before it was truly real. And where was the living together in this marriage even when they were in the same house?

The pendulum swung once more through its confusing arc. What if it were not her father behind Mara? What if it had been Dirk? Dirk pushing her down on the path, thrusting that rough bag over her head, fleeing before he could be recognized. This was the thing she had been holding away, refusing to face. Had she the courage to face it now, to seek the answer deliberately, to know for sure? When she knew the answer—what then? What of life and marriage and love, if this thing were true?

The telephone bell downstairs shattered the silence. Let it ring, Susan thought. There was no one she wanted to talk to. But she knew she could not ignore it. The ringing might bring Willi inside to see why she had not answered. Besides, to call at this hour, the person who phoned must have good reason.

She went downstairs and took the receiver from the hook, spoke into it.

"I miss you, darling," Dirk's voice said over the miles from Johannesburg.

Something in her quivered and responded with heedless joy. She had loved him so long ago as a little girl. And she loved him now as a woman. The shimmering melancholy of loneliness that had seemed to hang in the air fell away and there was in her only a longing for Dirk's arms and his love securely around her.

"Are you coming home tomorrow?" she cried. "I hate it here without you!"

He was reassuring and affectionate and regretful. The business her father had sent him on would take longer than he had expected. He might go on to Durban tomorrow and perhaps to Basutoland. So he would be gone for several days more.

"Father is planning a trip around the Cape," she told him wistfully, though she knew this was a child's coaxing. "He wanted you to drive."

Dirk's laughter had a dry sound. "At least I'll be spared the trip this year. Go with him, darling, and keep him happy. Let him tell you about every landmark along the way and explain about the shipwrecks and the storms. But not for me. Not this year. If you like, we'll do the trip again by ourselves later."

"I'd love that," she said. "We don't do enough things together." It was easier to talk to him over the miles of mountain and veld than when he was in the room beside her and so quick to grow impatient.

"I know," he said more warmly. "And we must mend that. Let's make a date right now, darling. You've wanted to go up the mountain—so I'll take you up the very day I get home. That's a promise."

Whether it was the mountain or something else, she did not care, just so she would be with Dirk.

"I love you," she said. "I'll be waiting."

When he rang off she put the phone down and went upstairs, warm now and tingling. No, it was not Dirk! Whatever was happening it was not because of Dirk. She had been in a gloomy mood because she was lonely. Love, after all, was not a steady flame. It burned sometimes high, sometimes low, depending on those concerned. So long as it always leapt up high and warm again, there was nothing to fear.

There was no reason to believe that anyone was behind Mara Bellman. Or, if anyone was, then it must be someone who had no connection with Protea Hill.

She went to a window and flung open the draperies that Willi had closed. The mountain was there, waiting, and stars hung brightly above it. She had heard that the top was like some strange landscape of the moon, bleak and awesome and vast. Had she lived here when she was older she would have climbed it, as all Cape Town children climbed it sooner or later, by way of the easy trails, if not up the precipices. For her first trip, however, she would gladly settle for the fun of the cable car with Dirk. And tea at the top.

"I'll be seeing you soon," she told the mountain and turned back to the room.

When Dirk came home she would tell him about Mara's coming here, searching this room. She would tell him about the stones she had found and entrusted to John Cornish's care. The pendulum had swung full arc again and, clinging to its high point, she could believe that this was where it would stay, improbably arrested at the peak of its flight and against all laws of gravity.

She slept well that night and there was no blue fire in her dreams.

During the next few days there was an interlude of calm while she waited for Dirk's return. An interlude during which she busied herself with small matters and thrust away whatever might disturb her or force her into thinking. It was not necessary to face these problems alone. When Dirk came home she would talk to him. He would help her. He would know what to do.

Toward the end of the week the spring weather turned cool and misty again and clouds lay over the table and hid the Lion's Head. A strong wind blew across Cape Town. At least it was not raining and Susan never minded misty weather. She put on her mackintosh and pulled its hood over her head. Then she set off for a walk downtown.

Today she chose Long Street because she liked its ironwork balconies and its two unexpected palm trees, around which traffic had to swerve. After a few blocks she cut across to Adderley, stopping along the way in a *boekwinkel* to see if they had John Cornish's book on Ghana. They had not, but took an order. Then she strolled beneath the arcades of Adderley and past van Riebeeck high on his pedestal surveying the town he had helped to create. Over in the Parade Ground hustlers picked up what change they could by making a great show of helping motorists to park.

Susan turned back on Adderley to her father's shop and stood looking into the always fascinating window. There was a display of beautifully carved animals: a rhinoceros with his great mouth gaping, a big-eared African elephant, a graceful springbok. She must ask Dirk to bring home some companions for the impala, she thought, walking on.

Little things were important, only little things. When the minor matters of the day became too inconsequential to dwell on, it meant that one's mind was troubled and depressed. Today she would not be depressed. She would remain in a state of pleasant suspension until Dirk came home.

Now she followed Adderley back toward the mountain till she reached the alley that housed the flower market. Here she would purchase more chinks to cheer up the house. She would bank it with flowers against Dirk's homecoming—which would be soon now, soon, though he had not yet told her when. But before she filled her arms with blooms she would take a few more pictures of the flower market to replace those on the film Willi had destroyed. Her mind flicked at the subject and winced quickly away. No, not today. This was the sort of thought she must guard against.

She gave herself over to reveling in color and scent and texture. She smiled at the colored women who offered her their wares, moved on to the far end of the market and turned about.

Niklaas van Pelt, leaning upon Thomas's arm, his cane in one hand, was entering from the Adderley Street end. This was perfect, Susan thought. Now she could retake the pictures of him in the midst of these flower stalls. She uncased her light meter to determine the exposure. Thomas did not see her down the length of the market. He left Niklaas at his usual place, touched his cap, and went away without glancing about.

Susan took a few steps down the long aisle of flowers, studying first the meter and then the subject. It was a gray day, lacking the shadows that gave a picture contrast and depth. But her film was fast and she would give it a try.

The same plump woman reached up to free Niklaas of his cane and he bent toward the nearest basin of flowers, absorbing their fragrance.

Susan stood stock still, suddenly arrested. The greeting which had risen to her lips was stilled. In a flash of searing clarity she understood how the second step of the smuggling was managed, and how cleverly and innocently it was done. No crude cigars were being used this time. This way was far better. She felt sick with the shock of knowledge, shaken to the point of nausea. And she could not bear to speak to her father.

Somehow she slipped past him, so close that she could have reached out and touched his arm. With the scent of the flowers all about, he would not catch her perfume today. No one noticed her except as a possible buyer of flowers, and in a moment she was on the street again, walking hurriedly toward the Avenue.

The mist was wet upon her cheeks—or was she crying? Crying because she had nearly found her father, only to lose him again. For good this time. Now she knew who had given the order to have that film destroyed. Thomas had seen her taking the pictures when he had come for Niklaas that day. He would have reported the fact, of course. The picture taken of Thomas on the library steps had nothing to do with the matter. The order had been relayed by way of Thomas to Willi. And again the order to stop her had been given when something had been missing from the cigar box. By whom, she knew now, and *to* whom did not matter. It was her father who had given both these orders. Perhaps to Mara, more likely to Thomas. Perhaps even to Dirk, if Dirk was aware of

179

these matters. Though she would not yet believe that Dirk would accept such an assignment. She would see him soon and would ask him for the truth.

Along the red dirt path of the Avenue were little puddles and the young oak trees dripped moisture on either side. The handsome white towers of the Jewish temple rose against a misty backdrop of mountain, and all about her the doves burbled and cooed. Only a few moments before the peace of this place would have suited her mood. Now she scarcely noted where she walked as she climbed the hill toward home. When she turned through the gate at the Aerie, she found the light meter still in her hands.

Willi heard her step on the walk and left her work to open the door.

"Your father rang up about an hour ago, Mrs. Hohenfield," Willi said. "He was disappointed not to catch you."

Susan scarcely heard her. There was nothing she wanted to say to her father, or to hear from him, at the moment.

Willi took her coat and followed her into the living room. "Mr. van Pelt asked me to give you a message. He said the weather should clear tomorrow and be fine, so he is planning to motor around the Cape. Mr. Cornish has offered to drive. Mr. van Pelt will have a picnic lunch packed and if you are ready at nine in the morning he will pick you up. If this suits your convenience, he said you need not ring him back."

She could not go, Susan thought. She could not face her father until she had thought this thing through, decided upon some course of action. No action at all was now inconceivable.

Willi was watching her, puzzled and a little anxious. Susan tried to smile.

"Thank you," she said. "I may call my father later."

But she did not call him. By evening she still had not called. She had nothing to say to him. She could not even bring herself to tell him that she could not accept his invitation for the trip around the Cape. If he asked for a reason, what was she to say?

After Willi had retired to her room, Susan sat listening for a long while to the radio, trying to think against the quieting background of music. Someone was singing a program of songs in Afrikaans—old folk tunes of the sort that Dirk often loved to whistle.

"Marching to Pretoria . . ."

It occurred to her abruptly that there was something she could do if she went tomorrow. She could tell John Cornish

180

what she had discovered. If she went on the trip, it was likely they might have a little time together while Niklaas rested. There was nothing else she could do, no one else to whom she could turn.

The weather report for the Union of South Africa came on and fine weather was promised. There was not even the hope that a storm would develop out of today's murk and enable her to do nothing, postpone all action, if that should be her wish.

By morning she knew that the weather report would hold true. She dressed in dark-green slacks with twin brown sweaters and a green kerchief tied in a band about her hair. Her every move was listless and the heaviness of her spirit could not have been greater.

When Willi came to say that Mr. Cornish was waiting downstairs for her, she picked up her camera, slung the heavy strap of her big leather bag indifferently over her shoulder, caught up a coat against the winds of the Cape, and went to face her father.

20

Niklaas van Pelt sat in the back seat of the car, his head turned in the direction of the house, as if he listened for his daughter's step. When she said, "Good morning," and started into the car beside him, he stopped her.

"Why not sit up in front with John, my dear? I have the lunch back here. Mara was too busy to join us today, but she had something packed for us."

John had come to open the car door and Susan was aware of his look as she got in. She knew he had sensed that something was wrong, even more wrong than before. But he said nothing and turned the car toward the Kloof Nek where they could go through the pass and drop down the other side to run out along the Marine Drive. They drove in silence past Camp's Bay, and Susan remembered walking across the sands with Dirk only a little while ago.

How much did Dirk know of what occurred in the flower

market? she wondered unhappily. Perhaps nothing. Surely he too had been fooled by the cleverness of Niklaas van Pelt. She must believe this, must hold to it until she saw him again and he could speak for himself.

As they followed the drive she watched the sea on one hand and the changing peaks on the other. Once she turned in her seat to look back at her father. He sat with his cane clasped between his hands, his head turning first toward the Atlantic, feeling the sea breeze against his face, then turning toward the mountains, as if he could sense their weight and presence. There was no gentleness in his face today, no betraying of thoughts behind the guard he had learned to wear.

How defenseless a blind person must feel, Susan thought. Those he could not see were free to study him as they pleased, intrude, perhaps, as a person with sight is never intruded upon. But Niklaas had learned to hide his secrets well behind the cold mask of his face, behind the dark glitter of his glasses. Only once had she surprised him without the mask— that time in the little garden for the blind. That day she had softened toward him as she could not soften now.

Niklaas spoke aloud, almost as if to himself. "Drake said it was the fairest of all capes, and Diaz called it the Cape of Storms."

"While we," John Cornish added, "call it, ironically, the Cape of Good Hope."

"Ironically?" Niklaas said.

"What good hope is there for South Africa?"

"That again? You must admit that our government has held down the disturbances," Niklaas said mildly.

"Toward what end result?" John was impatient. "You'd think we believed in the legend of the boy and the dike. If Hans stands long enough with his thumb in the crack the waters will recede. But any man of sense knows they won't. The pressure is building and the dike is going to be smashed flat, with chaos resulting. Nevertheless, Hans stands there stubbornly, shouting that others are interfering and he can hold back the waters alone in his own way."

Susan glanced at her father and saw that he was smiling.

"You think about these matters a great deal, don't you?" he asked John.

"How can I not?"

"Since you can do nothing, why not let events take their course and leave action to those who better understand the problem?"

"That's exactly what I mean to do," John said angrily. "Though I doubt that there's much understanding on the part of those in power."

Quietly Niklaas changed the subject, and Susan, whose sympathies were entirely with John's viewpoint, hardened a little further against her father.

"Where are we now?" Niklaas asked.

"Chapman's Peak is directly ahead," John told him. "Look your longest, Susan; this is the finest scenery of the Cape."

On their left the mountains rose in grandeur, jagged and steep, their stony slopes partly wooded. And where there were woods there were arum lilies—great white carpets of them—and everywhere wildflowers growing among the rocks. On the sea side the embankment dropped away in steep cliffs, gull haunted, with South Atlantic breakers rolling in at their base, roaring above the purr of the car.

"Here's a point where we can stop," John said and turned the car off the road beside a rocky lookout. He helped the old man from the car and led him gently to a place where he could stand with the sea wind in his face and the mountains massed behind him. Susan chose a spot a little away from the two. She did not want to be near her father or to touch him. The sickness of heart she had felt in the flower market yesterday had abated not at all.

John stood at the parapet, watching the frothing sea below, and his expression was grave and a little sad. "One has a curious feeling sometimes in returning to a familiar place. Earth and rocks and sea and mountains have such permanence. There's no change here, even though everything else in life may have changed."

Niklaas understood. "You came here last with Janet, didn't you?"

"Do you remember her?" John asked.

"Very well. A quiet, serene young woman. A good balance for you, I always thought. You were often too intense, too involved in the things you wrote about."

"Once it seemed a good thing to be involved," John said.

"But now," said Niklaas, "you are merely angry without being involved?"

John made a movement of impatience and spoke to Susan. "How is the picture series coming along?"

"It's not," she told him. "I'm still looking for scenes that will really tell the story."

"Perhaps I can help you," he said. "There are places I can

183

show you around Cape Town. The *pondokkies* on the Cape Flats, for instance, where squatters live in the most utter destitution."

The old man seemed to have heard enough. He put his hand upon the sun-warmed rock of the lookout point with an air of authority. "Enough of this talk for now, or I'm afraid our trip will be spoiled. Susan, I've been in this place before too. More than once with your mother. She used to enjoy the drive around the Cape."

Susan said nothing, refusing to be softened by this reference to her mother. He must have sensed the resistance in her, for when he went on the chill had returned to his voice.

"John has told me that you remember seeing Claire with a stone that must have been the Kimberley. That you were playing with the stone and she took it away from you. Have you recalled anything more about that occasion?"

She answered him shortly. "Nothing more. I don't know what she did with it after she hid it in the powder bowl."

She expected him to urge her to recall the rest, as Dirk had urged her, but he did not.

"Perhaps it's better to let it stay forgotten," he advised. "Better not try to remember. Shall we go on now?"

Once such advice from him would have reassured her. It did not now. She could only remember how important all concealment must be to him. Perhaps of the past as well as the present.

They returned to the car and followed the intricate curves of the coastline down the Cape Peninsula. The scenes were varied: small beaches of white sand and little fishing villages; breaks in the mountain rampart through which green inland valleys cupped by hills were visible. Then the road took a center course as the land flattened toward the farthest tip of the Cape. But not, John said, the farthest tip of Africa. Oddly enough, Cape of Good Hope was not the end of Africa. Cape Agulhas across False Bay stretched farther south. Yet it was the Cape of Good Hope—the Cape of Storms—a sailor sought to round, and warmer currents were met when the point was passed, even though the Indian Ocean began technically around the farther cape.

They had entered the nature reserve now and Susan began to watch for animals. While none of the larger beasts were to be found here, many smaller varieties roamed free under protection. She remembered from her childhood the exciting watch for the wild creatures that blended so well with rocks and vegetation that one had to look long to see him. Once, close beside the road, they came upon an elderly baboon. He remained where he was, staring them haughtily out of countenance. Several of his female companions ran skittishly off to hide themselves in a pile of rocks, but the male posed with great self-possession while Susan took his picture.

As they moved on, the Cape narrowed and grew rock-bound as it pointed into the sea. On either side of the paved road wildflowers grew in profusion. Cormorants perched on the sea rocks, and the *dassies*—those small-eared rock rabbits of South Africa—lay sunning themselves on landward outcroppings.

A rocky hill rising ahead was Cape Point itself. The car could go no farther.

John found a place to park and carried the basket lunch, while Niklaas took Susan's arm. They followed the lower road along the False Bay side, moving toward the new lighthouse. Above, on the peak of rock, was the older lighthouse, which had not been wholly successful, since ships had still wrecked themselves on the extending toe of rock below.

Here the sun was warm and pleasant and they were shielded from the Atlantic breeze. John found a big flat rock below the road and Susan helped him spread out blankets and cushions upon it. Soberly, with a distinct lack of picnic gaiety, she began to unpack the lunch.

Of the three, only Niklaas seemed contented and for the moment amiably disposed. He had remained unruffled by their earlier discussion, and while, as always, he seemed a little remote, he had clearly come on this trip to enjoy himself. They ate egg and sardine and watercress sandwiches, and nibbled sticky plum tarts.

In the distance the dim outline of Table Mountain was visible, and John nodded in its direction.

"From the top of the table you can see the entire Cape on a clear day," he told Susan. "Have you been up there yet?"

She shook her head. "Dirk has promised to take me up when he gets back from his trip."

"I'd planned to take you climbing up there by the time you were eight or nine," her father said. "Your mother disliked heights and would never go up the mountain. In the beginning when I was in prison I used to think about the time when I would be free again and you and your mother would return to South Africa. Then you and I would go up the mountain together."

Susan glanced at him uncomfortably. "But you never wanted us back. You never wrote."

He was quiet for a time. With one hand he reached out toward a scrubby bush beside the rock and plucked absently at its tough green spikes.

"I wrote," he said at length. "I wrote while I was in prison —to you as well as to your mother. And I wrote again when I was free."

Susan heard him in disbelief. "But there were no letters! Mother told me there were no letters."

He went on, paying no attention to her words. "When I sold the Johannesburg house and moved to Cape Town, I kept your room as it was in the hope that you would at least return for a visit. I suppose I kept it as a sort of hostage to fate. By that time I knew Claire would never return, but you still might if I kept it ready for you. I couldn't blame Claire. She was not one to be tied to a blind man."

"But she didn't know you were blind!" Susan cried. "Of course she never knew."

"She knew," Niklaas said quietly.

Susan stared at him, stricken. "But she never told me. She never said a word."

"Perhaps that was the kinder way, as far as you were concerned."

His tone was as cool and detached as though he spoke of some stranger whose wounds he could not feel, and Susan could not bear to hear him. She could not bear to be so torn herself. Torn between what she knew of him so recently and the anguish rising in her for what he had suffered in the past. How could she condemn him for what he was doing now when so much that was cruel had been done to him?

She had lost what appetite she had and now got up restlessly and sprang from the rock to the road. "If you don't mind, I think I'll climb to the old lighthouse. I'd like to take a few pictures."

"You were always snapping pictures as a little thing, too," Niklaas said. "I can remember how you treasured the small camera I gave you. And how devastated you were when you broke it."

Susan stood uncertain on the path, puzzled by his words. "But I never told you I had broken it," she said. "I can remember how frightened I was of letting you know. You always hated it when I broke anything and when you lost your temper I was terrified. So I never told you I'd broken it at all."

"Of course you told me," her father said. "You even

186

brought it to me one day in my study to show me the damage."

She continued to watch him uneasily, though she did not know what it was she tried to read in his face. How could she have been so convinced all these years that she had never shown him the broken camera? Something stirred vaguely in the dim reaches of the past. Something frightening, something shattering. In memory angry voices sounded again in rising fury and there was the shrillness of a telephone that rang and rang. She covered her face with her hands, swaying a little.

"Are you all right, Susan?" John called to her. He jumped down to the path and took her arm, steadying her.

The mists receded. "It's nothing," she said. "A moment's dizziness. Will you walk with me to the top?"

"Go with her," Niklaas said. "I shall be content here." He had taken a cigar from his pocket to clip and light, and they left him smoking peacefully.

John and Susan walked back to the place where a steep concrete pavement led straight to the top of the rocky hill. The road was closed to general traffic, but open to pedestrians and the jeeps that served the houses clustered at the top. Far above two slim radio towers pointed toward the sky.

When they had climbed to the enclosure around the old lighthouse, John drew her to a place where she could lean on the wall and follow with her eyes the sweep of the Cape around the wide curve of False Bay. The Hottentots Holland range was misty blue in the distance. John's thoughts, however, were not on the view.

"Something has happened, hasn't it?" he asked. "I knew the moment I saw you this morning that something was wrong."

She had been waiting for an opportunity to tell him what she had seen in the flower market yesterday. Yet now she held back the words, reluctant to speak. What good would it do to involve the lost, saddened man who was her father? How could she lift a finger to injure him further, no matter what he might be doing now?

"I can't tell you," she said. "I must think first. I need more time to think."

"I won't press you," he said. "But, Susan—" the concern in his voice deepened—"don't put yourself in some dangerous position."

"Dangerous?" She glanced at him quickly. "What danger could there be?"

"Knowledge can be dangerous if it puts someone else in

187

jeopardy. Are you sure this isn't something you ought to share for your own safety? Remember, there's been one attack upon you and there's someone still wondering whether you found those stones."

She shook her head, afraid to think of the stones, afraid to know the face of her assailant. John's eyes were kind and his mouth had lost its sober lines.

"Courage is something I admire," he said gently. "It's a quality I've sensed in you from the first. But don't let it carry you too far. Ask for help if you need it."

She looked into his face and saw more than kindness there, saw in him a hint of tenderness, as if she had been a very young person whom he wanted to protect. Did he mean the courage to hurt her father? she wondered. Or was there something else in his mind—something still more devastating?

"I don't know how much courage of any sort I have," she said. "All I know is that I'm confused. I'm not sure of my directions. I don't know yet which way I must turn."

Unexpectedly he put his hand beneath her chin and tilted her head so that his eyes held hers. What she saw in their depths made her a little afraid. More and more this man was coming to be a safe harbor—the one person to whom she could turn with confidence and trust. But this would not do. His face must not come between her and Dirk. She needed no such harbor. She turned abruptly from his touch, Dirk's image sharp and clear in her mind, and at once John drew back as if he too were aware of a barrier he must not pass.

She walked about the base of the lighthouse, peered down the rocky cliffs, made a great show of being interested in their surroundings, and John Cornish watched her in silence. When he spoke again his words startled her.

"Why do you have a *sjambok* on the wall of your living room?" he asked.

The suddenness of the question took her aback and she stammered a little in answering, not wanting him to know how much she hated the whip that Dirk had hung upon the wall.

"It—it belonged to Dirk's father, I believe. It was a—a whim of Dirk's to hang it on the wall. I'm not sure why."

"There are initials cut into the handle?" John asked. "The letters of his father's name?"

Susan's hands were still on the strap of her camera. "How did you know?"

"I've held the whip in my hands," John said. "I remember

188

it very well. This morning I saw it again on the wall of your living room."

There was something in his tone that caught her sensitive ear. "You know the story behind the whip? Will you tell me, please? Tell me what happened."

He made no attempt at evasion. "You and your mother were still in South Africa at the time, though you weren't at the farm in the veld when it happened. Janet and I had been recently married. We went there for a visit. One day your father used that whip in a flogging. I stopped him and took the whip away from him."

"But why would my father do such a thing?" Susan asked in dismay.

"He was capable of great anger when he was aroused. Life hadn't chastened him then. Once he was a strong and rather violent man. It's sad to see the fire burned out so that nothing rouses him now."

"Who was it he flogged?" Susan asked. "Someone who worked for him on the farm?"

John looked down toward the surf curling below the steep rocks of the point. He spoke without looking at her. "It was Dirk Hohenfield he whipped that day. Later your father thanked me for stopping him. For all his rage, he would never have injured Dirk when he was in his right senses."

Something turned painfully within Susan. "But what had Dirk done to cause my father to fly into a rage?"

John shook his head. "I never knew the reason. I didn't ask. I simply got the whip away from him and went into the house until everyone could cool off. I didn't see Dirk again before Janet and I left, and your father never mentioned the cause of what happened."

The surf far below had a chill sound as it broke about the rocks of the point. The South Atlantic held a steely glitter beneath the sun and the breeze had turned cold.

Susan could bear to hear no more. All feeling in her seemed drawn to a taut, thin strand that might snap at any minute.

"Remember that all this happened a very long time ago," John said. "Dirk was only a boy. Everyone has forgotten it by this time."

Dirk had not forgotten, she thought as they started down the steep roadway. Not with that whip upon the wall. But she did not want to think of that now. She wanted only to put the ugly memory of the whip from her mind.

Casually John caught her hand as they went down the walk

and she found the pressure of his fingers comforting. Had he come here with Janet too? she wondered, and felt a sudden pity for his loss and his loneliness.

"I'm sorry about your wife," she said softly.

"This trip has brought her back," John admitted. "I've been thinking of her a good deal ever since we left Cape Town. But all that belongs to another lifetime. Not to the one I'm living now."

She understood what he meant. All lives seemed to break into segments. Her own too. The segment of her childhood in South Africa. The growing-up years in Chicago. The new world of the newspaper and all that pertained to it. Then the world of Dirk that she was living now. She pressed John's fingers gently and slipped her hand from his.

They found the old man as they had left him, his cigar smoked to a stub, his attitude one of listening, as if he waited for their coming, ready to start home.

The three of them had little to say on the drive up the opposite side of the Cape. Susan curled herself in the front seat, watching the clean little towns and villages slip past. But her thoughts were not upon them. She was remembering what her father had told her of the day she had brought her broken camera to him. A day she had buried carefully in the past— for what reason she did not know. This time she would not try to shut the door.

Let it open—let it open fully! She was ready for the answer now. A purpose began to come clear in her mind. She knew very well what must be done. A new impatience seized her to reach home and be off on her own private mission as soon as possible.

21

When Niklaas said he had some errands downtown and asked John to drive him there, Susan felt an enormous relief. She did not request them to drop her at her true destination, preferring to let her purpose remain secret for the moment. When they left her at the Aerie and drove away, she went into the house only long enough to rid herself of her camera equipment. Then, still wearing her coat and with her big leather handbag slung over her shoulder, she set off for Protea Hill. The key to her old room was in her bag and she was sure now of the one object that would bring memory flooding back.

Somewhere she had built up a block against what had happened, but there would be a way to level the barrier, to remember fully. She must finish this before Dirk came home. Then she would know whether or not she must tell him what she had discovered about her father.

The maid was long in answering her ring. Susan greeted her a little breathlessly. Asking no permission, she ran past her up the stairs and down the hall. She hoped Mara would not be about today. This was something she wanted to achieve quickly without her knowledge.

To her surprise, the door of her childhood room stood open and a breeze blew into the hall from the windows. She paused in dismay in the doorway to see that the promised spring cleaning was under way and that the housemaid was working here under the supervision of Mara Bellman. Mara herself knelt on a cushion beside the toy chest, with articles from the big *kist* heaped on the floor beside her. In her hands she held the small box camera and she opened the back to peer into it as Susan came indignantly into the room.

For a breathless moment the two stared at each other in open antagonism. All the pent-up resentment and distrust and jealousy Susan had felt toward this woman surged up in an angry wave of feeling.

"What are you doing here?" she cried. "I haven't given you permission to go through my things!"

A flush tinted Mara's fair skin, but she did not rise from her position on the floor.

"It's a job long overdue," she said, waving a scornful hand at the toys she had heaped on the floor. "All this seems to be trash and I was sure you'd be willing to let us get rid of it."

"I'm not willing!" Susan spoke sharply. "My father has left everything in this room in my hands and I want it left alone. Will you go, please?"

Mara made no move to comply. She still held the camera with its back open and again she looked into the small black box curiously. She shook it as if she half expected something to rattle or fall out. Susan watched her in an agony of impatience, wondering what she would do if Mara chose to oppose her. But the other woman shrugged in elaborate indifference, set the camera back in the chest, and got slowly to her feet.

"As you like," she said, and nodded to the maid to come with her out of the room.

The moment they had gone, Susan swung the door shut and ran to the chest. She picked up the camera and then stood looking uncertainly about the room. Was there anything else? Any other object that would speak to her as she had felt the camera would? There seemed to be nothing and she went to the closed door and stood very still, listening for any sound she might catch from the hall beyond. All seemed to be quiet.

She opened the door cautiously. No one was in sight. The door of Mara's room stood closed. Moving almost stealthily, Susan hurried along the hall and down the stairs to the landing. At the newel post in the entry hall below Mara stood waiting for her. The flush had vanished from her cheeks and she was very pale. Her eyes went at once to the camera.

For an uneasy instant Susan wondered if she might try to take it from her, but her entire purpose had been keyed to this moment. She would not be stopped or delayed. She went down the stairs with all the stubbornness and determination of her father and passed Mara without a word. The other woman did not try to stop her, and she went directly to her father's study and closed its door behind her.

The room seemed empty and strange without his familiar figure behind the great desk. But this was where she wanted to be, and she must be here when he was not present. There was no key by which she could lock Mara out and she could only hope that the woman would not follow her here. Quietly she seated herself on a small footstool in one corner, the camera in her hands. Even the choice of the footstool as a place to sit seemed right, and part of a pattern in which she now seemed to move without volition or choice.

Her father had been right in what he had said today about the camera. She had indeed told him of dropping it and breaking the lens. He had summoned her into his study to lecture her on the subject of being more careful with her possessions. He had told her to sit on this very stool—which had been just her size. She could remember the way she had stared at the pattern in the carpet while he talked to her about her increasing carelessness.

She had been upset, but had not then been filled with paralyzing alarm. Indeed, she had been more uncomfortable listening to his words than she had been frightened. Mainly she had been sorry about the camera, which she had treasured, and hopeful that he might mend it or buy her a new one.

It developed quickly that he intended nothing of the kind: "When I was a boy," he said, "and I broke something out of carelessness, I was told that I must either mend it myself or do without. I believe we've come to the place where this rule must be applied to you, Susan. I'm afraid you must now mend your camera yourself or go without."

His words were a blow, but still not terrifying. She sat hunched upon the footstool with tears in her eyes, wondering if she could move him to pity so that he would relent. But she knew this was not likely. When the telephone on his desk rang, he picked it up calmly enough. Neither of them had known that the call would change everything in life for them, that afterwards nothing would be the same again.

She remembered watching him a little resentfully, waiting for the call to end, so that his attention could return to her. But it had not. His face had blanched and his voice turned cold as he answered the person on the wire. She could recall the very words he had spoken, but who it was she never knew—a friend? a business acquaintance? the police?

"What you are saying is impossible. I have no uncut diamonds in my possession. Neither here nor in Johannesburg."

The man on the other end of the wire went on and Susan saw her father's expression grow strained and grim as he listened. When he hung up the phone he touched the bell that summoned the maid and sent her to find Claire. He looked so coldly formidable that Susan edged her stool into a corner and sat very still so that she would not notice her and vent his anger upon her.

How well she remembered her mother coming gaily into the room. She was wearing a flowered green dress, the color of ferns, and in her hair a white rose. Then she had seen her husband's face and the smile had left her own. This was when the time of terror had begun.

Coldly Niklaas told her that, thanks to a lead from some outside source, his house in Johannesburg had been searched and a cache of uncut diamonds had been found there. What, he demanded, could she tell him of this? Claire began to weep and deny, but Niklaas persisted in cold accusation. When she would not answer, he left his desk and took her by her soft plump shoulders, shaking her until she went limp in his hands. Limp and ready to admit everything. Yes, she had managed to take the stones when she was working for the company. She had not wanted to give them up. They had meant safety

193

and security, no matter what happened. And diamonds were so pretty, so fascinating.

Neither had noticed the child in the corner, withered by the cruel anger, the accusations, and the rising voices. The telephone began to ring again, but Niklaas ignored it. He flung Claire from him roughly, so that she fell against the desk and bruised her arm. She had shown Susan the blue mark later as evidence of his cruelty. He had almost stepped on Susan, cowering in her corner, before he saw her. Then he had shouted at her to get out of this room and stay out. She had no business here. She was to leave at once!

Terrified, Susan fled from the room and upstairs, the camera still clutched in her hands. All her small world that was bounded so securely by her parents had been shivered into fearful splinters by those angry voices downstairs. Wounding splinters that pierced her spirit as glass might have pierced her flesh. Her father detested her, that was clear. He had looked at her with hatred in his eyes, and her mother had done nothing to come to her aid. Her mother, giving in to an excess of wild weeping, had forgotten she existed.

Her own room upstairs was lonely and the camera in her hands reproached her. The conviction was growing in her young mind that she had brought all these terrible things about when she had wickedly broken the camera her father had given her. For a while she sat on the bed in her room turning the small black box this way and that, wondering how she could fix the broken lens. If only she could mend it and make the camera work again, then surely her father would stop hating her and stop hating her mother. Her mother would stop crying and there would be no more angry words shouted between them.

Because of her enormous need, the answer came to her quite simply and clearly. It would take a very special sort of glass to make a lens, and it was possible that she knew where there was just such a piece she might use. Moving on tiptoe, without a sound, she ran into her mother's room and prodded with her fingers in the powder bowl. The stone was still there.

Now, so many years later, the grown-up Susan crouched on the footstool as the child had done, and her hands trembled as she opened the camera. Like Mara upstairs, she peered into the box. It was black inside and empty. There was nothing there. The film holder had long been lost and the camera was useless. She shook it hard as Mara had done and something shiny fell out in her lap. She picked it up and held it on the palm of her hand. It was only a piece of the broken lens.

Then she reached her fingers deep inside the box and felt behind the shutter. Nerves prickled at the back of her neck. Fumbling in her haste, she managed to pry up an end of sticky material that ripped loose when she pulled it. Stuck to her fingers was a strip of black mending tape that had been stuck crossways behind the shutter. Again her fingers searched and found the second crisscross of tape. When she pulled it loose something came with it, adhering to the material. Held in place as it had been by the covering of almost invisible black tape, it had lain hidden all these years. Susan stared in fascination at the stone she held in her hand.

It was colorless and transparent, perhaps an inch or more in length and somewhat less in thickness, cut in an oblong shape. In the shadowy room it lay lusterless upon her palm with none of the shimmer of a diamond. But diamonds, of course, once freed from the darkness of the inner earth where they were born in fire, could live only upon light.

She walked to the French doors and stepped through them. Bright daylight flooded the terrace. When she held out her hand the Kimberley Royal sprang magically to life. Light splintered into bright rainbows in its depths and glinted blue fire from the very heart of the stone. Yet it was a fire without warmth, and the stone was cold in her hand. It seemed to her a stone of evil omen and she was unable to suppress the quiver that touched her skin to gooseflesh.

Returning to the shadows, she sat in her father's chair with the camera before her on the desk. She could remember everything now. Men in uniform had come to the house and her father had gone away with them. There had been no time to show him the mended camera after all, so the bad fortune held, the evil she had done did not end. Her mother had cried endlessly, while the child, Susan, sat in her room and stared at the mountain until it seemed to lean menacingly toward her. Perhaps if she stared long enough, it would tip over and crush her—which was, no doubt, what she truly deserved.

So much she remembered!

How heavy the diamond seemed now in her hands, colder than any other stone, leaving her as chill as the stone itself.

There had been a further outburst from her mother when Claire had found the stone missing from her powder bowl. But she had not known whom to accuse or where to turn without betraying herself. She had questioned her daughter tearfully, but Susan by that time had been too frightened to confess what she had done. Besides, this was something for her father to see. Only he would understand about the camera.

She knew now why her mother had fled from Africa. Claire had been afraid that she would be the one to go to prison, and that was something she could not face. But Niklaas had taken her guilt upon his own shoulders and his "confession" had left her free to do as she pleased. The fact that the Kimberley was missing had not come to light until years later as far as the public was concerned. And in the meantime Claire had urged forgetfulness upon her daughter. "Forget, forget," her mother had said. "Don't try to remember what happened there." And Susan, confused, frightened, guilt-ridden almost to the point of illness, had drawn a merciful veil across her memory. Only now and then through the years had the veil fluttered, lifting away from the terror it had hidden. Whenever she dropped something or broke even the most trifling object, the gossamer shield would tremble, allowing incomprehensible fears to flow through her.

The sickness and hurt were back again in this moment, magnified many times over, though the guilt sense had faded. Her hurt was for her father now and all her love. She understood her mother's guilt and her father's innocence. Only that disturbing thing she had seen in the flower market stood unexplained in her mind, and because of what had happened in the past she would not now accept that without giving him a chance to answer for himself.

Distant voices sounded in another part of the house and she wondered if he had come home. She would wait for him here and when he came in she would give him the stone. He had paid for it with his own fortune. It belonged to him now. But more than that, she would tell him the things she had remembered and she would tell him what she had seen in the flower market.

Steps sounded in the hallway outside the door, but the footfall was firm and decisive, not the slightly shuffling sound of an elderly blind man's step. She had just time to slip the diamond into her handbag and click the camera shut before the door opened and Dirk came into the room.

There was an electric excitement in him, she saw at once. Something had happened to him that she did not understand and it made her wary. He swooped down upon her and pulled her out of the chair and into his arms.

"I *have* missed you!" he cried, his cheek against her bright hair.

When he kissed her she waited for the melting to run

through her, and the familiar warm response of her blood. But nothing happened. Only the wariness remained and a resistance to his arms. He sensed her lack of response and dropped his arms from about her, but he offered no reproach.

"I went home first," he told her, "and then phoned here. Mara said you were in the house, so I came right over. I wanted to surprise you." His eyes searched her face keenly."And I see that I have."

"You should have let me know, so I could be at the airport to meet you," she said, trying to cover whatever she might have betrayed. "I'm just home from the drive around the Cape with my father."

"And with John Cornish?" he said.

He reached past her across the desk and picked up the camera as she watched him uneasily. Her father must know before anyone else that she had found the stone. She had no intention of telling Dirk. He looked into the box almost idly and dropped it back on the desk. Had Mara told him of her sudden appearance in the room upstairs and of how she had taken the camera down to the study? But, though Mara had looked into the box, the black tape would have kept her from seeing anything. There was nothing she could have told Dirk except that his wife had carried away the camera.

"Are you ready to go up the mountain?" Dirk asked, still smiling in that oddly elated way.

"Up the mountain?" she echoed. "Now?"

"Why not? There's plenty of daylight left and the cars are running. I noticed on the way over. Remember—I promised to take you up there the very first thing when I got home."

"I've made one trip today," she objected feebly. "It's not as important as all that. Let's go tomorrow."

"It's important to me," he said, and she knew that the imperious mood when he would not be balked in his most trivial wish was once more upon him.

She shook her head helplessly, aware that opposition would only stiffen him in his purpose, yet not knowing what else to offer. She had no heart for the mountain now. She wanted only to sit at this desk and wait until her father and John Cornish came home.

"Of course we'll go now," he said. "You're dressed for it with low-heeled shoes, a warm coat, and slacks for climbing. Besides, we may not have time for this again."

There was an air of triumph in the puzzling words that made her stare at him.

"I've something to tell you," he said. "But let's get started first. We can talk about it at tea on the mountaintop. Come along, darling."

He held out his hand and took a step toward her. Then he paused, looking down at the carpet to see what he had stepped on. Lifting one foot, he examined the sole of his shoe. Susan watched as he peeled a black strip of sticky tape from the leather. Instead of discarding it, he turned it about in his fingers, studying it as if it had something to tell him.

Quite suddenly Susan was frightened. She did not want him to suspect that she had found the diamond or that she carried it in her bag. She did not know how he would take the discovery of so much wealth that her father did not know existed. What if he tried to persuade her not to tell Niklaas? She forced her fascinated gaze from the bit of black stuff in his fingers and stood up, her handbag flung carelessly by its strap over her shoulder, as if it could not possibly hold a fortune.

"All right," she said. "Since you're in the mood, let's go up the mountain."

He dropped the strip of tape into an ash tray and linked his arm through hers. "Good girl! We'll be up on top in no time at all. I'll show you the greatest sight in the world, and I'll tell you my news."

What did it matter? she thought. It would be better to make the trip up the mountain and get it out of the way since he wanted to go. Safer, really, than to sit here behaving in a way that was clearly odd, waiting for her father to come home.

Dirk called upstairs to Mara to tell her where they were going and they went out together to his car.

22

Once they were on their way she felt a little better. Now that she had given in to what he wanted, he was in a gay mood— cheerful and amusing and affectionate. If she had not been carrying a fortune in her handbag, she might have felt more at ease with him.

They left the car in the parking place at the foot of the cable house and went up the long flight of stairs inside the building. A car was about to leave and when Dirk had bought tickets, they hurried to join the group going through the door. On the walls of the cable house were huge pictures of British royalty visiting the top of Table Mountain—pictures of the younger princesses Elizabeth and Margaret coming down the steps from the landing platform with their mother, the Queen.

In the tunnel-like room there was a steady clanking of cable machinery, and ahead people were packing themselves into the small car. The guard had a South African accent, dropping his h's and blurring his syllables as he performed an obviously routine task. The holiday visitors to the mountaintop were a gay lot, the girls ready to laugh, the men showing off just a little.

There were small end seats in the car, but no one wanted to sit down. Part of the fun was to look out the windows as the car went up the mountain. Dirk was the last one in behind Susan. The door closed and the car slid gently away from the platform and began its smooth climb up the cable to the top. No one seemed to mind the fact that passengers leaned dizzily out the open windows. When Susan looked down at the steepening rock cliffs below she was glad to have Dirk's arm firmly about her.

She inched her handbag more securely up the shoulder away from the window and kept a hand upon its clasp. The thought of dropping the Kimberley Royal down a mountainside or of having her pocket picked made her feel quite hollow.

How small the car seemed against all this spread of nearby rock and distant hills and ocean. Even the tawny head of the Lion, with the sun dipping toward it, was left below as the car swept upward, its tiny shadow moving along the cliffs below. Murmurs from the passengers made Susan turn in time to see the sister car coming down, carrying its waving human freight. If only she could catch a little more of this holiday spirit and fill the queer hollow within, still the fearful shivering that had begun as the car moved up the mountain. It was not the height that frightened her, and the diamond was perfectly safe in her bag, so she was not sure why she trembled.

The trip took only a few minutes. As the car reached the final steep rampart of rock, Susan looked out dizzily to see a girl and boy in shorts and cleated boots, ropes tied about their waists, as they sought for toeholds in the sheer precipice. Again the quiver ran through her. Rock climbing, certainly, would never be for her. This ascent in a suspended car was quite enough.

Except for pointing out landmarks, Dirk had little to say on the way up and she was uncomfortably aware that he was watching her more than he watched the scenery. But, then, he had been up here many times and would naturally be interested in her reactions.

At the top the car slid into its cubicle in the tall white stone building that looked so small from below. A solid, squarish mass, the structure was, rooted in rock and undoubtedly able to withstand the gales that must belabor the mountain. They left the car to walk about the observation section behind guard rails, and Susan noted a warning sign: WHEN HEARING THE HOOTER PASSENGERS MUST PLEASE RETURN AT ONCE.

"Does anyone ever get left up here?" Susan asked.

"It's not uncommon," Dirk said. "Every year climbers get caught by sudden changes of the weather. Sometimes they spend a few cold, wet hours before they get down—if they're not close enough to reach the tearoom. Sometimes they get themselves stuck climbing up and have to be rescued. The Mountain Climbers Club is called upon for rescue duty every so often."

"I suppose there are falls too," Susan said, looking down over the dizzy cliffs of rock.

"The mountain still claims its sacrifices," Dirk said lightly.

She stood for a while studying the wide stretches of countryside spread out below. All of Cape Town could be seen, of course, and the far beaches beyond the Lion's Head. When they moved around to another vantage point, the entire Cape Peninsula stretched before them like a relief map. Susan could see clear to the distant point where she and John had stood earlier today. At the memory a queer regret touched her. How much more secure she would have felt if it had been John beside her now instead of Dirk, in whom she dared not confide.

The teahouse was built of stone and set in a hollow where tall boulders shielded it part way around and made it invisible from the ground below.

"This is a good day for the trip," Dirk said. "There's almost a dead calm up here. Let's have tea before we tackle the mountain itself," and he led her down a walk to the doorway.

They found a table in one of the stone-enclosed alcoves that occupied the corners of the dining room, and sat together on a cushioned bench curved about a round table. Windows circled the alcove, giving them a glimpse outside. However, what was going on inside was as interesting to Susan as the outdoors, and more reassuring.

A group of young people, barelegged, brown and rugged, had come in with their knapsacks and climbing shoes, to seat themselves at a table and compare climbing experiences over tea. There were small family groups as well, and older people who had come up by the cable car.

A waitress brought their order, and drinking hot English tea in the cheerful holiday atmosphere of the big room, Susan began to feel more relaxed. Soon they would go out to look at the mountaintop and see whatever views there were, and then they would be on the way down again. When she was back home she would manage to see her father as soon as possible.

"I want to tell you my news," Dirk said, lowering his voice so that those at the nearest table could not hear. "We're leaving South Africa very shortly."

She looked at him, startled, and he went on.

"This is no country to be living in now. Everyone knows there's a bad crackup coming. The government can hold things down for a while, but eventually—pfft! And it's not a country I want to live in if the blacks take over. So I've been making a few quiet arrangements outside."

"Wh-what are your plans?" she asked, feeling a little stunned. "You might have given me some warning."

He reached for her hand across the table and touched the pink diamond lightly. "Trust me a little, darling. You used to think everything I did was right and wonderful. Now you're puckering your nose and looking as though you might be obstinate. Give me a chance to show you what I can manage once we're out of South Africa."

Her fingers lay limp in his. This was too sudden and she could not respond. "Does my father know?"

"Certainly not," he said. "And you're not going to tell him. Or your friend John Cornish either."

"Do you think they would try to stop you?" she asked in bewilderment.

"Don't be melodramatic, darling. No one is going to stop me. Or even try. I mean to have it an accomplished fact before anyone knows I've taken the step permanently."

"But why must you do it that way? Why should you hurt Father with such secrecy? He trusts you and regards you as a son."

"You think he would be hurt?" Dirk made a derisive sound and let her hand go. "Niklaas has turned into a vegetable. There's no blood left in him. There's nothing left except cobweb dreams about saving the country."

Susan had never heard her father speak of such dreams. He

had always seemed content enough to defend the status quo. None of what Dirk was saying made any real sense.

"No one will try to stop me," he repeated grimly. "Your father wouldn't dare. Do you think I don't know what's going on? I would have only to say a word to the proper authorities and he would be back in prison in a flash. No, I think he will not lift a finger when the time comes."

Susan made a helpless gesture with upturned palms. "I don't understand what you're telling me or what it is you're planning."

"That's as it should be. When we're out of the country, starting a new life, I'll tell you anything you want to know."

She could think only of the cruel blow to her father that seemed so senseless, so needless.

"Father took care of you when you were young and had no one to turn to. He—"

"He took me after he had destroyed my father by turning him over to the English, who interned him. And he killed my mother with grief. Whatever he gave me he owed me. Don't imagine that there has ever been any sentimental love between us. And don't imagine that I haven't been waiting for this moment."

Susan closed her eyes. The tea grew cold in her cup and the toast she had nibbled turned leathery. Nowhere was there solid ground upon which she could stand.

"Is that why you hung the whip on the wall?" she asked. "Was that to remind you?"

"So you know about the whip?" he said. "Who told you?"

"John Cornish. Today when we were down at Cape Point. He said he took the whip away from my father when he was flogging you with it. Yet you've always seemed to hate John."

"I don't like an interferer. That's what he has always been. He's at it again now. He's poking around and getting suspicious. Because of him I've had to push up my arrangements and get out of the country sooner than I wanted to."

Her mind was still upon the flogging. "What had you done that Father should take such fierce measures with you? You were only a boy—sixteen or less."

Dirk's laughter was unpleasant. "That's the ridiculous part of the whole thing. That he should have flogged *me* because I had taken my father's whip to punish disobedience. But let me tell you this—your father didn't stop me as quickly as John stopped him. Sometime you might ask Thomas Scott to show you the scars on his back."

Susan drew in her breath with a quick, shocked gasp. At

every turn Dirk had seemed to place an enormous concentration upon her father, and she had always taken this for devotion. Now she knew better. Now she knew it to be something twisted and corrosive, building only toward destruction—something symbolized by the reminder of that whip.

"Now you will be able to help me with what I plan," he said.

It was strange, she thought, studying him almost remotely, that although she was sickened, she felt no real pain over this final destruction of the illusion she had been in love with. Something in her that she had not been willing to face had always known this day was coming.

"I will help you with nothing," she said evenly. "I am going home now and I am going directly to my father."

He laughed almost gayly. "And bring the whole house of cards crashing down about his head? Do you think his position isn't precarious on every score? Do you want to send him to prison again in his last years? I have only to tip off the police to finish him. And not only because of the odd lot of visitors he has at times."

She was beginning to understand now. An edge of cruel, clear light had begun to sweep across all that had bewildered her. She remembered the cigars with the diamonds hidden in them—sent to Niklaas van Pelt, so that he would be incriminated if they were discovered, but intercepted by Mara, as all packages were in that house. No, it had not been Thomas who had pushed her down on the path that night, even though it was he who had phoned Willi to destroy the picture she had taken of Niklaas in the market. Yet here was confusion again.

"Surely Thomas can't love you," she said. "How can you make him do what you want him to? And Willi through him?"

"Because he has been foolish enough to trust one white man—your father," Dirk said with biting scorn. "Thus he is involved—he's caught. His word would mean nothing in defense of your father, of course. He can only take whatever steps may keep Niklaas protected for the time being. So he does what I say. If I leave the country as quietly as I plan, no harm will come to your father. But if anyone tries to stop me—"

She did not believe him. She could not believe now that he would spare her father anything of the payment he had meant all these years to extract.

She spoke softly, her words hardly more than a whisper. "I saw—in the flower market. That is part of it too, isn't it? To weave the trap about my father, while you take the rewards?"

"You're far too clever, darling," he told her, his smile a little chill. "I'm afraid I've always underestimated you. I should have made you an ally from the first. Then we'd be in this together."

"As Mara is an ally?" she said.

"It's not exactly the same," he told her. "You, after all, are my wife."

"So it *is* you who have been smuggling diamonds?"

"Not alone, I assure you," he said mockingly. "Much as I have disliked the idea, I have had to accept certain—assistants, shall we say? But mine are the wits behind the operation. It would get nowhere without me. It's a tidy little sum I have being held for me when I get out of South Africa for good. We'll live moderately well, my dear. Not as well as I had hoped—industrials are not the most profitable commodity, but there have been a few gems to help out."

"What happens to them after the flower market?" Susan asked.

"You know enough for the moment, I think. Let's leave a little for you to puzzle out. I promise that you'll know everything once we've reached safety."

She wanted to repeat that she would not go with him, but now she dared not. The thought of the Kimberley in her handbag returned sharply to mind, and she barely held her hand from making an involuntary gesture. Whatever happened now, he mustn't dream that she had it in her possession. She had no illusion about how quickly he would take it from her and hold her to silence with threats against her father.

"Was it you on the path that day?" she asked him wearily.

For the first time he looked uncomfortable. "That was a necessary action. And I took care not to injure you, darling. After you came to the study and chattered naïvely about dropping the box of cigars, Mara called me out of the study to let me know something was missing. I dropped over the terrace wall and got out of sight on the path ahead of you."

She shivered, remembering rough hands pushing her down, the brutal thrusting of the bag over her head.

"By the way," he asked, "what did you do with the industrials you found that day? Where did you hide them?"

"I gave them to John Cornish," she said. "You aren't completely in the clear, you know. He does have some idea of what's going on."

"You have been a little fool," he said.

"Let's go home." She spoke dully. "It will be sunset soon and too dusky to see anything up here."

"There's still plenty to see," he assured her. "The lights at night are miraculous from the table. However, I promise not to keep you up here after dark, if you'd rather go down. At least you must see the top of the mountain, now that you're here."

She did not want to go with him, but she felt too limp and beaten at the moment to struggle any further. For the moment there were only two things left for which she must fight. The knowledge of the diamond must remain hidden. It belonged to her father, and to no one else. And the fact that when Dirk left South Africa she would not go with him.

When he had paid for their tea, he took her arm in a mockery of affection and drew her up the rough rock ledges and out into the open at the top. The sky was still light and tinged with sunset colors over the ocean, but at the far end of this enormous bleak plain of tumbled boulders a hint of gray dusk had begun to settle.

She knew now what people meant when they said this was like a landscape of the moon. The great plain at the top of the mountain was longer and wider and far vaster in its spread than she had ever imagined. From where they stood at one end and near the center there was no view except the tops of nearby hills and in the very distance the Hottentots Holland was being swallowed in blue mist. The drop-off on every hand was too far away to be seen, and in a sense this was reassuring. She had no desire to go close to that dizzy edge.

"Come," Dirk said and took her hand. "Watch your step, my darling. Up here a fall might hurt you badly."

Near the teahouse concrete had been poured to make a sort of path, but as they ventured out upon the mountain there was only a vague way of dirty white sand strewn between rocks. After a few years, the path was mainly guesswork and they had to pick their way. What looked from the ground to be an utterly flat slab of even rock across the table proved now to be anything but flat. On every side great black boulders, speckled with white and scabrous with age, rolled away over the great plain that had once been the bottom of an ocean. Scrubby green brush grew here and there, and once more there were the bright little wildflowers, finding sustenance in precarious crevices between the age-old rocks.

For all that there were a good many people up here, the table seemed to swallow everything human as soon as the teahouse was left behind. The place was huge enough for thousands, and the little parties scattered and were lost to each other at once. She noted with an odd relief that voices carried well up here, and that even those that seemed far away could be heard distinctly. At least she and Dirk were not really alone.

The air was clear and exhilarating and the dead calm had lifted. A slight, cold wind had begun to blow and Susan found herself wishing it would increase to a gale, so that everyone would be sent down from the mountain at once, summoned back by the hooter.

Dirk was pulling her along faster than she wanted to go, and she hung back, stumbling over rocks, stepping now and then into some pool of stagnant water held in a rocky basin. Once they ventured upon the edge of a slimy green bog and Dirk changed his course to circumvent it. Far away and out of sight someone was testing the echoes, shouting down toward the cliffs behind the mountain, then waiting while strange wild voices shouted back.

The boulders grew larger now, crouching like black animal shapes, eerie against the fading light in the sky. It became necessary to leap from one rock to another, instead of clambering laboriously up and down.

"Where are we going?" Susan pleaded. "I don't want to go any farther. It's all ugly and difficult. There's nothing to see."

"There will be soon," Dirk promised her. "But we must move along quickly or it will be getting dark and we'll have to go down."

She stood stubbornly where she was, refusing to budge another foot. He looked all around them and then capitulated suddenly.

"All right. This place will do as well as any. I don't want to tire you. Sit down and get your breath. You needn't worry. We'll go back in a moment. I know this tabletop like the palm of my hand."

She did not want to rest. She wanted only to turn back at once, to join the other groups that must by now be streaming back toward the cable house before the light should fade completely. But she was out of breath and when Dirk drew her down to sit beside him on a flat slab of rock she gave in. At least for the moment he was not hurrying her on.

"We're not far from the edge now," he said. "If you look over there you can see the lights beginning to come on in Cape Town."

She shivered at the sight and drew her coat more closely about her. The wind was growing bitter.

Dirk leaned forward to take hold of the strap of her handbag, tugging at it gently. "Will you tell me the truth now, darling? You found the diamond, didn't you? It was in the camera, of course. Mara was suspicious about your interest in that little camera, though she couldn't see anything when she looked into it. We'd both been through that toy chest before, of course, but the camera seemed to offer nothing. I didn't guess until I picked up that bit of black tape on the floor of your father's study. Why don't you tell me the whole story now, Susan dear?"

She forced words between teeth that had a tendency to chatter. "I d-don't know what you're talking about."

"You know very well," he said. "Will you trust me with the diamond or must I take it away from you?"

"It's for—for my father," she said. "It doesn't belong to you!"

"It belongs to whoever holds it," he said softly. "Do be reasonable about this, darling. With the Kimberley in our hands we'll be in the strongest position possible. The world will give us anything we want. There's a rich, wonderful life ahead of us. For you and me, darling."

Susan steadied her trembling and forced the shiver from her voice. "Father knew my mother had taken the stone. Just as she took the others that were found in the Johannesburg house. Perhaps he still believes she took it out of the country. He impoverished himself to pay for it and save her reputation. He loved her deeply and I think she was incapable of loving him as much. The stone belongs to him. He has paid for it with a good deal of his life."

"You leave me very little choice," Dirk said, and the mockery of affection was gone from his voice. "I can get out of the country by ship tomorrow if necessary. The signals are ready to be given. I mean to take the diamond with me. You don't want to spend the night alone on the mountain, do you?"

Before she could speak, a sound pierced the air across the mountaintop. That was the hooter, the signal for everyone to go down. Susan stumbled to her feet, wrenching the strap of her handbag from Dirk's grasp. But before she had managed to get two boulders away, he was after her, whirling her about to face him, his hand across her mouth.

"Don't make a sound," he said. "If you scream, the edge is very close. They'll think you slipped and fell, and screamed in falling. I'll have tried hard to catch you—and only saved your handbag. A great tragedy, my dear. And especially sad for your father."

She saw his eyes, bright in the fading light from the west. The shining brightness she had loved was upon him—the brightness of a diamond and, like a diamond, hard. He would do as he said. Against his desire for the diamond her life was nothing.

When he saw that she would not move or scream, his grip relaxed a little.

"Don't be frightened," he said more gently, and she trusted gentleness in him less than she did cold force. "It will take a while for everyone to get in. There's plenty of time to join the last car. Or, if we have to stay, I know a fairly easy way down. There's even a hut we can take shelter in on the far side of the mountain if that should be necessary. But we can leave at once if you'll open your bag and give me the diamond. That's the sensible way to manage it, Susan. I'm fond of you, my dear. I'd never want to hurt you."

She looked at him with unconcealed loathing. With her eyes she told him the truth—that she despised him now as much as she had once loved him. That there would never be any life for them together anywhere. That she would betray him at the first opportunity and stop him, defeat him, if she could.

He read her look and reached grimly into his pocket. "My first plan won't do, after all. I can see I couldn't trust you, even with the diamond in my possession. So now we will have to arrange something else. It's your own fault, my dear. You leave me no choice."

He drew his hand from his pocket and she half expected to see a gun in it. But what he held was a looping of metal that looked vaguely familiar as he began to slap it back and forth across his hand in a speculative manner. A finger of fear traced itself up the back of her neck.

"Do you know what this is?" Dirk asked, once more at ease and even faintly amused.

He held the metal strand out for her to see and she recognized it as a looped bicycle chain.

"A favorite weapon of the Cape Town skollies," he said.

Skollies, she knew, were the young toughs who hung around District Six in gangs. Hypnotized, she stared at the links of chain being stroked across Dirk's palm.

"Do you see how cleverly this has been fitted for use?" he said and showed her how an end of the chain had been folded back and forth to make a handle, then bound with workman's tape so that it would not slip in the fingers. The remaining loop made a flexible lash.

"It can even be adjusted to the reach of an arm," Dirk said pleasantly, as if he were rather enjoying himself now. "A man with a long arm doesn't need as great a reach of chain. A shorter man can extend his reach by letting out the loop. It's pretty lethal as a weapon, and far quieter than a gun."

He took a step toward her and she saw death in his eyes.

"Open your bag," he said.

It was strange now that her hands did not tremble. She opened the clasp easily and reached into the copious depths for the stone. When she felt it in her fingers she drew it out and would have tossed it wide over the edge of the precipice, but he was too quick for her. His left hand closed about her wrist and he swung her about toward the rocky edge of the mountain. The hand with the chain in it was behind her now and she closed her eyes against the blow that was sure to come. She felt her fingers opening beneath pressure and the stone dropped into his grasp.

The moment her hand was free she whirled away from him, and saw in a terrified flash that she was on the brink of the mountain. The lights of Cape Town moved in a blur across her vision and she flung herself wildly back from the edge, flung her arms about Dirk, more terrified now of the precipice than she was of him. She was in his arms, closed in a deadly embrace, and she could not tell whether he was urging her toward the cliff or drawing her back from it. She felt her feet slipping over nothingness—and suddenly they were falling together, scraping against stone, rolling over the edge, sliding, falling, locked in each other's arms.

23

The blackness and the cold crushed down upon her. Behind her closed lids the world was made up of darkness, and there was pain everywhere. She seemed to hurt all over and it was hard to breathe. Someone was leaning over her, murmuring her name over and over, calling her back, though she did not want to come. She was being held in someone's arms, cradled there, rocked and grieved over—yet there was no comfort for her in the fact.

Painfully she opened her eyes and looked into Dirk's face bent close above her own in the last faint light before darkness came down. With the sight of him, memory swept back in frightening intensity and she tried to struggle away from him.

He held her still and there was a tenderness in his voice that startled her.

"Lie quiet, darling," he said.

But she pulled herself out of his arms and sat up. She was sore and scraped raw along one thigh, though her coat and slacks must have saved her to some extent. Her arms and legs seemed to move normally when she tried them, though she knew she would be black and blue tomorrow. If there was to be a tomorrow.

She saw now where they were. They had rolled together over the edge, it was true, but only to be caught several feet down on an earthen ledge cupped in rock extending below the upper table. A sloping buttress of rock down which they had slid had broken the full impact of the fall. The ledge which held them was fairly wide, but it sloped unevenly to the real drop-off of the farther pitch. Susan edged back against the rock buttress and stared at the spreading lights of Cape Town so very far below, yet so dreadfully close.

"You would have thrown me over!" Her voice was choked with horror. "You would have struck me with that chain. You tried to kill me!"

She had drawn as far from Dirk as she could on the ledge and he made no further move to touch her.

"No," he said, "I never meant to kill you. I knew there were ledges all along the edge of the mountain. I've climbed down to this very place before. I knew you wouldn't fall far." He watched her strangely. "At the last minute I couldn't let you go. I was afraid you might roll or hurt yourself seriously on the rock. I tried to pull you back—and we fell together."

There was no mockery in him now, but only a stark despair, and she knew he spoke the truth. But she no longer wished for his affection.

"What are we to do?" she asked dully.

"I can get back up," he said. "It would be harder for you alone. Impossible, perhaps."

"Then," she said, "if you still have the diamond, why don't you go?"

He had been kneeling on the ledge, now he stood up, and looked down at her.

"I have the diamond." He showed it to her in his hand and then put it away in a pocket of his jacket. "Susan, I want you to come with me."

She shook her head violently and pain throbbed at the back of her skull. "You know that's impossible. I can stay here. I have my coat. Tomorrow they'll find me and get me up. If you want to get away, go."

She could sense hesitation in him, an uncertainty that was unlike him. It was not part of his plans to be thinking first of someone else. And he was not able to do it for long.

"It's perfectly true that you'll be all right," he said. "I can get down alone, even in the dark, and tomorrow I'll be out of the country."

She expected him to turn and start up the sloping buttress of rock, but instead he knelt beside her again and suddenly his hands covered his face and his head was bent. A memory of the boy she had known so long ago seared through her and something in her twisted in pain. She reached out to touch his fair hair lightly, though she could not see its brightness now, and felt the ring on her finger. With a quick gesture she pulled it off and held it out to him, nudged him with it.

"I'm giving you back your luck, Dirk. The pink stone belongs to you. I'll never wear it again."

The finality of her tone must have reached him. He raised his head and took the ring from her, dropped it into the pocket of his jacket with the other. As he moved his foot struck something on the ledge and he picked up the bicycle chain.

"I may need this," he said dryly and looped it into a neat and compact form before he thrust it into a pocket.

A steady repetition of sound had begun to penetrate Susan's daze and confusion. She recognized it for cars being started, driving away somewhere down the mountain. Unsteadily she stood up and looked directly over the edge. On the highway near the cable house far below and half the length the mountain to her left, people who had ridden up were still getting into their cars, still leaving. If she screamed they might hear her, come to her help. Those in the cable house might hear her cries.

Dirk sensed what she intended. "Don't," he said wearily. "What good would it do you? It might take hours of hunting to find you. I couldn't let you scream more than once. Isn't it better for everyone if I get away from Cape Town? Better for your father. Better for you, Susan."

She felt too weak to struggle against him any further. And what he said was true. Whatever the cost to herself, this was the best way. He sensed her agreement and turned toward the rocky wall, began to pull himself up.

She waited fearfully, not sure whether she wanted most to see him go or to have him stay so that she would not be doomed to spend the dark hours alone in this dreadful place. Once she thought of pleading with him to help her get up from the ledge, to at least leave her on the mountaintop. But she knew without trying that such a plea would do her no good. Here she could make little trouble for him. On top he could not trust her.

He was good at rock climbing, he had done it all his life, and he found the toeholds, the crevices for his fingers. There was a man's strength in his arms and he went up and over the top.

She closed her eyes and sat very still and quiet against the buttress, listening for his departure. His voice came down to her.

"Good-by, my darling. I won't forget you."

He was whistling softly as he turned away, but the sound was melancholy and without cheer. Remembered words ran through her mind: "I'll ride all night . . . when the moon is bright . . ." and tears stung her eyelids. She heard his steps high above, heard a small stone roll as his foot struck it. Then all the mountain was quiet and she was alone. Even the sound of cars on the highway below had come to an end. Tears squeezed between her closed lids and a small sob shook her. Not for fear of her predicament or because of the long ordeal ahead of her, but for sorrow at the ending of love. So empty she was, so lost and lonely. Yet the man she had loved was someone who had never truly existed.

Her tears were brief, they dried quickly. She stood up with her back against the wall. Once more she stretched her legs and arms gingerly to try them out, and felt the sore place along her thigh. She was lucky, lucky. She might be dead by now. Her back could have been broken. She could have rolled on over the edge. She was safe and she was unhurt and she must remember only these things and hold to her courage for the night ahead. How cold and bright and deceptively close the lights of Cape Town seemed. So very close, so very far away. And how dark the bay beyond. It was strange to think of people down there, dining happily in hotels and restaurants and homes, never knowing that a girl crouched up here on a mountain ledge, cold and frightened and helpless in this darkly evil place. Out there on the Cape Flats were the *pondok-kies* and a longer-lived misery than her own. Those people too had no thought for her shivering here, and perhaps would not have cared had they known.

All these years the mountain had waited for her. Even as a child she had sensed its malignant purpose, had known that it bided its time. Awesome and tremendous and enormously cruel it could be—cruel as the old dark gods who had ruled it long ago and who would be satisfied only when blood was spilled upon the black stones.

She crossed her arms about her body and held herself in a tight embrace, rocking back and forth. This was no place for such vivid imaginings to possess her. If she stayed quietly where she was no harm would come to her. Only her own mind could betray and injure her now. She had been shocked and shaken and held under a frightening strain. It was only natural that her thoughts should run wild in reaction, very nearly out of control. But not entirely. There was still something left in command. She laid her hands upon the reins of her galloping thoughts and pulled them in.

She must think only of physical things and her own immediate comfort and safety. She must be thankful that the full blast of sharp wind, sweeping away the warmer air of the day, blew over her head and did not strike her fully on this ledge. With the wind upon her, she would have been much worse off. She wished now that she had drunk all her tea, finished her toast. Wished for the remains of the lunch she had discarded today at Cape Point. Food would have helped to fortify her against this long night. Better not think of it.

Feeling for her watch, she found the crystal broken and one of the hands missing. It did not matter; she could not see the dial clearly anyway, and to watch the time would only make the night seem longer.

What was her father doing now? And John Cornish? The thought of John was steadying. He would surely come for her when he knew she had not returned and must be up here. This was a thought to hold to with all her might. In the morning he would come up the mountain—and he would find her. She had only to wait until then.

Her body was sore and achingly tired. Rest was the answer. If only she could sleep, dull her senses to discomfort, and sleep until it was morning and something could be done about her predicament. Carefully she began to feel about on the slanting ledge, groping with her hands for small stones that would hurt her body. At first she tossed them over the edge, but they made a sickening sound as they crashed on the stony slopes far below, and she took to piling them out of the way instead. At least there was a space of earth here, so her bed would not be wholly rock. Setting her big leather bag down for a pillow, she wrapped her coat about her, turning up her collar, and curled herself on the ledge. She was glad now for her two sweaters underneath. The night had turned very cold, and it would probably grow even colder.

For a time she lay quiet, her eyes open, watching the darkness, listening to the wind. The doves of Cape Town had quieted for the night and city traffic noises had lessened and were far away. Once she heard the sound of a car and raised her head to see headlights moving up the long slant of highway toward Signal Hill, where she and John had traveled together—so very long ago! The Lion's Head was a black knob against the sky. She stared at it until she began to feel drowsy.

She slept in rough snatches, waking, drowsing, dropping off into some wild dream, fighting out of it to a waking state, only to find that it was still night and nothing had changed.

Not much time had passed, she suspected, when she sensed a difference in the sky overhead. Below her the lights of Cape Town were still bright. They had not winked out into midnight thinness. But overhead there were no stars, no moon had risen. There was a damp smell on the air and as she stared upward something soft and white drifted like smoke along the lip of the rocky cliff. Clouds had come down upon the mountain and the knowledge shocked her fully awake.

The sight of that misty softness was terrifying. Darkness was one thing, but the cloth of cloud that could blanket the mountain was another. In mist there was no hope of escape, no hope of being found. Mist might cover the mountain for days and then no one could find her.

Frightened now, she stood up and began to call, remembering how sound had traveled earlier on the mountaintop. Dirk had said the people who ran the teahouse lived up here all the time. Perhaps they might hear her in their distant hollow at the end of the mountain. But the fog soaked up her voice like blotting paper, changed the sound of it in her own ears.

Yet now she knew she must not stay here. Perhaps the clouds had not thickened fully on top as yet. Here on her ledge the mist that crept down the mountain was still thin as a gossamer veil. There was no way down over this sheer precipice, so she must go up as Dirk had gone up. If he could do it, so could she, granted the will and the urgent need.

Her first assault on the buttress of rock was foolish and wild. She flung herself upon it and tried to claw her way up, succeeding only in scraping her sore hands further, yet finding nothing to cling to, no tiniest ledge for her fingers. It could not be managed that way, she realized, and drew back for a more careful examination of her position. Dirk had been given the advantage of at least a dim light. She had no light at all. Whatever was to be found she must discover by means of her hands, her fingers, her toes.

She leaned forward against the slanting buttress and reached upward as far as she could stretch, but she could not touch the edge of the mountain above her head. Yet if she could pull herself up even a little way, the edge could not be far out of reach. Its heavy rocks might give her a handhold and a leverage. Carefully, trying to be patient, she patted her hands over all the surface she could reach, and then moved around the buttress a little and repeated the process. Now, at the very height of her reach, she could feel a rough projection, a jutting of rock, and here, somewhat below, but too high for her foot was a tiny ledge that would surely give her a toehold if she could get to it. But she could not grasp the projection—it remained just out of reach and there was no way to use the promise it offered.

There must be a way up. There must be a way to do it. That was what her wits were for. Now was the time to use that wild imagination of hers and find some way of getting up. She turned about on the slanting buttress and leaned against it. In dismay she saw that the mists had thickened and Cape Town had vanished except for a faint glow. This was going to be even worse than she had feared.

Her foot had struck her handbag as she turned and she bent to pick it up, slung the strap over her shoulder. In an instant the possibility came to her. Eagerly now she stood on tiptoe, reaching toward the rough, just-out-of-reach projection overhead. When she had located it, she stood under it and looped the long strap of her handbag into a noose. Awkwardly she jumped and reached the noose up the wall above her. Twice she missed, and then the loop caught, hooked securely over the horny irregularity in the buttress.

With each hand she grasped one side of the strap and pulled herself up, praying that the leather would hold her weight. With almost ridiculous ease she walked up the buttress a few steps to the place where she could stand on the tiny ledge. Holding to the loop with one hand, she reached with the other and found the edge of the mountain only a little way above. She had no need for the strap now. She flung her handbag on top ahead of her and pulled herself up the remaining few feet, crawling breathlessly onto a flat slab of rock. She was once more on top of the mountain.

For a few moments she lay upon the cold stone, breathing hard with relief. Then she crawled away from the edge to safety and stood up in a pocket of rock to look about and plan a course of action. Now, surely, it would be possible to reach the teahouse and get help and a telephone. If she could find the way.

If.

She had never seen mist so thick. No lights were visible anywhere and there was an eerie stillness. Even the wind which had brought cold air into warm and created this heavy fog had stopped blowing and could not be counted on to clear the mountain of this quilting of cloud. The important thing was to keep her sense of direction. Behind her as she stood lay Cape Town, so she must move to her right. If she kept going in a more or less straight line she would reach the end of the mountain where safety lay.

But in the mists were no landmarks to enable her to hold to a straight line. Laboriously she felt her way, clambering over rocks, edging around them, stumbling now and then, moving ahead. But there were boulders too large to climb and the mists blotted out what lay behind her and in ten minutes she knew she had lost all sense of direction.

It was a dreadful feeling. The plain was so vast that she could wander on it for days if her directions were confused and she moved in circles. And there was always the danger of finding another precipice and this time falling to her death. Despairing and defeated, she sat down upon a low rock and leaned her head upon her knees, trying to think, praying for guidance. But now no inventive notion came to mind. There was nothing to do but sit where she was until the clouds thinned enough so that she could regain a sense of direction. Now there was no earthy ledge to lie upon, but only hard damp rock on every hand, rough and porous to her touch. Indeed, she was lost on the bottom of a prehistoric ocean bed and the world she knew had vanished from existence.

24

At first the faint glow in the mist at her left meant nothing. She supposed the clouds had drifted a little thinner there. Then she sat up with a start, realizing that a light was indeed moving about, shedding a faint radiance far away in the fog. She jumped to her feet and cupped her hands around her mouth, calling, shouting, unnerving herself by the very urgency of her unexpected hope.

Had Dirk come back for her? But he would not have carried a light.

The fourth time she called the answer reached her faintly and she wondered if she heard only an echo. Then the sound of a voice came distinctly through the mist. Someone was calling her name.

"I'm over here!" she shouted. "Here, here!"

The voice reached her more clearly, and the intensity of light increased. She knew the voice now—it was John's. He had not waited till morning, he had come up through the dark and the mist. He had come for her!

When he loomed out of the fog close by, she saw that he was not alone. Another man had come with him. Thomas Scott leaped lightly down from a high boulder and stood beside him.

Susan waited on no ceremony. She flung herself into John's arms and felt them close about her securely. She wept in relief against his shoulder and he held her there, stroking her hair gently. She had seen tenderness in his eyes earlier today and had turned away from it. Now she wanted it safely around her.

"You're all right now," he said. "I couldn't have made it up here without Thomas, but he knew the way, and the mist isn't so bad down below."

She lifted her head to smile at Thomas. He held his own flashlight toward the ground, but his face was lighted indirectly by the torch John carried and there was a grim, unsmiling look in his eyes.

217

"Dirk left you up here deliberately, didn't he?" John said,

"Yes!" She did not want to stir from the security of his arms. "It's such a long story. I'll give it to you later. But he didn't try to hurt me. He only took the diamond away from me and went down the mountain."

"The diamond?" John said and looked at Thomas.

Reluctantly Susan drew herself out of his arms. There had been enough of weak relief and it was time to regain her self-possession.

"Yes. I found the diamond earlier down at Protea Hill. Dirk suspected that I had it and he made me give it to him. He's gone now—down the mountain. He means to get out of the country with it. I was caught on a ledge up here—"

"Don't try to tell us everything now," John said. "Do you feel a little better? Strong enough to try the way down?"

"The way down? Can't we go to the teahouse first? Why must we go down now?"

Again John and Thomas exchanged glances.

"The story isn't as long a one to tell as you think, Susan," John said gently. "We know some of it. Another batch of diamonds came to the house today. I'd warned Thomas to keep a lookout for any sort of package that Miss Bellman took charge of. Tell her, Thomas."

The colored man spoke in an expressionless monotone. "It was a package of drugs addressed to Mr. van Pelt. I watched and saw Miss Bellman take it up to her room before I went out today. When Mr. Cornish came home, I let him know."

"Mara had to talk," John said, sounding grim. "There was nothing else she could do. So we got a picture of the whole scheme. Almost any convenient means was used for smuggling the diamonds to Cape Town, but always in a way that would point to Niklaas if they were discovered. From what Mara said, I gather Dirk intended to involve him deliberately just before he got out of the country. She turned a bit hysterical then and told me about your going up the mountain with Dirk. She said you'd never come down. So Thomas and I drove to the cable house and watched the last cars empty. We checked every man and woman who came down those steps until the cars stopped running. Then we drove to the place where an easy trail starts up and left the car." He held out his hand to her. "Come along, Susan."

Someone else had said that to her tonight. "Come along, Susan." But now the words were different, comforting. She could go with confidence and trust. She did not understand

218

why the climb down the mountain was necessary when she felt so sore and weary, but she would do as John said.

Thomas moved a little ahead to choose the way, holding his flashlight downward to light the rocks immediately at their feet. The mist did not defeat him as it had Susan.

"Dirk has the diamond now," she repeated dully as they started over the rocks. Somehow this was the only clear thought her mind clung to.

"Don't worry about it," John said. "Let's think of nothing except getting down the mountain. The police will have to come into this now and your father hasn't a notion of what's up. Before we call them in, he must know the whole story. That's why we're not going to the teahouse first."

Thomas seemed to have a sixth sense about direction or else there were landmarks he knew even on this desolate sea bottom. She kept thinking of it that way—as the bottom of the sea. It was only a mountaintop when you could see across it and know there was a world somewhere lower down.

The easy trail was not very easy in darkness and mist, but no fog was so thick that it could hide the immediate ground beneath her feet, and the flashlights made it possible to proceed a few steps at a time. John's hand was always firmly about her own and she did not slip or fall. As they descended the mists began to thin. The tablecloth lay only across the top of the mountain. Now and then, through trees growing in the cleft of ravine they followed, lights far below were visible.

Once, for Susan's sake, they stopped to rest. She sat upon a grassy slope and tried to catch her breath and gather her wits. Somehow she felt a little numb and capable of only one or two persistent thoughts.

"Will the police stop Dirk tomorrow?" she asked. "Perhaps it would be better if he could just get away." Better for everyone, she thought, remembering the threats he had made against her father. "He has the diamond now—what more can he want?"

Thomas moved impatiently. "Tell her. It's better to tell her."

John nodded. "Thomas is right. You'll have to know and it's better to tell you now. This is the trail by which Dirk chose to come down. We met him—not very far from the top."

Susan sat still and tense, listening as he made her see what had happened.

Thomas had been climbing ahead, finding the way. Dirk

219

must have heard him coming up, and he stepped off the trail to let him go by.

"I doubt if he knew who it was," John said. "But I was throwing my light close to my feet and it reflected upward so he must have recognized me. We didn't realize he was there. He had only to wait till I went by and he could have had the trail to himself. But he didn't wait. He came at me swinging a bicycle chain before I had time to get out of his way."

Susan winced, remembering the chain.

John had ducked just in time. The chain had cut him across the face, but it had not knocked him out as Dirk intended. And John still knew his commando tricks. Dizzy though he was from the blow, he dived in for a hold and made Dirk drop the chain. After that a fair fight might have been possible, but Thomas, hearing the sounds, had run back down the trail. His flashlight caught the shine of metal on the ground and he picked up the bicycle chain.

"That was when Dirk saw him," John said. "He forgot me as though I didn't exist. My torch was on the ground and it showed Thomas standing there looking at Dirk with that chain in his hand."

John paused and glanced at Thomas, listening grimly to his words.

"This is the hard part to tell you, Susan," John said.

Susan spoke softly. "Dirk hated you. I think he would have killed you if he could. Tell me what happened."

"Thomas never touched him with the chain," John went on. "Or in any other way, for that matter. I didn't need help at that point. But Dirk saw him and I think his own conscience did the rest. I've seen frightened men before and Dirk was frightened. He knew the things he had done in the past and I think he expected no mercy from a man whose skin was dark. He thought Thomas meant to kill him with that chain and he was more afraid of him than he would have been of me or any white man. Because there was so much reason. That time with the *sjambok*, perhaps, and other times as well."

Susan could see the picture as John made it clear. Dirk had stood frozen in fear, staring at the chain in Thomas's hands. He said something like "Don't!" but the word choked in his throat. Thomas had known what was happening to him. Scornfully he threw the chain at Dirk's feet, knowing the white man could not use it.

"Dirk picked up the chain," John went on. "But his hands were shaking and his eyes never left Thomas. I said, 'Drop that!' but instead he stuffed it into his jacket pocket. Then he lost his head and turned to run. He fled without sense or reason—and we were still high upon the mountain and it was dark."

John took Susan's cold hands into his own warm ones and held them.

"He fell a long way," Thomas said quietly. "Down into a rock gully."

"We climbed down to where he was," John said. "But there was nothing we could do. He was dead when we got to him. We had to go on to the top after you. We emptied his pockets so he wouldn't be robbed in the event that anyone found him before the police could reach him in the morning. Then we covered him with his jacket and climbed to the top. Thomas has everything in his pockets. We can show you when we reach Protea Hill."

Susan was glad that John was holding her hands so tightly. Now she could think only of Dirk's fair head bent before her up there on the mountain ledge. And of Dirk as a boy down at Camp's Bay, laughing at a little girl who wanted to take his picture with a broken camera. All else was wiped away. There were no tears, only a thickness of old grief in her throat. She was aware that both John and Thomas were watching her.

"I'll be all right," she told them. They could not know that she had lost Dirk long before this and that her pity now was only for a man who might have been so much more than he was. A man who had been destroyed by what he had become. "Let's go down," she said. "Let's get back to my father."

Later she remembered few details of that climb down the trail in the dark. It was a relief when they came out at the bottom and found Niklaas's car where Thomas had left it at the foot of the path. It was Thomas who drove them home. Susan sat in the back seat with John's arm about her and they talked not at all.

Niklaas van Pelt was waiting in his study when they reached the house. They went in at once to see him.

"I've been waiting," Niklaas said. "Something has happened, hasn't it? Something is wrong. I think Mara has gone away."

"She can't get far," John said. "The police will pick her up tomorrow."

He told the story then as simply as he could and there was a deep sadness in her father's face as he learned of the smuggling of diamonds that had gone on in this very house, with himself as a shield. Now Susan could tell what she had seen in the flower market.

She picked up his heavy cane with the three flags embossed upon the silver head and ran her fingers down to the tip. The reinforced lower section was difficult to turn; no casual hand would have found the secret compartment. But when she unscrewed it the tube was revealed, where diamonds could be hidden. Under the shelter of the bench that held her tubs of flowers, the woman in the market had been able to remove the tiny industrial stones from their hiding place. This had been the next step on the way out of Cape Town—and again Dirk would have seemed free of any involvement and Niklaas van Pelt would have been incriminated if there had been a slip. No wonder Mara and Dirk, learning of the pictures Susan had taken, had been worried. Mara must have persuaded Thomas that the pictures could injure Niklaas in some way, and he had told Willi to destroy them.

But now it was over. Now the police could learn the truth without danger to her father.

While Susan told him about the cane, Niklaas took it into his hands and found the hiding place for himself. Sorrow lay heavy upon him and Susan knew that, no matter what Dirk might have thought, Niklaas had loved him and now grieved over what he had done.

"Diamonds have been destroying men ever since they were discovered," he said softly; "women too," and Susan knew he was thinking of Claire. "But there's something more important that concerns me now. John, have you made up your mind? Have the things I've told you this afternoon convinced you?"

"You have convinced me," John said gravely. "You and Thomas."

"Can we use him, Thomas?" Niklaas asked.

Listening in bewilderment, Susan looked from one to the other, and Dirk's puzzling words on the mountaintop about her father's notion of helping the country returned to her mind.

"We can use any who will work with us in good faith," Thomas said. There was an air of quiet invincibility about him.

"Men like you, John," Niklaas pointed out, "can't run away from South Africa in its time of greatest need just because you dislike some of the things that are happening here."

"I know that now," John answered gravely. "I mean to stay."

"But doing what?" Susan asked in bewilderment. "What is there anyone can do?"

"There's no such thing as a situation in which nothing can be done," her father said. "Not while there are men of courage. There are those in South Africa today, both black and white, who are in need of aid. A few of these have found a haven in this house. And it has been a quiet place for men to come and talk. And plan. There are more of us who believe in freedom than you might think—among Afrikaners as well as English-speaking South Africans. Many who believe that the only hope for the country is to act in whatever way we can against despotism and prejudice. And to make sure our numbers grow. There's work for you too, Susan. Perhaps through your pictures. The pressure of outside opinion matters more than it ever has before. Even Hans with his thumb in the dike must listen eventually. So, will you stay? Here in his house?"

"South Africa is my home now," Susan answered simply.

She was beginning to understand many things: her father's long and careful testing of John, his arguments that seemed to take the wrong course in order to challenge the younger man. Behind her eyes there was a stinging of tears, but they were tears of pride and love for her father. There was something tremendous about him and she could delight now in being his daughter.

"You brought Dirk's things?" John asked Thomas. "We might have a look at them before the police come."

Thomas reached into his pocket. One at a time he placed upon Niklaas's desk the articles that had been in Dirk's pocket. His billfold and loose change. His cigarette case and lighter. Then something that clanked as he set it down on the polished surface—the coiled bicycle chain. And after that a small gold ring with an orchid-pink stone in its setting. Susan looked quickly away at the sight of it. It had not brought Dirk the luck he needed, after all.

The last article Thomas drew from his pocket was a folded handkerchief and Susan knew what it contained. All that had happened had driven the thought of the diamond from her mind. But now she wanted to be the one to put it into her father's hands.

"Please," she said, "let me."

Carefully she turned back the folds of the handkerchief. For just an instant the great diamond seemed to glitter in the lamplight in all its brilliance—yellow rather than blue because of the reflected light. Then Susan touched the handkerchief and, as they watched, the stone separated into a Y-shaped break before their eyes and lay upon the cloth in three pieces.

Susan gasped and could not speak.

"What is it?" Niklaas asked impatiently. "What has happened?"

John picked up the shattered diamond and put it into the old man's hands.

"It's the Kimberley," he said. "Or it *was* the Kimberley. It was in Dirk's pocket when he fell."

Niklaas turned the pieces knowingly in his fingers. "Yes, this could happen. He fell upon rock, you say. The point of the diamond could have struck and if there was something hard in his pocket—"

"There was this," John said and pushed the chain toward the old man's hand.

Niklaas touched it and nodded. "Yes, it could have happened that way." He thrust the bits of stone aside and reached for the telephone. "It does not matter. It's time now to ring the police. We can wait no longer."

As casually as that he pushed the thought of a lost fortune from him and Susan, watching him, knew that it truly did not matter. There were other affairs to occupy her father.

While he was telephoning, she stood up and stretched her sore and weary body. There was still the ordeal of the police to endure before she could rest. She moved toward the French doors to look out at the night and Thomas came quietly to open them for her.

She smiled at him. "Will you phone Willi when you can? She'll be worried about us all."

He nodded and there was a moment of understanding and sympathy between them. Then Susan stepped through to the terrace and stood looking out over Cape Town.

It was past midnight and the lights were fewer and more scattered than they had been from the mountaintop. She heard John come to stand beside her and she turned to look up at the mist-hidden mountain.

"I was there," she said softly, unbelievingly. "I was up there tonight."

He did not touch her or speak. But he was close beside her and she knew he would wait until the time was right. They would work together through whatever dark times lay ahead. If only there were enough like John and her father and Thomas—enough who would stay, and who would listen and think and consult, persuading quietly, working for the good of all—then perhaps there would truly be a time of honor and glory in this lovely land of South Africa.